NANCY CURTEMAN

MURDER
ON THE
EMERALD
ISLE

Nancy Curteman

ISBN-978-0-9834631-5-3

First Edition: November 2019

Dedication

Larry, Jerry and Juli

Nancy Curteman

Acknowledgements

First, my sincere appreciation to my husband, Larry, for his loving encouragement.

Much appreciation to my Irish supporters. Sergeant Rod Craig of the Ballymena Police Service of Northern Ireland for acting as an excellent source for all my many questions about police procedures. Séamas McAleenan, County Antrim Camogie Coordinator for taking time to respond to all my technical questions regarding the sport. I'm grateful to John McSparran and John Robbin of Cushendun, County Antrim Northern Ireland for sharing with me everyday life in the beautiful Glens of Antrim.

Special thanks to members of my writing group, Art Carey, Chris Dews and Caroline Ahlswede. They taught me the basics. I couldn't have written this book without their powerful suggestions.

Thank you to my two book clubs. Champagne and Chapters members: Laurel Gonzales, Sandy Grandbois, Janyce Hummel, Kim Kelly, Trudie Mathiesen, Trish Murray, Catherine Rost, AnneMarie Sylva and Carol Wilson. Book Babes members: Georgette Buriani, Devora Carson, Carrie Douglas, Lynn Fox, Leslie Traber, and Barbara Wong. They were my cheerleaders. They gave me the courage I needed to try.

Finally, a big vote of thanks to Lynn Fox for the excellent job she did editing this novel.

Murder on the Emerald Isle

Chapter 1

We waited for the silent hour, the hour between midnight and one. The rain had ceased, and a cold mist replaced it. Now we could go.

It took our combined strength to drag the dead weight shrouded in an old sleeping bag. Strained back and arm muscles throbbed from exertion and a hoarse whistling sound wheezed in my chest with each gulp of frigid air. Despite the cold, sweat ran down my forehead into my eyes and obscured the muddy path.

An owl's call startled me. I almost dropped my end of the bag. We glanced at each other but did not speak.

I ignored my increasing exhaustion because we had no choice but to make it across the road to an old shed behind an abandoned farmhouse.

How had it come to this? Everything had happened so fast— insane demands, a lightning punch in the face, the sickening thud of a cast iron pan. Murder.

I shivered as we approached the road. Only a few more meters.

Suddenly, car headlights flashed lighting up the moonless night. We dropped to the ground, stopped breathing and waited until the swish of tires sloshing on wet pavement faded. What was someone doing on this narrow country road at well past midnight?

And more important, had they seen us?

Nancy Curteman

Chapter 2

Lysi Weston, snug in a blue down jacket and tailored wool slacks, stood on the curb in front of Dublin airport's Terminal Two holding a sign with large letters printed in black felt pen that read: Pennington.

Maynard Christie in a light jacket and cotton chinos stood next to her shifting from one foot to the other, arms wrapped tight across his chest, teeth chattering. Lysi pressed against her tall Australian husband. "Are you okay?"

"Freezing. Otherwise fine," Maynard said. "That pilot had it right when he announced San Francisco's March weather would feel like summer compared to Dublin's 5° C."

"San Francisco temps can dip down to the forties." Lysi didn't remind him that she'd cautioned he might need something warmer than his light Australian Bush jacket though it definitely suited him. Her pulse rate still quickened each time her eyes roamed over his broad shoulders, narrow hips and long legs.

Maynard doffed his outback bush hat and dragged his fingers through thick black hair. He shook his head and blew out a lungful of air. "I must have had a few kangaroos loose in my top paddock to let you talk me into coming along to this ice house."

Lysi failed to suppress a smile as an uncharitable urge for revenge crossed her mind. She remembered her first trip to Maynard's Outback sheep station near Alice Springs. She'd almost passed out in the 104° heat. He'd joked that thorny devils, a kind of ugly Australian lizard, shared her dislike of hot weather.

"Thorny devils would share your dislike of chilly weather too, wouldn't they?" Lysi said in as serious a tone as she could manage.

Maynard turned to face her, paused, then burst into good-natured laughter and said, "Touché"

She'd made her point.

Within a few minutes a shiny black limo swerved to the curb. The driver stretched across to the passenger window and flashed a card with Weston printed on it.

"This is our ride," Lysi said.

Maynard picked up the bags and loaded them into the limo trunk then followed Lysi into the backseat, his teeth still chattering.

With an unsmiling nod the driver started the engine and headed toward the Dublin city center. He drove to Eastlink Road then made his way to M50 South followed by several short jaunts on regional roads with names like Shelbourne Road, Clanwilliam Place, and Mount Street. After threading his way through bumper to bumper traffic he arrived at the five-star Merrion Hotel on Upper Merrion Street about 9 miles and 50 minutes later, a trip that would have taken only 22 minutes during non-commute hours.

Grace Wright, who had just arrived herself, and Chesterfield Pennington met the limo at the curb. Lysi did a quick assessment of the Georgian style hotel before she scooted from the car. Its perfect symmetry appealed to the orderly side of her nature. Identical wrought iron fences flanked the steps that led up to paneled doors with twin pillars on each side. The triangular tympanum that crowned the doors reminded her of a Greek temple except for the red brick walls. Even the two potted evergreens on each side of the door matched to perfection. The balance would have been flawless if instead of only one uniformed doorman there were two, one on each side of the door. Still, very nice.

Grace threw open her arms and encircled Lysi in a big bear hug. "Hey girlfriend. I sure missed you."

"Me, too." Lysi smiled at her tall African American friend whom she hadn't seen since Grace left San Francisco to visit her family in Harlem seven months ago. She hadn't changed— shimmering, shoulder-length black hair, thick lashes framing large brown eyes, full lips painted the same bright red as the pantsuit that caressed her slim figure. Lysi always imagined that Makeda, the Queen of Sheba, must have looked like Grace.

Long-time colleagues at Stellar Corporate Development, Lysi and Grace had traveled all over the world conducting management training sessions. Lysi looked forward to working the Dublin assignment with Grace.

Chess shook hands with Maynard and slapped him on the back. "Good to see you bro." In a sympathetic tone he added, "I better get you inside so you can thaw out."

The first time Lysi met Chess in Paris she decided he was a Denzel Washington look-alike with the body of six-foot-ten-inch Kevin Durant of Oakland Warrior basketball fame. She could see how he would conquer any woman's heart.

Chess kissed Lysi on the cheek then took her arm and guided her into the Merrion's Italian marble-filled lobby. On their way to the elevators they passed several drawing rooms decorated with French crystal chandeliers, plush period furniture and a parade of paintings by famous Irish artists including Paul Henry, Jack Yeats and John Doherty.

"Chess, you outdid yourself with these accommodations," Lysi said. "The Irish sure know how to pamper business visitors."

She'd been a little hesitant when Chess asked Grace and her to do a sexual harassment management training seminar at Cadigan Construction Tools, his newest customer. She and Maynard had just finished a six month stay in Australia and had planned to return to San Francisco in March, the month Chess needed the seminar.

When she and Maynard married, they had agreed to spend half each year on Maynard's Outback sheep station near Alice Springs and half the year in San Francisco. Lysi was looking forward to returning to her city by the Bay, but a trip to the Emerald Isles sounded pretty exciting.

The Dublin company had contracted with Vermillion, Chess' software company, to build a corporate website and communication system that connected all aspects of manufacturing from production control to materials handling to automation. Vermillion's contract also included training employees to use the system. It was a lucrative contract Chess couldn't pass up. When the male-dominated company recently hired several female supervisors at various levels, sexual harassment reared its ugly head. Hence, the need for Lysi and Grace's management training seminar.

"Get settled into your rooms," Chess said. "Later we'll meet for dinner and talk about the company." He handed Maynard a keycard. "Room 306."

"Has Billy arrived yet," Lysi asked. As soon as Billy Weston, Lysi's uncle had heard about her assignment in Ireland he booked a ticket insisting this would be a great opportunity for him to introduce Lysi to all her Irish relatives in County Antrim.

"Oh yeah." Chess burst into a fit of laughter. "He arrived yesterday and immediately turned into a leprechaun. Called me and said he caught a Goldline coach right outside the Dublin airport terminal and headed straight for Belfast. He's already settled into his cousin's farmhouse in a small village called Beechgrove."

Chess turned to Grace. "We're in 308, Gracie."

"How are the beds?" Grace asked. "I'm tired, hungry and cranky. Seven hours on a plane is not my idea of great.

"Seven hours?" Lysi said. "Try nineteen hours in coach. Old Stoneface was too cheap to fly me business class." Lysi used the special name she and Grace had coined for their Stellar Corporate Development boss, Charles Stone.

"Want me to come up with you and check that bed out?" Chess winked at Grace, gave her a quick kiss and turned to go. "We'll test it out together later. Work beckons."

Chapter 3

Along the road from Belfast to the village of Beechgrove, Billy Weston watched the passing Irish countryside from the side window of his second cousin, Ryan O'Rourke's, old Ford Ranger pickup. It spluttered and coughed and made a terrible grinding sound each time Ryan shifted down to navigate a hill.

Despite the racket, Billy's thoughts waxed poetic as he gazed at the lush green rolling hills. Ah ... the Emerald Isle. Perfect name. Seems like there are a hundred shades of green—dells and knolls draped in velvety green, stands of trees and shrubs shimmering in jade, cows grazing in pastures the color of shamrocks—all beneath a cornflower blue sky. He thought the sporadic appearance of quaint farmhouses enhanced the pristine paradise.

Billy felt very Irish in a new tweed flat cap perched at a rakish angle over his right eyebrow, and a traditional cream-colored Aran cardigan with pewter buttons that strained to contain his ample stomach. He patted his belly, still surprised he could have gotten so out of shape since retiring from his job as San Francisco District Attorney five years ago. It had been thirty years since his last visit to Northern Ireland. What would his Irish relatives think of him? He bet they probably didn't look so great either. He glanced at Ryan. No belly but also no hair. At least Billy still had a full head of red hair complete with thick sideburns.

Ryan O'Rourke turned off A52/Crumlin Road onto A26/Tully Road. The ride seemed a bit smoother now—until Ryan slammed on the brakes.

"What the ..." Billy shouted.

"Ah it's a new driver ahead of us. See that R on the license plate? That means he's a restricted driver and can't drive over 45 miles per hour. That law endangers other drivers in my opinion."

"Good point," Billy said then settled back into his nostalgic thoughts.

About a mile down the road Billy spotted a conglomeration of motor homes and campers in a grassy field. Unlike the quaint farmhouses, they did not enhance the countryside. Men and women sat outside on plastic lawn chairs and at aluminum camp tables. Children kicked a soccer ball around or skipped rope.

"Ryan, what is that? Looks like some sort of campsite."

"Ah, that's an unauthorized site for itinerant Irish Travellers."

Billy looked quizzical.

"You know … gypsies. The government encourages farmers to allow them to live on these sites, but they're a bit of a problem for us."

"A problem?" Billy said noticing a tall man in a dark sweater and black fedora standing by the road watching cars pass.

"Aye, many Travellers spend summers on the road then halt as they like—carparks, public gardens, church lots, farmers' fields. I've heard some farmers, desperate to get rid of them so they can work their fields, have taken to spreading pig slurry whenever Travellers camp on their land." Ryan wrinkled his nose in disgust.

"Really." Billy didn't know what pig slurry was, but he guessed it must be smelly.

"Aye, and there's tension between Travellers and some of the locals because folks believe most Travellers are given to thievery and the rest live off the taxes of hardworking people. Few are employed and those who do work only have 'cash jobs' like laying tarmac on roads or selling scrap metal they collect. Most live on government social benefits. The government authorizes public housing and caravan halting sites for them but there's not enough official spaces so most of us tolerate the unauthorized sites in our neighborhoods." Ryan shrugged. "Travellers still say we discriminate against them."

"How so?"

"Travellers keep to themselves claiming they're disrespected by the rest of society. I suppose in some villages it's true, but not Beechgrove people. You'll sometimes see Travellers in our stores, cafes and pubs. We treat them humanely."

"Irish gypsies. Fancy that," Billy said. As the settlement disappeared from view he had relaxed into his pleasant musings when suddenly he was hurled forward when Ryan slammed on the brakes.

Not again!

"Damnation!" Ryan rolled down a window. "Bugger off, you *divil.*"

Billy peered through the insect-splattered windshield at a pair of soft brown eyes and a black muzzle leisurely chewing cud as if no one was around.

Ryan jumped from the truck, ran to the cow and slapped her several times on the rump until she turned and meandered off to the side of the road. He got back in the truck. "Bloody cows can't tell the road from a pasture. Probably got spooked at that faerie hill."

"Fairy hill?" Billy looked in the direction Ryan pointed.

"Now Billy, you haven't forgotten our Great Uncle Sean McCarthy who was lost to the faeries, so?"

"Lost to the fairies?" Billy had no recollection of great Uncle Sean McCarthy or fairies.

"Sure, he made the mistake of climbing a faerie hill after dark, something you should never do."

"Really? And why would that be?"

"Because that's when the small people are up and about playing the hornpipe and dancing."

"Uh huh."

Now the story goes that Great Uncle Sean joined their dancing, another thing you should never do."

Now the story got interesting. "Because ?"

"Because humans who dance with the Shee are lost." Ryan lowered his voice as if the small people on faerie hill might be listening. "No one ever saw Great Uncle Sean again."

Billy smiled. Fairy hill. Dancing small people. What a charming bit of Irish legend. He almost wished fairies really did exist.

Three miles later Billy saw a sign at the entrance to a small village that read Beechgrove printed beneath an image of a dark green beech tree. Below the village name Ryan read the Irish words aloud: "'Céad Míle Fáilte.' It means a hundred thousand welcomes."

"Nice," Billy said with a contented sigh.

At the edge of the village Billy spotted an exquisitely maintained grass field with H-shaped goals at each end. About a dozen or more young men wearing green and black uniforms and green helmets with some kind of metal face guards raced up and down the field swinging sticks at something on the ground. Ryan noticed him peering out the window and answered his question before he asked it.

"Hurling. A popular Irish sport. Our Beechgrove team won the championship this year. Our captain, Rory McScally accepted the cup with a speech so long the lot of us dozed off." Billy could hear the pride in Ryan's voice.

"Hurling. Sounds familiar. We may have teams in California," Billy said.

"Hurling is like a religion here in Beechgrove. It's one of the oldest Irish games—over 300 years old. My grandfather played, my father played, and I used to play." A note of nostalgia tinged Ryan's voice. "The idea of the game is for players to use those hurley—"

"Hurley?" Billy said.

"Aye, hurley. See those sticks curved outward on the ends. So, they use the hurley to drive that ball, called a sliotar, through the goals or over the bar to score." Ryan's explanation sounded as if he was a spectator cheering for a team. "Our girls play, too. Pretty much the same game but a different name, camogie."

"Never watched a game. I'd enjoy seeing one," Billy said.

"Good as done! I'll arrange it with Dr. McStarran, one of our coaches." Ryan said.

The village main street, barely wide enough for two cars to pass, was lined with a few pebbledash structures housing small shops—a pharmacy/post office, a deep pink colored B&B, a grocery and a white-washed pub advertising food, wine and spirits. A stone church, St. Brigid according to a sign, stood sentry over a small cemetery at the end of the street near a cobblestone square lined with benches and shade trees. Compared to San Francisco, Beechgrove was a pint-sized place. You could wander its entirety in a few minutes.

"Billy, did you see that pub we just passed?" Ryan spoke in an animated voice. "That's Mary McClone's Bar and Restaurant. She's a grand Irish lass and a dab hand in the kitchen is Mary. We'll pay her a visit tomorrow evening."

"Sounds great." Billy said anxious to try some good Irish bangers and mash. He noted a sparkle in Ryan's blue eyes at the mention of Mary McClone and wondered if Ryan might like more about the woman than her food. Ryan had lost his wife ten years ago and hadn't remarried. Could he have tired of life alone on a small farm?

They passed through Beechgrove almost as soon as they'd entered it and turned onto a paved boreen, a narrow country road lined with shrubs and drystone fences. More than once Ryan slowed the pickup to a crawl to allow sheep to cross the road. Near a junction he had to drive two of the truck's wheels up on a verge to allow a tractor pulling a wain to pass. Just another day in the Irish countryside, Billy mused contentedly.

As they bumped along Ryan pointed out several small parcels of land on which Holstein dairy cows grazed.

"Healthy looking cows," Billy said, though he knew nothing about bovine health.

"Aye," Ryan said. "Someday I plan to get myself a wee Moiley."

"Is that a breed of cow?" Billy asked.

"What?" Ryan jerked his face towards Billy and almost swerved off the boreen into a stone wall. "You've never heard of the famous Irish Moiled Cow? Why the rare breed is known throughout the world. It's indigenous to Ireland. We even have societies to protect it."

"I don't recall seeing any in San Francisco." Billy laughed at his own joke.

Billy noticed Ryan's pastures were interspersed with stone fences and straight rows of some kind of shrubs. "Why do you have these fences running through the middle of your pastures?"

"No fences running through my pastures," Ryan explained. "Each stone fence is a border between pastures owned by different farmers. Land Acts of the early 19th century granted an acre of land to tenant farmers. Some of them made it in farming, some didn't. Over the years my relatives bought the acre plots from farmers who couldn't make it. Many of the plots are not adjacent."

"And those rows of shrubs?" Billy said. "Some kind of Irish fruit?"

"You're looking at whins or gorse. Not for eating." Ryan laughed. "It's a dense evergreen shrub, very spiny and prickly. We use them as fences to keep cattle from leaving their pasture."

Fifteen slow minutes later Ryan turned into a gravel drive and parked in front of a pebbledash-coated stone farmhouse. As he got out of the car, a black and white Border collie jumped up to his chest greeting him with a series of sloppy kisses. "Enough," Ryan said scratching the dog's ears with both hands.

While Billy stepped from the pickup and looked around, Ryan grabbed his suitcase and motioned him to a gravel path bordered with early blooming daffodils that led to the cottage. A bench sat beside the cottage door in front of blooming pansies planted in four flowerpots anchored randomly to the cottage wall.

"Ryan," Billy said. "I had no idea you had such a green thumb."

Ryan reddened slightly and mumbled. "No green thumb for me. Mary McClone has the green thumb."

Mary McClone again. Billy wanted to enquire a bit more about her, but Ryan hurried ahead.

The collie sniffed at Billy's heels all the way to the house. They entered through an old-style Dutch half door. Billy's eyes wandered around the 300-year-old stone cottage—an open plan room with exposed beams, white-washed stone walls and floor. He wondered how many generations had lived in the ancient cottage and who might have built it. He would get answers to his questions tomorrow. Overcome with jet lag now, all he wanted to do was go to bed.

*

Billy Weston listened to rain pound the roof of the cottage. Not a great start to his first morning in nirvana. He sat at an oilcloth-covered table, the Border collie at his feet. Both he and the dog watched Ryan O'Rourke prepare tea on a small cook range next to an old beehive oven with an electric space heater sitting inside. "Where's the turf fire?" Billy asked.

"Most of us don't use turf anymore. Lot of environmental worries about the depletion of peat bogs." Ryan set two cups of tea and a plate of Irish shortbread biscuits on the table. He pulled out an old Súgan chair with a straw-rope seat, and with a loud grunt, dropped down opposite Billy. "Too much work to cut the peat, haul it from the bog, dry and stack it. Burns too fast and too smoky. No, the range is better."

Billy remembered warming himself next to a turf fire the last time he visited Belfast. So much for that. He hoped not too many other things had changed. He fingered an old Aran nickel-mounted pipe perched on the table next to an antique wood tobacco jar and smiled. Some of old Ireland still hangs on.

"You know, we had some excitement around here." Ryan stirred his tea and took a sip. "Last week a dead body turned up a few fields from here. Looks like Beechgrove's first murder."

"No!" Billy had come to Ireland seeking a kind of Gaelic version of Paradise Lost. He couldn't imagine a murder in this pristine environment. Murders happened in cities like San Francisco, Oakland, New York and Chicago not in this quiet village.

"Aye, Sean Kavanagh by name." Ryan crunched down on a shortbread biscuit scattering a dusty film of powdered sugar on the table.

"You sure this isn't one of your blarney stories?" Billy chuckled half hoping it was.

"No, it's the Lord's truth. If Liam Maguire hadn't decided to plow that field, we'd not have found Sean Kavanagh's wretched remains until God only knows when. Maguire spotted Kavanagh's red muffler and stopped his tractor just in the nick of time or he'd have plowed Sean right into the ground."

"Any suspects?" Billy reached for a biscuit.

"Nearly everyone in the village."

"Really?"

"Our area PSNI Chief Inspector has no idea where to begin investigating."

"PSNI?"

"The Police Service of Northern Ireland."

Ryan took another sip of tea then squinted at Billy. "No one deserved to die more than him. A scoundrel he was."

"How so?" His interest piqued, Billy's investigative nature kicked in.

"Kavanagh was the divil himself. Never a civil word to anyone. He was the only snake St. Paddy left in Ireland. Sure, and I could have offed him myself."

Chapter 4

The limo stopped in front of a one-story building on Naas Road in the western outskirts of Dublin. Cadigan Construction Tools, Ltd. printed in foot-high red letters identified it as the factory's corporate office. The swarthy limo driver hurried from the car and with a salacious grin opened the door for Lysi and Grace. Lysi felt his hungry eyes devouring them as they followed the short walkway to the building entrance.

"Grace," Lysi said. "That limo driver has ogled us ever since we left the Merrion."

"Yeah, well what do you expect? We're a couple of hotties. Especially me after my Merrion spa treatment this morning—full body massage, facial, manicure, pedicure. And that Indian head massage, whoa!"

"Worth getting up at five A.M. for?" Lysi asked.

"Oh yeah. After that flight from New York I was ready for a whole lot of pamper time. I feel great. I'm going to give Chess a real treat tonight."

"No need to share the details right now." Lysi hoped Grace could keep her mind off Chess long enough to plan the seminar.

They entered the Cadigan reception area through double glass doors. A receptionist with skin the color of rich espresso and big brown doe eyes raised a bottle blonde head from behind a computer monitor. "May I help you?"

"We have an appointment with Chesterfield Pennington at 4:30," Lysi said.

"Oh, yes. Chessie—" The receptionist's fingers flew to her lips and she giggled. "I mean Mr. Pennington. He said to have you wait in Mr. Murphy's office and he would be there soon." She pointed to an open door at the left of her desk.

"Chessie?" Grace's explosive outburst caused the receptionist to jump "It's Mr. Chesterfield to you."

Lysi saw Grace's nostrils flare and her eyes darken. She quickly hooked an arm through Grace's and dragged her into the office.

Grace jerked her arm from Lysi's hold. "Where does that big-boobed, bleached-out air head get off calling him 'Chessie?'" she said.

"Honey, it's nothing," Lysi said. "You know Chess would never even look at a gushy specimen like that. Now retract your claws and let's focus on our job." But Lysi realized it was indeed something. Grace, the love-'em-and-leave-'em poster child was jealous. Could Chess mean more to Grace than her usual boy toy?

Grace shot air through her teeth. "Okay. But this is not over."

"Right." A catastrophe averted for the moment. Lysi wondered if Chess would still reap the benefits of Grace's spa treatment tonight.

Lysi looked around the office. "Hmmm. Leather, tobacco, sports and liquor. Looks like a man's world."

"Not very subtle," Grace said. "Portable mini bar. Oversized leather couch. Big honking he-man desk."

Lysi pointed at three paintings of sweaty, bare-chested boxers sporting gloves poised ready to punch. "Why am I not surprised to see those?"

"Hey, the center one is Joe Louis, the Brown Bomber. He was world heavyweight champion for 12 years. My dad saw him fight in Madison Square Garden once." Grace's eyes sparkled. "I had no idea he was Irish."

Lysi laughed. "I'm not sure he is."

"He was American. Born in Alabama." They turned at the familiar voice. Chess, wearing a congenial smile, entered the office with two men and a woman. He didn't seem to notice Grace's icy glare. "Lysi ... Grace ... I hope we haven't kept you waiting too long."

Grace opened her mouth but Lysi, fearful of what Grace might say, jumped in first. "No, no. We just arrived."

"Please take a seat." Chess gestured towards a long conference table and waited until everyone sat. "Introductions first then down to business." Chess spoke in a formal business tone Lysi hadn't heard him use before. "May I present Lysi Weston and Grace Wright, Management Trainers with Stellar Corporate Development. Grace and Lysi nodded.

Chess pointed to a man with graying hair wearing a tweed suit jacket and an open-collared white shirt. The man sat leaning back with an arm draped over the back of his chair and an ankle resting on one knee. "Killian Murphy, Cadigan CEO," Chess said.

"Call me Killie. Nice to meet you girls," Killian Murphy said with a grin and a wink.

Lysi and Grace exchanged glances at his patronizing wink and use of the word "girls."

"Next to him is Caitlin O'Connor, the company's Executive Director of Human Resources," Chess said.

The dark-haired woman in a royal blue pantsuit that matched her serious blue eyes nodded and smiled. "So nice to meet you."

"Dylan Doyle is the Operations Supervisor," Chess said pointing to the second man.

Doyle nodded but didn't smile. Suntan pants and a work shirt with sleeves rolled up above the elbows tagged Dylan Doyle as a down-in-the-trenches kind of guy. Lysi noted the sparsely clad girlie tattoos on his arms.

"Caitlin." Chess turned the meeting over to O'Connor.

"As you can imagine, from the company name Cadigan's products have been directed toward a male market for years," Caitlin O'Connor began. "The company has recently hired about thirty women in jobs ranging from assembly to supervisorial positions. This brings me to the reason I needed to contract you to do a sexual harassment training session. In some departments male employees have had considerable difficulty transitioning to a female boss and female coworkers, and—"

"Ah Caitlin, what are you on about?" Dylan Doyle interrupted. "Sure a lot of this is in the imagination of female bosses unused to supervising males, and the girls on the floor knowing nothing about tools."

Caitlin O'Connor glanced at Doyle, raised an eyebrow and exhaled.

Lysi's eyes strayed to Killian Murphy. She didn't like his patriarchal grin. "Killian, where do you stand on this issue?" Lysi knew where he stood. An uninvolved CEO complying with a bellyaching employee's silly whim just to shut her up.

"Ah, I just want to keep the peace. Nothing's more irritating than whiney employees."

Lysi translated Killian's insensitive reference to "whiney employees" to mean "whiney women." Oh yes indeed. Cadigan Construction Tools, Ltd. needed a corporate training session on sexual harassment, alright.

"Brilliant, now." Killian Murphy stood, stretched and checked his watch. "I have an appointment. How about I let Caitlin show you girls around the plant and make arrangements for this ... training session."

"Aye." Dylan Doyle popped up from the table. "I got to get back on the yard."

"Uh-huh," Grace said. "You are busy little boys aren't you."

Neither man smiled. Chess shot Grace a warning look then said, "Caitlin after the tour, you can meet in here for your planning conference if you like."

Caitlin O'Connor led Lysi and Grace from the office onto a wide area of blacktop bordered by buildings on two sides and a car park full of large trucks opposite the office.

"The company produces cutting and drilling tools for the construction industries," Caitlin said.

Lysi looked quizzical. Grace looked bored.

Caitlin motioned towards two long Quonset hut-shaped buildings. "We design and manufacture cutting tools in Building 1—concrete chainsaws, road saws and grinders.

"Drilling tools are manufactured in Building 2—diamond blades, diamond core bits and core drills, porcelain tile drills and grinding cups. We also provide safety training in tool use."

"Interesting," Lysi said. Grace rolled her eyes.

"Let's take a walk through the buildings to give you a feel for the plant," Caitlin said.

Caitlin led them through both buildings and introduced them to the area supervisors. Men and women working on various levels of tool construction and assembly raised their heads but didn't acknowledge the visitors.

After the plant tour, Caitlin guided them into a small auditorium with plush theatre seats and a raised stage. Lysi envisioned Killian Murphy on the stage with his employees gathered together to hear him deliver an annual 'atta boy' talk for the purpose of motivating them to increase production.

Lysi sank onto a chair and Grace plopped down next to her, kicked off her spike heels and exhaled. "I thought that tour would never end. Let's get on with planning the sexual harassment training session."

Caitlin ran a video of the Cadigan manufacturing, sales and delivery process then ushered Lysi and Grace into a room off the auditorium where Cadigan products were on display. "Here are some examples of our tools," Caitlin said, naming each tool and explaining its function.

Lysi felt inundated by the flood of information Caitlin provided. She knew Grace had already stopped listening back in Building 1.

"You really know your company," Lysi said anxious to turn to a familiar topic. "Now let's talk about the seminar."

"You saw some indication of the problem when we first met in the office," Caitlin said with exasperation. "Killian doesn't see a problem. He listens to complaints then does nothing. Dylan just wants all women out. He considers construction tools a male purview. When women complain about male workers making crude comments and even touching them inappropriately, Dylan says the guys are just being friendly. When males hang vulgar calendars and posters in the break room, he says boys will be boys. When women complain about men making derogatory comments about their female supervisors and female colleagues, Dylan tells them not to be so sensitive, that they have to expect these things in this kind of job. He tells complainers if they can't take life in a man's world, then they should get out."

"Sounds like Dylan could use a little lesson in manners," Grace said. "I think I could provide some individualized sensitivity training for him. Where is he?"

"Grace, not now." Lysi knew Dylan Doyle would be lucky to survive Grace's individualized sensitivity training.

The three women scheduled a week's training session, two full days for managers and supervisors to learn to identify sexual harassment and develop a plan to eradicate it. Three half days of worker release time to attend sessions that would enable them to understand that sexual harassment includes groping, fondling, lewd comments, suggestive jokes, and obscene graffiti. They would train all employees in appropriate behavior in the workplace.

"Sounds grand," Caitlin said.

As Lysi and Grace passed through the lobby area the receptionist flashed a gushy smile. "Have a nice—"

"Shut up, gush mouth," Grace said under her breath.

Chapter 5

Mary McClone's pub was everything Billy Weston had envisioned. A golden den of twinkling lights and antique mirrors that gilded the white vaulted ceilings. Wide plank floors darkened by years of smoke and boots. A roaring turf fire and a fiddler playing traditional Irish music completed Billy's image of a real Irish pub.

"Perfect," he said taking in the warmth and smoky sweet smell of burning peat mixed with the yeasty scent of beer. The oniony mouth-watering aroma of the evening's special—sausage and creamy champ—generated a memory of his mother glopping a heaping spoon full of the buttery mashed potatoes and onions onto his plate and saying, "Eat. Talk doesn't fill the empty stomach."

Billy scanned the comical pub posters that competed for space on the wood-paneled walls. He laughed out loud at a large poster of Mona Lia with white foam on her upper lip holding a beer with a caption that read "Got beer?" Is nothing sacred? Next to Mona Lisa hung a smaller poster of two very tipsy identical leprechauns, with the words "Party 'til you see double." On the wall above the bar, Billy spotted a colorful print of two bottles of green beer, a leprechaun in each bottle with the words "St Paddy's Brewing Company, a little leprechaun in every swig" scrawled beneath them.

Ryan O'Rourke pushed his way onto a bench at a crowded table. "Move over and make room for two lads who can handle more pints than the lot of you put together without getting blootered."

"Blootered?" Billy said.

All eyes fell on Billy. After a silent beat a volley of shouts rose from the men gathered at the table. "Soused, smashed, plastered, tanked, sloshed, crocked, legless."

Billy raised his hand in a cop's stop-the-traffic position and added, "Drunk."

Rough hands slapped the table along with raucous laughter and approving nods.

"Meet my cousin Billy Weston," Ryan said. "Come all the way from America to try our good Irish stout."

Four men in wool sweaters, two from each side of the rough wood table stood, leaned forward and took turns shaking Billy's hand. No sooner had Billy sat then a tousle haired, twenty-something waiter plopped pints in front of him and Ryan. Billy picked up his glass and took a sip.

"Ah, Holy Mother Mary," shouted a red-cheeked young man seated next to Billy. "Ryan, you've not had the decency to show your own flesh and blood the proper way to drink a Guinness?"

Everyone at the table moaned and two men crossed themselves.

"Billy, meet Liam Maguire who fancies himself a master of the art of imbibing, so he does," Ryan said.

Billy remembered the name Liam Maguire, the guy Ryan had told him discovered the dead body while plowing his field. At the possibility of a murder, Billy's old D.A. investigative instinct kicked in and he made a mental note to talk to Ryan about the Kavanagh cadaver.

"So, the educating of Billy Weston falls to me." Liam Maguire snatched Billy's mug from him and banged it on the table spilling bubbly froth down the side of the glass.

Liam pointed to the mug. "Lesson one: keep your eyes on the glass, Billy."

Billy watched as the beer darkened and the rest of the froth bubbled to the top.

"Now, you see that rich dark color? Now you know your Guinness is ready to drink," Liam said.

Billy nodded and reached for the glass.

"Liam grabbed Billy's beer just as his fingers touched the glass. "Lesson two: Watch." Liam gulped down at least a quarter of Billy's Guinness and swiped the back of his hand across his mouth. "Guinness is not for sipping. It's for swigging. Now, would you be needin' another demonstration, Billy Weston?"

Billy laughed. He grabbed his beer from Liam's hand. "No need. I think I got it."

"Well then, get you round that," Liam said. "sláinte."

"Sláinte," Billy repeated the toast to good health and took a big gulp that left less than a quarter of beer in the glass. "The next round is on me."

Liam slapped Billy on the back amid boisterous laughter and shouts of "Good lad. Then the next shout is yours."

A gust of cold air swept through the room when the pub door opened revealing a tall man in a black sweater and black fedora. The man's thin face was cadaverous, but his features were sharp. Billy recognized the man he'd seen standing by the road when Ryan drove past the gypsy camp.

The Traveller didn't enter but his searching eyes swept around the room then he said in a Derry accent, "My brother Paddy is missing. Have any of you seen him?"

No one responded.

"If he should turn up, I'd appreciate you letting me know." The Traveller nodded then turned and disappeared out the door.

Billy turned curious eyes to Ryan.

"His name is Michael Doherty. A good enough lad. Works when he can. Now his brother, Paddy— a dodgy sort, usually up to no good. Michael is always having to clean up after him." Ryan shook his head.

Billy wanted to know more but his attention was drawn to a pleasingly plump, middle-aged woman with silver-streaked red hair wearing a ruffled green apron and a giant grin. She butted, rump first through swinging doors from a kitchen located to the left of the bar. She carried a large wicker basket filled with snack-size packages of Tayto cheese & onion crisps and stationed herself behind the oak bar beside a larger than life black and white Guinness Toucan with a brilliant orange bill.

"Ryan O'Rourke, would you be willin' to pass around these crisps to everyone? On the house, of course. We've got something to celebrate tonight."

Ryan jumped to his feet nearly falling backward over the bench and his cheeks turned crimson. "It'd be my pleasure, Mary."

Billy caught Ryan's schoolboy crush behavior. He could see what attracted Ryan to Mary. Her dimpled cheeks, twinkling blue eyes and soft curves would catch any man's eye. A comfortable woman, the kind to warm a man's bed and his heart.

Billy had asked about Mary McClone's pub on the way to the village from Ryan's cottage. Ryan, always ready with a good story, went into some historical detail. He explained that Mary McClone's great grandmother, Ada, emigrated to Canada and worked as an au pair for a wealthy family for many years. When the mother passed, she bequeathed a large sum of money to Ada who returned to Beechgrove, purchased a wee bit of land on Main Street and had a restaurant built with living quarters upstairs.

On Sunday afternoons Ada and her two daughters dressed up in formals and served tea with wee sandwiches, scones and biscuits. People came from as far off as Belfast to partake of the tea. The daughters continued the tradition after Ada passed until one of them married and moved to Australia. The remaining daughter, Mary's mother, turned the restaurant into a pub. Mary has managed it ever since."

Ryan took the basket of crisps from Mary and distributed them to eager pub patrons.

"And what would we be celebrating Mary McClone?" The question came from a bearded man seated by the wall under a green poster of a leprechaun holding a pint. Black letters beneath the Leprechaun read: "Experienced beer drinkers only."

Everyone burst out laughing at the question. Billy didn't laugh. The question seemed perfectly reasonable to him and he wanted to know the answer.

"Could it be the recent passing of the good Sean Kavanagh?" This question came from an elderly woman seated at a table near Billy, holding a pint aloft. The comment ignited another round of laughter.

"Now how did you know that?" Mary asked. She crossed herself, bowed her head and failed to stifle a grin. "I'm thinking it isn't proper to joke about the dead. So, before you open your crisps, would anyone be willin' to say a kind word about the recently departed Sean Kavanagh?"

Mary raised her eyes and looked around the room. Not a sound. Even the fiddler lowered his bow. "Well then. I'll say a word. I appreciate that Sean Kavanagh was good enough to die and leave the fine people of Beechgrove in peace. Sure, and he's gone to his well-deserved reward."

Again, rollicking laughter as the customers opened their crisps amid several comments. "Thank you, Sean, for providing an occasion for the crisps" and "Hell will welcome you, Sean" and "We'll be missing you like a rotted tooth." A chorus of "Here, Here," followed each comment.

Ryan returned to the table and Billy immediately asked about what he had witnessed.

"Look around this room, Billy. Pick anyone. They all have their own reason to celebrate the demise of Sean Kavanagh."

Nancy Curteman

Chapter 6

Grace could feel Chess watching as she swirled the ice in her drink. She didn't look at him but kept her eyes glued to the deep green walls in Merrion's No. 23 cocktail lounge. The dark room and heavy furniture seemed to reflect her downcast mood. She responded in monosyllables to every effort Chess made to engage her in conversation.

All evening images of the gushy receptionist's gooey smile, big vacant brown eyes and dangling bleached-out curls kept parading through Grace's mind. And that little girl voice purring, 'Chessie.' How saccharine was that? How could Chess even look at a woman like her?

After a few more attempts at light conversation Chess lapsed into an awkward silence, downed his drink and signaled the waiter. He gestured at Grace's almost empty glass. "Another?"

Grace shook her head. "No."

When Chess reached for her hand, she pulled it away and picked up her drink. Chess knitted his brow and blinked several times. "Grace, you seem so far away. Are you okay?"

"I'm fine, Chess." She still didn't look at him. Grace was not fine. She grappled with unfamiliar, conflicting feelings. She tried to work on herself. What had happened to her carefree philosophy—enjoy men but keep it casual? The one time she'd deviated from this protective philosophy she almost ended up married to an obsessive-compulsive, egocentric South African businessman. Well thank goodness the subject of marriage hadn't come up with Chess.

The words of a favorite show tune played in her mind, "When I'm not with the man I love, I love the man I'm with." Hey, what Chess did when she wasn't with him was his business. What she did when Chess wasn't around was her business. Right? Out of sight out of mind. Don't get serious. Don't commit. Don't care. Don't ... But she did care, damn it. And she hated that she cared.

The waiter appeared wearing a white jacket, a comical green bowtie and a jovial smile that irritated the hell out of Grace.

"Yes, sir?" he said to Chess as his admiring eyes drifted to Grace. She'd worn a figure-hugging black dress with a plunging neckline that exposed a tantalizing bit of cleavage. A rhinestone belt accented her small waist. She wanted Chess to see what he might lose.

Chess pointed to his glass. "One more scotch, and this time make it neat and a double." His tone broadcasted growing frustration.

The waiter nodded toward Grace's empty glass. Chess shook his head and waved him off.

Grace wondered if the waiter had detected the coolness between Chess and her. She shrugged. Didn't matter. Not anymore.

Why did she care about that stupid woman calling Chess 'Chessie?' Grace gave herself a mental slap. She needed to get centered. Of course, Lysi was right. Chess probably hadn't even noticed that wad of cotton candy and if he had, she probably meant nothing to him. Grace assumed Chess considered Cadigan employees business acquaintances like any of his other accounts. Still, she'd seen fawning women like that receptionist in action with men before. First the big fluttery cow eyes, then the soft stroke on the guy's arm accompanied by breathy compliments about his big muscles or beautiful smile or brilliant comments. Yuk! What sickened Grace was that even intelligent men like Chess almost always seemed to fall for the syrupy slop.

The waiter set a scotch in front of Chess. "Run a tab," Chess said and took a big swallow of his drink. He leaned back, looked at Grace and shook his head.

On a rational level Grace understood Chess' frustration. They hadn't seen each other for over a month while she visited her family in Harlem, and he negotiated plans for the Cadigan project in Dublin. Her eyes sparked. Plenty of time for him to get to know the bimbo. She exhaled through her teeth. Stop! she shouted in her head.

Grace knew she should stop. But she couldn't. She detested the way she felt. No way should she feel competition with that moronic, bleached out blonde dodo bird. But she did.

"So ... how do you like working with Cadigan people?" Grace ventured without making eye contact with Chess.

"I like most of them, but they could treat their female employees better."

Grace could tell from Chess' expression that he reasoned he'd said just the thing she would like to hear. Normally he would be right, but not this time. That ditsy receptionist deserved to be walked on. "So, you feel sympathy for the women?"

"Yeah, the men treat them like they don't know anything. The women I talked to seem as smart and even smarter than the men." Chess looked like he'd found the perfect words to please Grace.

Wrong!

"Oh yeah, how about that lusty, busty, brainless receptionist. The one who calls you, 'Chessie?'" There, she said it.

Chess' eyes widened. Grace could see his confusion was real. After a moment he said, "You mean that redhead who sits at the front desk?"

Redhead. Oh no. He hadn't even paid enough attention to her to notice her hair color. Oh God. I should have listened to Lysi. Grace struggled to hide the embarrassment coloring her cheeks while at the same time an ocean of relief flooded her body.

Chess stared at her in silence as a trace of a smile tickled the corner of his mouth. His eyes almost twinkled. He leaned close to Grace and planted a kiss on her burning cheek.

"I ... a ... that is ...." Grace struggled to find words to excuse her outburst about the receptionist.

"Grace, you're jealous!" Chess laughed so loudly couples at the other tables turned to see the ruckus.

"No I'm not."

"Yeah, come to think of it that little receptionist is kind of cute. I'm not really into red-haired black women, but I think it looks fetching on her." Chess jiggled his eyebrows up and down several times.

"Stop it Chess. I was just testing to see if you included lower-caste women in your opinion of the high level of Cadigan women employees' intelligence." That excuse sounded weak and nasty even to Grace. She wished she could take back the words, but it was too late.

Chess reached over and took her hand. This time she didn't pull away. His warm touch felt like a low-voltage current as he casually rubbed her fingers. She felt the smoldering sexual signals that always made the air crackle between them.

"I think you're still recovering from jet lag. Shall we go up to the room?" He smiled and added in an erotic whisper, "I can offer my version of a little nightcap to help you sleep."

Grace knew what he meant and felt her body tense at the thought. She was hungry for him.

*

In the elevator Chess pulled Grace close and kissed her. She caught the fragrance of his soap, the trace of mint on his breath, the spicy tones of his aftershave. By the time they got to the room, they were both breathing hard. Grace barely got the door closed before Chess was unzipping her dress, kissing her lips, neck and shoulders

She unbuttoned his shirt, pulled it open, and ran her fingers through the hair on his muscular chest.

Somehow, they made it to the bed. They made love more than once. At first, there was so much hunger, so much heat. Then he raised himself up on his elbow and kissed her long and sweet and it began all over again. This time a slow rise to almost intolerable intensity.

"Grace, I've never wanted anyone the way I want you," Chess whispered between heavy breaths. "Never forget that."

She nodded just before her mind emptied of all thought replaced by a sudden gust of pure incredible sensation.

Chapter 7

An overcast sky and moisture-laden breeze threatened a chilly day. Hoping for a little sunshine, Lysi and Maynard braved a stroll through the cobble stone streets of Dublin's Temple Bar section.

"This area reminds me of New Orleans' French quarter with all the historic buildings, theatres, galleries, and pubs," Lysi said, her voice oozing with enthusiasm.

Maynard smiled and seemed to enjoy Lysi's excitement.

"And look at all those unique shops. You can find everything from clothes to jewelry to souvenirs and antiques." Lysi's head shifted from side to side taking in window boxes filled with daffodils and pansies, colorful bunting-decorated pubs and the plaques on old buildings listing construction dates and titles. Live music filled the air as buskers and street performers entertained appreciative crowds of adults and rosy-cheeked children on every corner.

When they reached Grafton, Dublin's world-famous shopping street, Lysi remarked on all the expensive, high-end stores. "This is a shopper's paradise. Grace will love this street."

Maynard looked up at the gray clouds darkening the sky. "May not be the best day for shopping."

"Right, I may need an umbrella," Lysi said, noticing the entrance to Brown Thomas Department store, the Irish version of Selfridges. "Let's pop in here and see what's available."

When they left the store a short time later, Lysi did not have an umbrella. She hadn't even looked for one, but Maynard sported a new merino wool sweater under his Bush jacket. He'd fought against the purchase but Lysi insisted. "You didn't plan to buy an umbrella at all, did you?" he said.

"Now why do you think that," Lysi said with a wink.

Maynard had to admit he felt much warmer.

"On to more important things," Lysi said. "I discovered this street was named after Charles II's illegitimate son, Henry, Duke of Grafton." She held up a green guidebook. As usual she had done research on her destination city and, as usual Maynard was always a good audience for her.

"Interesting," he said. "Those kings had it pretty good with all those mistresses."

Lysi gave him a playful slap and poked her nose into her guidebook. "Grafton Street runs from Fusilier's Arch of St. Stephen's Green to College Green near Trinity College. St Stephen's Green is a Victorian park started in 1663." She looked up at Maynard, a surprised expression on her face. "Wow, says here there are bullet holes on the Fusilier's Arch from the 1916 Easter Rising when the Irish Citizen's Army tried to overthrow the British powers."

Eyes back on her book and not on the street, she stumbled on an uneven cobblestone. Maynard caught her arm to steady her. "Lysi, I want to hear what you learned about Dublin, but it'd be better to wait until we're sitting down."

Lysi sighed and tucked her book into an oversized purse. "You're right."

Maynard stopped at one of the flower vendors, bought a nosegay of pansies and handed it to her. "Thanks for the sweater."

She smiled and squeezed his arm.

The sun parted the clouds and its warm rays dried the breeze. They entered a small café, found a vacant table by a window, and did a little people watching as they sipped lattes. The sun's glow seemed to lighten the spirits of passersby who peeled off their jackets and scarves. A street musician appeared strumming his guitar and singing an Irish folk song.

"He's singing 'Molly Malone,'" Lysi said. "That's the unofficial hymn of Dublin. According to my guide, the Dubliners adopted it because of the first line—'In Dublin fair city where girls are so pretty'. The story goes Molly sold fish right here on Grafton Street in the 17th century."

"Australians know the song and story," Maynard said. He took a sip of latte then returned to a topic he'd mentioned earlier. "Are you sure you're all right with me doing an overnight car trip with Chess? I'm really interested in seeing one of the Irish sheep stations in Galway."

It tickled Lysi to hear Maynard call Irish sheep farms 'stations.' The comparison of Australia's 300,000-acre sheep stations with Ireland's average 80-acre farms seemed ludicrous.

"You know Galway's Ireland's second biggest sheep raising county," Maynard continued. "Chess says we'll see the indigenous Galway sheep." Maynard leaned forward. "And March is the beginning of the lambing season on the Hillary Guest Farm where we'll be staying."

"No problem," Lysi said. "I have to get with Grace to finalize our Cadigan presentation. I also plan to drag her to Dublin Castle." She flipped to a bookmarked page in her guidebook. "It's a Norman castle built in 1230. Imagine that! It—"

Lysi's cellphone chirped. She checked the screen. "It's Billy." She put the phone on speaker.

"Hey Lysi. You've got to come to Beechgrove for St. Paddy's week. I'm staying with our cousin in a 300-year-old stone cottage. You got to see it."

"Well—" Lysi tried to get a word or two in but Billy didn't seem to hear her.

"Bring Grace. She'll get a big kick out of pub life here. They got this great little pub called Mary McClone's. It's got an inn above it. You could spend the week there."

Lysi's brain immediately began to tick off the pros and cons of a visit to Belfast. She'd planned a visit to Dublin Castle and shopping with Grace. Two things not high on Maynard's to-do list. While he was gone would be a good time for her to visit the castle and shop. Best not waste the opportunity. But … while Maynard was off on an overnight excursion would be a good time to visit Belfast and meet her distant relatives.

No, not a good idea. There's work to do on the upcoming management training assignment. But ... on the other hand, if Grace came along, what would prevent them from taking a couple of hours out to polish their presentation.

No, bad timing. Grace might be afraid to leave Chess alone in Dublin with that silly receptionist. But ... it might be good for Grace to stop moping and get away for a little fun.

Definitely no. She wanted to visit the Northern Ireland city with Maynard. She'd visited Belfast many years ago with her father and was anxious to share it with Maynard. Also, it would be nice to celebrate St. Patrick's Day with Maynard. But ... couldn't Maynard come after he returned from his overnight?

"Well, Lysi," Billy said. "Are you coming?"

Lysi hesitated. "I ... I don't know. I ... "

Maynard nodded approval several times.

"I guess I'll come," Lysi said.

"Good," Billy said. "I'll have a special surprise for you when you arrive."

Chapter 8

Billy downed his last bite of porridge and spooned up the rest of the thick cream remaining in the bowl. He could smell bacon cooking in the kitchen of the small Corner Cafe and debated asking Ryan to order a couple of slices.

"Well now," Ryan said. "You did a grand job of finishing that porridge. Would you be ready to have a go at a wee Ulster Fry now?"

"You bet your shillelagh." Billy felt relief that he hadn't had to ask for a couple more slices of bacon. Didn't want to seem too pushy.

Billy liked the casual atmosphere of the restaurant—day's specials scribbled on a chalkboard, small wood tables, unmatched chairs painted blue, white and yellow—a local hangout.

A young waiter still in his teens appeared holding two large plates. "Two Ulster Frys. Enjoy them but no need to lick your plates. We have more."

Billy stared at the plate the waiter set in front of him. It wasn't a wee plate at all. It was the size of a Thanksgiving turkey platter. The two eggs, thick bacon strips, sausage, and tomatoes were familiar to him, but he had no idea what the slice of stiff white stuff was nor what kind of strange triangle-shaped bread lay on his plate. He poked his fork in the white stuff. "Tell me about this."

Ryan smiled. "Why, that's white pudding. Delicious. A mix of pork and fat, suet, bread and oatmeal. You got two kinds of fried bread there, soda farls and potato farls."

Well, Billy thought as he attacked the fat-laden feast, this is a heart attack in the making. A big eater as evidenced by his ample stomach, he still had difficulty finishing the "wee" Ulster Fry. He didn't look forward to lunch.

On the drive home from Beechgrove Ryan and Billy passed a plot of land with a for sale sign posted on it. A stone wall separated it from the adjacent fields. An old shed stood a few meters off the road with a series of empty bins in front of it. A sign on the shed read "Saxon Potatoes Here." A tractor that looked as if it had stalled in the middle of plowing, sat idle in the field.

"That's Liam Maguire's place. Sean Kavanagh put it up for sale." Ryan spit out Kavanagh's name. "Death was too good for that gobshite."

Billy flashed Ryan a questioning look.

Ryan pulled the Ford pickup to the side of the road. The old engine coughed and sputtered before shutting down.

"See that tree in the center section of the field?" Ryan said pointing to a tree about ten feet tall with dark green leaves. "That's the reason Kavanagh's burning in hell."

Billy's eyebrows shot up at Ryan's weird comment. He stared at the tree, the only one in the field. He noticed a large boulder near the tree's gnarled trunk. Tall grass grew around the tree while the rest of the field was perfectly cultivated. Curious. Why had the farmer plowed the entire field leaving a circular area around the tree untouched?

"You need to explain that a bit more," Billy said.

"Ah Billy. Have you been away so long that the faery trees have faded from your brain?"

"Refresh me," Billy said.

"Throughout Northern Ireland we have untouchable trees that have stood alone unharmed for generations. We call them the Faery Thorn. They often sit on a small rise we call a faery hill. The base of the faery tree is piled high with stones just to make sure no one dares disturb it."

Ryan lowered his voice. "Each tree guards a hallowed place, the entry to the faery world. That's why farmers never cut them down but always plow around them."

Scary trees, fairies, other worlds. Billy couldn't tell if Ryan was kidding or serious. He decided to turn the conversation back to Kavanagh.

"What would a tree have to do with Kavanagh's death?"

"Misfortune visits those who risk disturbing the faery tree. Kavanagh disrespected it. Liam Maguire says he saw him kick the boulder, rip a branch from the tree, toss it in the dirt and stomp on it."

"Oh?'" Billy said.

"After crushing the branch, Kavanagh shouted up to the Heavens that the existence of faeries was nothing more than a ridiculous Irish myth." Ryan shook his head. "Sure and the faeries had to have heard him."

"Why do you say that?"

Ryan lowered his voice to barely a whisper and looked deep into Billy's eyes. "Because not long after that Kavanagh's body turned up dead in this very field."

"So you think the faeries murdered him?" Billy sounded incredulous.

"Aye, they have their ways of seeing to a death—accidents, sickness, murders."

Billy, accustomed to dealing with concrete facts as prosecutor, did not feel comfortable with the idea of fairies committing murder. He did have an interest in the illegal sale of land.

"Okay, another question. How could this Kavanagh have put a farm that didn't belong to him up for sale?" The more Billy heard about Sean Kavanagh the less he liked him.

"I'll do better than answer your question," Ryan said. "You'll be wanting to ask Liam MaGuire himself. His father owns the plot next door. Liam had to move in with his dad when he lost his land. We'll call on him. Liam can tell you the story. I'll just say Liam thinks he'll soon end up a murder suspect. Being a district attorney and all maybe you can help him."

Billy remembered Liam MaGuire from the beer-drinking lesson in the pub. He had liked him. But, would he be able to help him?

*

Liam brought a chair from the kitchen and sat on it facing Ryan and Billy who sat on a well-used faux leather couch in the small living room. Liam's father, a slim wiry, sun-burned man running to bald, placed two cups of tea and a tray of biscuits on the coffee table. Billy was ready for the tea. He hoped it would dilute the fat from the Ulster Fry.

"Liam," Billy said. "Ryan tells me you're having some legal problems. I'm a retired district attorney. Maybe I can offer some advice."

"I'm thinking I'll soon be accused of murder. It's me own fault for trusting a cheating rogue like Kavanagh." Liam spoke in a working-class dialect.

"How's that?" Billy said.

"I ran onto hard times. Couldn't make me land payment to the bank because of a small harvest. I grow potatoes—mainly Saxons and a few acres of Lumpers. Kavanagh loaned me money to pay me mortgage and buy seed potatoes. The next year the harvest was better but still small. I couldn't pay Kavanagh's loan. Could barely pay the bank mortgage."

"We could have paid the principal on Kavanagh's loan but the interest was too much," Liam's father said.

Liam nodded. "Kavanagh said he'd give me a year to pay if I put up me land as collateral. Well with the increased size of the loan due to the added interest, I couldn't pay. He took me land and I had to move in with me da."

Billy frowned. "Liam, if the loan wasn't collateralized to begin with, the lender can't take the land.

Liam looked incredulous, furrowed his brow and scratched his head. "It was a gentleman's agreement. We shook hands on it."

Billy stared back at Liam with the same incredulous expression. No use trying to reason him out of that position. Just deal with the situation that exists.

"Liam, you found the body?" Billy said.

"In me da's field. I was plowing and I spied a bit of red cloth a few yards in front of me plow. I stopped and ran to it. I saw a body. I turned it over to see if I could help. It was himself. Sean Kavanagh. Dead."

"What did you do then?"

"I called 999 and a PSNI officer from the Serious Crimes department came."

"Go on."

"They put Kavanagh in a bag and an ambulance took him away. They put crime tape around the area.

"That's pretty standard," Billy said.

"The PSNI know about Kavanagh taking me land. The whole village knows." Liam hung his head. "I think they'll be accusing me of killing him."

Billy did not tell Liam MaGuire he thought there was a very good chance he would become a murder suspect.

Nancy Curteman

Chapter 9

Lysi and Grace stood outside the front entrance to the Merrion Hotel and scrutinized the shiny red compact Volkswagen Chess had rented for them. Lysi knew he'd rented it under protest, having failed in his frantic effort to talk Grace and her into taking the train to Belfast instead of driving. Lysi felt a tiny pang of guilt when she recalled his futile attempts to deter them, but the adventure of driving in a foreign country trumped a boring train ride.

When he'd said the more than two-hour drive would exhaust them, Lysi assured him they'd stop for tea along the way.

When he warned them about the poorly marked road direction signs, Lysi pulled out her phone and showed him the Google Maps UK/Ireland navigation app she'd bought in the U.S.

When he cautioned them about the difficulty of driving on the left side of the road and added that the Irish were notorious for their reckless driving habits, Grace told him she'd driven on the left in South Africa and joked that she could out-reckless drive any Irishman on the road.

When he raised his voice and produced a frustrated litany of the less-than-perfect road conditions—narrow lanes, sharp curves, steep hills, thick shrubbery, deep potholes, grass medians, livestock, cyclists, pedestrians—Grace laughed. She asked if he'd ever driven in a South African township, and asserted she'd spent a lot of time on comparable roads dodging animals and people when she and Lysi visited an old college roommate in Cape Town's Ikhaya Township. Chess admitted he'd never driven in South Africa but got the picture.

Lysi informed him he was describing R-Route and L-Local roads. She pointed out they'd be driving on N1, a primary road and M1, a motorway. Both roads were paved and had at least two lanes in each direction.

Thwarted at every turn Chess had thrown in the towel and rented the safest car he could find.

"Pretty nice," Lysi said circling the car. "Ya done good, Chess, honey."

He didn't smile but tightened his lips and remained silent.

Lysi kissed him on the cheek. "Don't worry, I'll take good care of Grace."

"It's not Grace I'm worried about, it's you. Just don't let her behind the wheel," he said, shaking his finger in warning.

"Love the color," Grace said completing her circuit around the car. "Can't wait to drive this baby. Color matches my outfit." Grace's shimmery silk jumpsuit almost outshone the gleaming car.

"It's all yours," Lysi said to Grace, avoiding eye contact with Chess. "I'll navigate."

They slid into the front seats of the Volkswagen.

Chess shook his head and shot a loud burst of air through his teeth. He tossed their overnight bags into the backseat, went to Lysi's window and handed her an envelope. "This is permission from the rental agency to take the car into Northern Ireland. It's illegal to cross the border in a rented car without it."

He went around the car to Grace's window. "I know it's ludicrous to say this but drive carefully."

"Yeah, yeah," Grace said. "You know me."

"That's the problem." He gave Grace a quick kiss.

Lysi set Belfast as the destination on her phone. Grace pressed on the brake, pumped the clutch and caressed the standard shift knob with the loving tenderness a mother reserves for a newborn. "I adore driving a stick shift. So much more zip."

Chess swallowed hard.

He watched Grace finger all the essential control knobs and locate the dials. "Windshield wiper, heater, radio, fuel gauge," she said. "I'm ready to take command."

"Wait a minute Grace. Aren't you forgetting something?" Chess grasped the window ledge as if he could prevent the car from moving.

"Don't think so." Grace perused the dashboard and smiled at Chess. "Nope."

"The speedometer, Grace. The speedometer." Sweat broke out on Chess' forehead.

"Oh, right. I knew that."

Grace started the engine, shifted into gear and peeled away from the curb leaving black streaks on the pavement. Chess lowered his head into his hands and shook it.

The doorman came down the steps and stood next to Chess. In a consoling voice he said, "Not to worry, sir. I'm sure they'll be fine."

Lysi looked over at Grace with affection, happy to see her back to her old self. She'd encouraged Grace to make the trip in hopes of getting her mind off the "Chessie" incident. It hadn't been necessary. Grace said the whole thing had been a silly mistake, that Chess hadn't even noticed the receptionist.

"Get this, he thought the bimbo had red hair," Grace had guffawed. "I can't believe he missed that bleached out pile of straw on her head."

Lysi tilted her seat back and relaxed. Everything had worked out just fine for the trip. Chess and Grace had resolved their misunderstanding. Maynard would be gone on the Galway overnight trip with Chess. Even the weather cooperated—cool and sunny. Yes, a perfect time for her to go to Belfast.

Lysi's contented state was short-lived. As soon as Grace hit the M1 Motorway she pushed the car to the maximum speed limit of 120 km/h and kept it at that speed for the next 79 kilometers except when someone passed her. Then she sped up to match that car's speed. Lysi tried to keep her mind off Grace's driving by focusing on the Irish countryside as they passed through flat fields of farmland and low rolling hills of grain. Green shrubs alternated with flaming yellow furze along the motorway. Lovely.

*

After about an hour of driving, Grace said she needed a potty break. She took the next exit, Julianstown, toward the town of Drogheda.

"Over there." Lysi pointed to a small café with a gravel parking lot in front. "We can grab a quick coffee and get right back on the motorway without getting lost."

Grace swerved into one of the four parking spaces in front of the Celtic Café.

A bell over the door jangled as they entered the café. It was empty except for two teenage boys who cast bored glances at them before turning back to their sandwiches. Grace found her way to the unisex bathroom while Lysi sat at the counter and studied a menu on the wall—King Crisp Sandwich, Fifteens, Coddle, Black Pudding, Taytos. Unfamiliar with the fare she decided to stick with tea.

A few minutes later Grace returned with a disgusted look on her face, "Yuk. The john's seat was up."

A waiter who looked about ten years old wiped the countertop in front of them with a well-used rag and said, "What'll it be?" Lysi ordered a cup of tea. Grace ordered Irish coffee.

"No Grace," Lysi said. "No alcohol."

"Hey, in Ireland you order Irish coffee. Right?" she said to the kid waiter.

"I would. It's almost our national drink." The young waiter grinned flashing a dimple in each cheek.

"Okay. Then I'll drive." Lysi knew Grace would rather starve than give up the wheel.

"Forget it," Grace said. "Plain coffee."

The waiter shrugged.

After they finished their drinks and returned to the car, Grace started toward the entrance to the Motorway then reversed and headed toward Drogheda civic center. Lysi looked confused.

"Just a quick tour," Grace said. "I want to get a look at one of the oldest towns in Ireland."

"We'll get lost." Lysi said. It surprised her that Grace had even listened to the description of Drogheda when Lysi read it to her.

"No, I've got a great sense of direction."

Lysi resignedly opened her tour book again and read to Grace. "Okay, since we're going to get lost anyway, here's a Drogheda site worth seeing: Millmount Fort, an old Norman castle built before 1186."

"Where is it?"

"Up there." Lysi pointed to a giant concrete structure atop a huge grassy mound so large it was probably visible from anywhere in the city.

Lysi read that the highlight of the old fort was a museum that housed a unique collection of old Guild Banners more than 200 years old. The collection included weavers', carpenters', shoemakers', and Boyne Fishermens' banners.

"Let's hit the museum," Lysi said once they'd arrived at the fort. She headed towards it. Grace reluctantly lagged behind until she spotted the craft studios.

"Hey, look at that," she said. "Jewelry and hand painted silks. You go ahead to the museum. I'll be along."

Lysi knew once Grace went into the craft shops she'd never get to the museum. "Is shopping all you ever think about?"

"No, I also think about sex—sometimes even when I'm shopping."

"Not funny, Grace. I'll meet you in the jewelry shop in about an hour."

*

They had had no trouble finding Millmount Fort because perched on a mound all you needed to do was look up. They had simply followed Mary Street up to it.

Getting back to the highway was not so easy. As soon as they descended the mound, they could no longer see the motorway. Lysi didn't want to use her phone GPS because the battery had run low and she had no cable to plug into the car's charger. Besides, she reasoned, in Drogheda they could find a place to ask directions. Once on the motorway between towns there'd be no place to stop. She needed to save the power for the rest of the trip. As a result, they soon found themselves caught in a maze of narrow streets some lined with a jumble of small shops, some that looped back to the street they'd just left, and some that dead-ended forcing them to retrace their way more than once.

"We'll eventually find the motorway," Lysi said. "Just take streets that go downhill."

"How about Shelly Lane?" Grace said.

Lysi shrugged. "Why not. It goes downhill."

Less than a block down narrow Shelly Lane a horn screamed, tires screeched, and shouts rang out. They would have collided with an oncoming car if Grace hadn't stood on the brake. Both Grace and Lysi sat with their palms pressed to their chests amid loud hollers from the car facing them. "Are you daft? One-way street, eejit. Back up!"

Grace's eyes sparked and she thrust her head out the window, "Hey dork, who you calling an idiot?"

"Grace," Lysi shouted. "Shut up and back up."

After that, Grace drove in an aimless fashion dodging road construction sites and avoiding one-way streets while trying to maintain a downhill direction.

On Laurence Street they stopped in front of a dark stone, three-story medieval castle type gate between two fifty-foot towers. "What is that?" Grace asked.

"It's a barbican, a medieval defense for a walled town." Lysi read a direction sign pointing toward the gate, "Laurence's Gate. Drogheda was a walled city. How exciting is that?"

"Not exciting. We're totally lost," Grace said.

"We're not lost," Lysi said. "We're touring. Turn down Constitution Hill."

Grace made a quick turn just missing a bicyclist who shouted something about a bloody culchie.

Grace bristled.

"Just keep driving," Lysi said.

On Trinity Street Lysi spotted a pub with a sign on the front that claimed it was the oldest pub in Drogheda.

"Pull over there, Grace," Lysi said pointing to the pub. "We may as well see the oldest pub in Drogheda since we're touring. And, we can ask directions to the motorway."

Grace parked in front of the pub called Noley's and they entered.

"We'd better order something, too. Don't want to be rude," Lysi said.

As soon as they walked in Lysi noticed only men sitting at tables and at the bar. She looked into several pairs of eyes, some curious, some disapproving, some annoyed. She hoped this wasn't just a pub for men. No ladies allowed.

They sat at a wood table near the window and turned their eyes to the drink menu on the wall.

"Wow, look at that list of Irish whiskeys," Grace said. "Jameson … good stuff. Bushmills, yeah, good. John Powers, ho hum. Paddys, hmm, never tried that. Grace licked her lips. When an elderly waiter with a bald head as round as a basketball approached the table, Grace said, "Give me a shot of Paddy's, neat."

Lysi heard a low rumble of positive comments from the men. Some grinned. Some nodded approval. "No Grace. You order that whiskey and you won't even think of driving."

The waiter stood with a pencil poised on his pad. "Do you need more time?"

"No. We'd like to try a local cider." That should be safe enough Lysi thought.

Approving male faces immediately morphed into derisive smirks accompanied by grumbles and laughter.

The bar tender pointed to Bulmers on the menu above the bar. Lysi and Grace ordered two half-pint bottles of Bulmers that came with a glass of ice. Lysi ordered the sparkly apple flavor. Grace ordered Berry Berry and took a big gulp from the bottle. "Yum."

Lysi looked suspicious as she poured her drink over the ice in her glass while Grace took another swig. Lysi tasted hers. Oh no. Hard cider. "Grace!"

"C'mon, Lysi. A half pint? A hamster couldn't get a buzz from that amount."

Lysi knew Grace was right. It would probably take a couple of quarts to get Grace tipsy.

After a couple sips of Bulmers Lysi signaled the waiter. "We're looking for the best way to get to the M1 heading towards Belfast."

"Easy," the waiter said and schpeeled off a set of confusing directions that neither Lysi nor Grace could get their heads around even after asking him to repeat them more than once.

As if speaking to kindergartners the waiter said, "Look, you can get a map at the petrol station on the corner. That might make it easier for you to understand."

"Hold on McGarrity." The scratchy voice came from a middle-aged man in a tan work shirt seated at a table near the window. He stood. "I happen to be goin' to the M1. I'd be more than willin' to lead these two fine ladies to the slip road."

Lysi and Grace fell all over themselves thanking the man.

They had no trouble following the Guinness delivery truck loaded with kegs. The man led them across the Boyne River, zigzagged to the M1 entrance and doffed his hat at them through the open window.

A few miles down the motorway just past Junction 7 Lysi saw a large blue sign that read M1 Toll €1.80. The tollbooth attendant held out his hand and Grace dropped coins into it.

"A toll road just like our New York Thruway," Grace said.

A bit further, a green sign told them they were on the N1. They passed a sign that read, Welcome to Northern Ireland, and the road name changed to A1. Less than an hour later they pulled into the outskirts of Belfast and were lost again.

Chapter 10

Clouds overhead looked like dark gray fluff, and rain had begun to polka dot the sidewalk by the time Lysi and Grace found a place to park on a Belfast street named Chichester.

To Lysi, Belfast seemed different than when she'd traveled there so long ago. As she scanned the neighborhood her thoughts wandered back to her last visit. Gone were most of the old narrow-fronted, red-brick terrace row houses that crowded the working-class sections of Belfast. Lysi's Irish friends had called them two up and two downs meaning a kitchen and sitting room downstairs, two bedrooms upstairs. They'd housed large families.

Soldiers marched through her memories. Soldiers everywhere. Soldiers in green and brown uniforms armed with rifles. patrolling the airport and streets, posted at numerous checkpoints.

A collage of vivid images burst into her consciousness—litter-covered sidewalks, broken windows, gashed concrete, walls plastered with sectarian graffiti, large oil drums in front of shops to prevent men in cars from swerving in and tossing bombs through store windows.

How Belfast had changed. No graffiti. No soldiers. No oil drums. A busy bustling city. Modern buildings. Clean sidewalks. High tech companies.

Outside the Volkswagen, taxis, cars and pink city buses blared horns as drivers fought for space. Passersby scurried along as if anxious to get to their destinations before one of the sudden downpours typical of Northern Ireland. So different from what Lysi remembered.

"What now? Grace said.

Lysi blinked as the unexpected sound of Grace's voice invaded her reverie. "We find our way to Beechgrove." She took out her phone and searched for directions. Nothing. "I think we have a problem. Looks like Beechgrove doesn't exist in GPS land."

"We could nip into a pub and ask directions," Grace said and jiggled her eyebrows.

"Or we could just call Billy for directions." Lysi did not want Grace anywhere near another pub. Nip? Odd to hear Grace use that word. So Irish.

"What? Are you worried a peeler might nab us? A hamster couldn't—"

"I know—couldn't get high on one Bulmers Cider." It struck Lysi as curious that Grace knew peeler meant cop in Ireland. She brushed the thought aside and punched in Billy's cell phone number. "Billy, we're here in Belfast."

"Lysi girl, here already?" Lysi could hear the smile in Billy's voice. "What'd you do? Fly?"

"Almost." Lysi glared at Grace. "Now I need directions to Ryan's cottage. Beechgrove's not on my phone's GPS."

"Okay love, would you be kind enough to wait a wee moment while I get Ryan on the phone?"

Oh boy, Chess was right, Lysi thought. Billy has turned into a leprechaun. She looked at Grace. Looks like Grace is turning into one, too.

"Hello Cousin Lysi. Bout ye? I hope you're okay after the long drive. Looking forward to meeting you," Ryan said.

Ryan didn't give Lysi a chance to say a word.

"I'm afraid you won't find my cottage on your phone. No address, only a house name. My father christened our place The Cottage. Same name as hundreds of other houses in Northern Ireland."

Lysi didn't say how impractical she considered this address system.

"But let's get you to Beechgrove," Ryan added. "Then we'll come get you at Mary MClone's Pub."

"Okay. We're on Chichester Street." Lysi guessed her pronunciation chich-ester was probably wrong but it was the best she could do.

"Aw, you're near Victoria Square where my brother, Kevin used to live." Ryan politely ignored her fractured pronunciation. "A26 is not too far. Easy."

"Good," Lysi said recalling their frustrating jaunt around Drogheda and the waiter's confusing directions.

"Go to Victoria," Ryan said. "Then take A1 and A12 to Clifton. Right soon a roundabout comes up and it's a wee bit tricky. You got to take the third exit from the roundabout onto Crumlin/A55. A lot of tourists take the second exit. Even my brother used to get confused."

"Your brother? You mean Kevin?" Lysi squinted at Grace.

"Aye, Kevin. My younger brother. He now lives in Beechgrove. Anyway, A55 turns into A52/Crumlin but if it doesn't, you probably took the wrong exit. Just go back to Clifton and start over again. Right?"

"Right." Lysi pursed her lips and shook her head at Grace.

"Good lass. Now stay on A52 until you get to Nutts Corner Roundabout. That's where you catch A/26. So far so good?"

"A … a …." Lysi's brain felt like scrambled eggs. She could hear Billy chortling in the background.

Grace whispered, "You have my permission to kill him."

Lysi nodded and grinned. She thought back to when she and Billy were kids. As soon as he'd discovered that directionality was not one of her strongpoints, he never let her forget it. He still enjoyed telling people that if you took Lysi a block away from home she couldn't find her way back.

"Good," Ryan said. "Now, take A26/Crumlin and go straight until you see a sign that says Beechgrove. Mind you, traffic will be heavy on this Dual Carriage Road."

"Dual Carriage Road?" Lysi said.

"Not important," Ryan said. "Now listen. Park in front of Mary McClone's Pub. Not McGarrity's B&B which is pink. We'll meet you there. Easy eh."

"Uh, right. Easy." Lysi had stopped listening after the first roundabout. She entered A26/Crumlin Road into her phone's GPS. "Got it," she mouthed to Grace. "Hey Ryan, thanks for the directions. We're on our way."

Lysi and Grace had no trouble finding Mary McClone's Pub. It sat right next to a chemist/post office. Their trouble started when Ryan arrived to lead them to his cottage.

*

Lysi sat white-faced and silent clutching the car's armrests as Grace tried to keep up with Ryan's dilapidated Ford pickup as it juddered over a slippery, unpaved boreen. Stone fences or yellow flowering gorse bordered each side of the narrow lane, and a strip of grass formed a straggly median. The Volkswagen skidded on loose gravel at each curve and splashed through puddles overflowing with muddy water from the recent rain.

"How can two cars pass on this old narrow road?" Lysi said.

"You tell me," Grace said. "It must have been laid out back in aught-six when two horses abreast seemed about the right width needed."

The car banged over a cattle grid. Grace startled at the clunkity-clank and shouted, "What was that?"

"A stock grid," Lysi said. She'd seen plenty of them in Australia's Outback. "They keep livestock from straying down the road."

"Great," Grace said. "Now I have to worry about running into cows as well as cars."

Grace struggled to find the sweet spot on the narrow lane where she wouldn't trim hedges or exchange side mirrors with oncoming cars and could still dodge some of the mudholes. To Lysi's relief, she had pretty much mastered driving on the boreen until the lane narrowed even more. No way now to avoid a head-on collision if they encountered an oncoming car.

A moment later, Grace slammed on the brakes and skidded into a patch of briars. Lysi's hands slammed against the dashboard. She was ready to shout at Grace when she saw that Ryan had come to a full stop in front of her and was flailing his arm signaling Grace to back up. He rolled down his window and shouted, "Back up. Back up and pull into that side road.

"What side road?" Grace shouted back.

Lysi looked out the back window. "I think he means that kind of foot path a few yards back."

Grace snorted, shifted into reverse and screeched back until she came to the side road. Ryan backed up and motioned her into the side road and followed her in. A Kia buzzed by at a dangerous speed and gave Ryan a thumbs up and an amused grin.

"That's it," Grace said. She got out of the car and stormed to Ryan's window. "Next time we meet a car, it backs up! Got that?"

Ryan, mouth agape nodded at her. Billy laughed.

Grace stomped back to the car. To Lysi's intense relief they didn't encounter another car or cow or sheep the rest of the trip.

Ten minutes later they followed Ryan and Billy as they made a left turn into a short driveway and parked in front of a white-washed, pebbledash-coated stone cottage. As soon as the car stopped, Lysi leaned back and took a deep breath. A boreen was scarier than any San Francisco freeway.

"I'd say these roads are a match for the South African township streets." Grace patted Lysi's shoulder. "Breathe girl, we did it."

Inside the cottage they all sat around a small kitchen table. Lysi, struggling to be courteous so as not to offend Ryan said, "Is the road we just drove the only way to get to your cottage?"

Ryan leaned forward and opened his mouth but before he could get a word out, Grace broke in. "Ryan, honey, I got to tell you. That's no road. That's a cow trail. No. Wait. It's a chicken trail. If that's the only way to get here, you better move before you end up road kill."

Ryan grinned, set out four tumblers and poured a generous shot of Irish whisky into each. "You girls look like you had a bout with some ill-tempered leprechauns. Drink up, it's sure the pair of you could use it."

"Well, what do you think of your ancestral homeland, Lysi?" Billy asked.

"Belfast looks so different from the time I travelled here with my father years ago when I was a teenager.

"What's different?" Billy asked.

"For one thing, we came in the middle of the Conflict," Lysi said.

"Aye, the Troubles," Ryan said. "A sad bit of our history it was."

"Troubles?" Grace asked, a puzzled expression on her face.

"That's what the Irish labeled the conflict over the constitutional status of Northern Ireland," Ryan said. "The Republicans, mostly Catholic, fought to force Northern Ireland to join a united Ireland but the Loyalists, mostly Protestant, battled to keep Northern Ireland part of the United Kingdom. More than 3,600 good Irish souls died and as many as 50,000 people were injured or maimed before it ended in 1998. Bad feelings still exist among the old timers."

"The Good Friday Agreement ended the conflict, right?" Lysi said.

"Supposedly," Ryan said. "Even today many villages and towns are considered to be either majority Catholic or Protestant. Sometimes towns are split. You drive through one section and you'll see the Union Jack flying. Drive through another section and the Tricolor will be waving. Take Belfast. It's still divided, Catholics live on the west side. Protestants on the East. Some neighborhoods are still separated by Peace Walls."

"Peace Walls?" Lysi said.

"Aye, they were constructed during the Troubles to separate the Catholic and Protestant neighborhoods to avoid street fighting. Some are still needed."

Everyone around the table stared at Ryan in silence. The image of the lighthearted Irish had weakened.

"Aye, it's true. Dissident splinter groups like the New Irish Republican Army and Loyalist paramilitary groups have formed." He shook his head.

Lysi felt sympathy for Ryan. She could only imagine how he felt about the deep divisions in his country. Americans who lived through the Civil War must have suffered the same pain.

"Ah now, enough talk about the Troubles," Ryan said. "You girls must be starving. I've arranged for you to stay in a room above Mary's Pub. Let's get you settled in and you can freshen up a bit before we treat you to the best meal in Beechgrove.

Chapter 11

Lysi leaned against an oversized pillow on a twin bed covered with a crisp white duvet, and surveyed the room above Mary McClone's pub— two twin beds separated by an antique oak nightstand, a matching dresser with four drawers, a tall dark mahogany wardrobe and a desk, perfect for their laptop. Modest but comfortable.

She could hear Grace splashing water in the small bathroom and singing "When Irish Eyes are Smiling" in a throaty gospel voice. What on earth could be taking her so long to get ready for a casual dinner? "Hey Grace, are you setting up housekeeping in there?"

The door popped open wide and so did Lysi's mouth.

"Are you planning to wear that?" Lysi asked. A stupid question. The black, wet-look leggings and 4-inch silver spike heels were typical Grace. But not the green T-shirt. Probably not a good choice.

"Like it?" Grace asked sliding her palms over the shirt.

"Green is good." Lysi chose her words carefully. "But ... I think ... the message expressed by those silver letters blazing across your chest might be a bit over the top."

Grace looked puzzled. "I don't know what you mean."

"Well ... a ..." Lysi struggled to find the words to make her case against the shirt without dampening Grace's enthusiasm. "Do you think Chess would like it?"

"Oh, he'd love it." Grace preened in front of the dresser mirror. "Come on Lysi. Loosen up." She stretched the T-shirt over her well-endowed chest. The words, Hug me I'm Irish, doubled in size.

Lysi sighed. Once Grace made up her mind, lesser mortals had no choice but to go along.

Lysi slipped a conservative white wool jacket over a mint green satin shell and black Armani pants. She got up and stood beside Grace in front of the mirror. Next to Grace's supernova look she felt like a garden-variety rock.

Smiling at her good friend, Lysi thought it must be true. Opposites attract—she was understated, Grace was flamboyant. She a planner, Grace an improviser. She conservative, Grace audacious. Yet, as the song goes their friendship was "a perfect blendship." She hooked arms with Grace. "Come on girlfriend, let's go knock 'em dead."

*

When Lysi and Grace entered the noisy pub, heads turned towards them one after another in a kind of domino effect. A man about to toss a dart at a board with a picture of a mug of beer in the middle, stood with his throwing arm in the air. A young waiter tipped a tray of mugs overflowing with beer. At a table in the corner, a woman dealing cards dropped the deck. Both men and women looked past Lysi to Grace, their eyes scanning her up and down. Even Billy looked taken aback. He recovered quickly and called to them from a table near a glowing turf fire, "Come on over here, girls."

Lysi nudged Grace. "I guess my white jacket was a hit."

Grace laughed. "News flash, girl. I'm the star here."

Ryan gulped, sprang to his feet and pulled out two chairs. He blinked several times but still stared at the tall black woman who smiled down on him.

"'Bout ye, Cousin Ryan," Grace said. "I'm ready for a pint and some good craic."

"How do you do, Grace?" Ryan said translating 'bout ye for Billy. "You won't find better craic in any other pub in Northern Ireland, so enjoy our special Beechgrove gossip and chatter."

'Bout ye? Craic? Lysi cast a suspicious glance in Grace's direction. She's loving acting Irish as much as Billy. There she goes again with that Irish slang. She's got to have an Irish phrase book stashed somewhere. Lysi squinted at Grace's oversized, silver handbag. She bet the book was inside. She'd find out later.

Lysi watched her friend conquer the room. She knew Grace would hold royal court for the evening.

"So good to be here in Beechgrove." Lysi hugged Ryan. "Looking forward to meeting my extended family here in County Antrim. Billy has told me so much about them."

A short, skinny, slightly tipsy kid about 18 with black hair and milky white skin staggered over to Grace before she could sit down. More than a head shorter than her he looked up through big, blurry blue eyes, and said, "Just wondering, since you're Irish and all and want a hug, would you be willin' for me to accommodate you?"

"Pay no need Grace. He's half cut," Ryan said and ordered the lad to bugger off.

"Aye, me fine lad," Grace said ignoring Ryan. "Step up on that chair and we'll have a go at it."

The kid lost his balance scrambling onto the chair. Grace grabbed his right arm and steadied him. "There's a good fellow."

She opened her arms and encircled him in a big hug. A hearty rumble of laughter, cheers and clapping broke out in the room.

Mary McClone bumped through the kitchen's swinging door and crossed herself. "Saints preserve us. What's all that clatter? Am I facing a donnybrook out here?"

Ryan jumped up, his cheeks turned pink and his eyes turned soft. "Mary, meet my cousin Lysi and her friend Grace."

"Good to meet you both. I see my assistant, Brigid got you settled into your room." Mary eyed Grace's T-shirt and laughed. She shook hands with Lysi and gave Grace an enthusiastic hug. "Now enough with the hugs, it's time for food." She pointed to the menu posted on the wall above the bar.

"Mary, no need to consult the menu," Ryan said. "Bring four of your wonderful bangers and mash plates for me and our American guests."

Mary reddened. "Get away with you Ryan O'Rourke." She swished off to the kitchen.

*

"Earlier we were just discussing a recent death here in Beechgrove," Billy said cutting off a hunk of sausage and dipping it into his mashed potatoes. "Knew you'd like to hear about it, Lysi."

"Why would I want to hear about a death? Was it one of our relatives?" Lysi asked. "Is that the surprise you mentioned?"

"No, not a relative according to Ryan," Billy said. "But that's not your surprise. The surprise is that people in the village believe the death was a homicide. I know how much you love to dabble in murder cases."

Grace's eyes jerked to Billy. She spoke through clenched teeth. "That has nothing to do with us."

"Just letting you know as you'll probably hear about it." Billy forked the last bite of sausage and mash into his mouth and chewed through a mischievous grin.

Grace did not smile. She shook her fork at Lysi. "Lysi, I'm warning you. Stay out of it."

"Grace is right. It has nothing to do with us," Lysi said, determined not to get involved. She understood Grace's apprehension. Poor thing probably still smarted from the last murder case Lysi had dragged her through in San Francisco where she had to fend off a gang attack. Of course, the San Francisco case hadn't endangered Grace as much as the Paris homicide where she had to fight off an attacker with nothing but a stiletto heel. No, it wouldn't be right to put Grace through another risky episode.

"Did I mention the victim was stabbed?" Billy said with a wink.

"Really," Lysi said. On the other hand, it wouldn't hurt to ask a question or two about the murder. In fact, it would be rather rude to show no interest at all.

"Are there any suspects?"

Chapter 12

"Bonzer," Maynard said gazing out a gigantic floor-to-ceiling window. He sat at a round table next to Chess in the Guinness Rooftop Bar and marveled at the 360° view of Dublin from seven stories above the city. Maynard and Chess had just finished a two-hour Guinness history and brewing process tour. Maynard raised his glass and watched the tiny bubbles circulate in the dark liquid. "I never thought beer could be so interesting."

People crowded around the huge circular bar in the center of the room collecting the free pints included in the tour. Most of them ordered more pints. Maynard noticed the more pints they ordered, the more jovial they became. More than one happy imbiber paused at Chess and Maynard's table to offer a friendly toast. Sláinte reverberated around the room.

"Who'd believe such a fantastic site would be housed in one of the oldest industrial complexes in the city," Maynard said. "From the looks of it, James Street isn't exactly the Champs Elysée."

"If you look past the inner-city apartment complexes and cheap shops, the view is incomparable," Chess said pointing out sights. "Phoenix Park, Irish Museum, the River Liffey. Off in the distance, those are the Dublin Mountains. The view changes on every side."

Maynard held up an empty Guinness glass and examined the golden harp above the word Guinness. "The harp is kind of interesting. Sort of unusual for beer, though. Do you know the origin?"

"That's a good question. I understand it appeared in 1862 on the label of the first bottled Guinness, over a hundred years after the first brew in 1759. Arthur Guinness patterned it after a 14th century Gaelic harp. You can actually see the original harp in the Trinity College long room."

"Interesting." Maynard finished off his pint.

"The harp is also the official national emblem of the Republic of Ireland," Chess continued. "The only difference is the emblem's harp has its straight edge to the right and the one on the Guinness label has its straight edge to the left."

"How do you know all that?"

"I make it my business to find out all I can about the values and traditions of a city where I contract to design a corporate website and communication system." Chess smiled. "Ireland's state flower is the Shamrock, animal is the stag. Want to hear the Irish Republic's National Anthem?"

Chess didn't wait for Maynard to reply. In a deep bass voice he burst into The Soldiers' Song. "Soldiers are we whose lives are pledged to Ireland ...."

The room quieted, and heads turned towards Chess who continued to sing. Several people rose, placed a hand over their heart and joined in the anthem. After singing, they bobbed their heads and gave Chess thumbs up.

Maynard admired Chess' outgoing personality, a perfect match to Grace. He also appreciated Chess' innovative ideas, entrepreneurial spirit and tireless drive; all traits that Maynard knew must have led to the great success of Vermillion, his company.

"Okay, okay. I get your point. Now that you've sung for your supper, let's try that Guinness beef stew and maybe even the Guinness chocolate mousse." Maynard couldn't quite feature beer-flavored chocolate but why not give it a whirl?

"I'm ready. Let's head downstairs to the 1837 Bar and Brasserie." Chess swallowed the last drop of beer and stood.

Maynard's phone rang before he could get up. He looked at the screen and a quizzical expression spread over his face. "It's Grace."

Chess sat back down and returned a puzzled look that seemed to ask why Grace would call Maynard instead of him.

"Grace? Maynard here. You must have misdialed. I'll pass the phone to Chess."

"No, no wait Maynard! It's you I called and I only have a minute. You need to talk to Lysi." Grace spoke in a half whisper.

"I need to do what?" Maynard pressed the phone tighter to his ear. "Speak up. I can't hear you."

"I can't. Just listen. There was a murder here in Beechgrove."

"What?" Maynard stopped breathing. "Is … Lysi okay?"

"She's fine," Grace said sounding frustrated "What I'm worried about is that Lysi "Miss Marple" Weston is going to jump into the middle of said murder and drag me with her."

"Wait! Slow down and speak in a normal voice. What are we talking about here? Where's Lysi?" Maynard tried to sort out Grace's meaning.

"She's in the pub with Billy Weston and cousin Ryan. They're talking about a murder. You have to stop her."

Billy and Lysi discussing a homicide? Now Maynard understood. He remembered Billy involving Lysi in the investigation of the Elizabeth Simmons murder case in San Francisco. Next thing he knew, Lysi had dragged Grace into her amateur sleuthing caper almost getting them both killed. No wonder Grace seemed anxious.

"Don't tell her I called you." Grace sounded urgent. "Just talk her out of turning into "Miss Marple." She'll listen to you. Talk to her."

Maynard started to reply when Lysi's voice echoed through the phone. "Grace, are you okay?"

"Oops, gotta go." Grace said.

Maynard heard a toilet flush, a stall door slam and high heels clicking on tile. Then the phone went silent.

Chess looked curious. "What did she want?"

"I'm not exactly sure. Something about a murder in Beechgrove. She thinks Lysi might get involved. She wants me to talk her out of it."

"Yeah, that's gonna happen," Chess said rolling his eyes.

Nancy Curteman

Chapter 13

Lysi watched Mary McClone hang the closed sign in the pub window, pull the shades, and lock the front door. Her eyes followed Mary as she removed her apron, stepped behind the bar and pulled out a bottle of amber liquid. White letters on its red label spelled out Red Bush Irish Whiskey. Lysi flashed a grin. "Grace, look what we have here."

"Yes indeedy," Grace said, licking her lips and jiggling her toes. She'd slipped off her stilettos and rested her feet on a chair.

"The Old Bushmill Distillery in the village of Bushmill, right here in County Antrim has distilled our famous whiskey for 400 years," Mary said. "The distillery is only an hour's drive North of Belfast. We're pretty proud of it. Would you be willing to try a wee bit of our home brew?"

"That would be grand," Grace said smoothing the creases on her "Hug me, I'm Irish" shirt.

Lysi nodded. "With pleasure." Whiskey wasn't her preferred drink, she was more a California chardonnay person. But she'd try some to please Mary towards whom she had felt an immediate affinity. Mary combined independence with warmth, intelligence with respect, acceptance with considerateness. Her Irish humor and carefree attitude clearly endeared her to pub patrons. Yet, Lysi detected an occasional cloud of sadness in Mary's blue eyes. Someone or something had hurt her deeply at some time in her life. Lysi wondered what or who.

Mary dropped a couple of ice cubes into three tulip-shaped tumblers and picked up the bottle.

"A ... Mary?" Grace said. "Would you mind leaving out the ice in mine? I always drink my whiskey neat. It's a mortal sin to dilute perfection."

Of course," Mary said with a twinkle in her eyes. "You drink your whiskey like a pro. Connoisseurs claim it's best drunk without ice, even a tad warm." She dumped the ice from one glass then poured whiskey into all three and brought them to the table. The three women clinked glasses. "Sláinte," Mary said.

"Sláinte," Lysi and Grace chorused.

Grace took a swallow and smacked her lips again. "Smooth as a shamrock leaf."

"Brilliant," Lysi said. She decided she might as well join Grace in her Irish brogue although the "shamrock leaf" simile didn't quite work for Lysi.

After a couple of sips, Lysi asked, "Mary, did you know the murdered man?"

Grace bristled. Lysi caught her look of disapproval and, not to be cowed, scowled back. Good grief, all she'd done was ask a simple question. It's not like she'd begun an in-depth investigation. Why did Grace always overreact?

"Aye, I knew the bastard, so I did. Sean Kavanagh by name." Mary's happy-go-lucky demeanor disappeared as she spit out his name like a mouthful of something disgusting. "The gutter would have been a step up for that maggot."

The cloud of sadness Lysi had noticed appeared in Mary's eyes along with intense hatred.

"Women avoided him. He had a reputation for being loose with his hands." Mary closed her eyes and bit her lip then in a quavering voice added, "Truth be told, he nearly ruined my life." She began to shake wrapping her arms around herself.

Both Lysi and Grace swallowed hard. Lysi spoke first. "I'm so sorry to hear that. Do ... do you want to share what happened?"

Mary hesitated. She stirred the ice in her drink with a finger and licked it. "It's not easy to talk about, but maybe you would understand seeing as how you know a wee bit about sexual harassment."

"Did he harass you?" Lysi understood Mary's reluctance to talk about her experience. Many women feel they're at fault when men harass them. That they somehow encouraged men to take liberties with them by what they wore or by not objecting in an effort not to offend. "Mary, you must understand that you were not to blame for anything he said to you."

"Yeah," Grace said. "Some men are predatory rats who mistake a woman's reluctance to speak out about their dirty mouths as consent and even complicity."

Lysi saw anger in Grace's eyes. Always a strong advocate for women, Grace couldn't stomach any form of sexual harassment. She'd seen Grace confront police officers, politicians and even CEOs about their suggestive innuendos. It always amused Lysi to watch self-professed powerful males back off when Grace switched from her soft, professional diction to coarse Harlem street slang and called them on their off-color remarks. Lysi's favorite "Graceism" happened in a boardroom in Sydney, Australia when a company executive commented on Grace's voluptuous figure. Grace rose to her full height and leaned over the short paunchy guy. "Listen up, little man. If I want your opinion, I'll ask for it. And a word of advice, being a total dick doesn't make yours any bigger!" Grace paused while the guy licked his wounds then she added, "I trust we understand each other."

Everyone in the room stared in silence. Grace smiled and said, "Now, where were we? Oh yes, you wanted a definition of sexual harassment." She pointed at the pudgy exec. "You just got one."

"Grace is right," Lysi said. "Women need to stand against vulgar treatment."

Mary McClone picked up the Bushmill bottle and refilled the glasses. She took a sip and after a deep breath, spoke. "The old divil tried more than once to have a go at me." She looked up at Lysi and Grace with fire in her eyes. "Of course I would have none of it."

Lysi and Grace remained silent. Experience told them what might have happened. Kavanagh probably did all kinds of things "accidentally"—brushed against her when he passed by, slapped her on the butt when she served his table, eyed her breasts, pawed her, made suggestive jokes and comments to or about her. Oh yes, they knew the sexual harasser's playbook.

"Then one night after closing," Mary's eyes flashed and her breathing increased. "I was cleaning up and he snuck through the back door. He grabbed me from behind, knocked me to the floor and tugged off my knickers. I struggled against him but the filthy swine was too strong."

Mary's eyes filled with tears and she seemed to beg to be believed. Now Lysi knew the origin of the sadness that occasionally clouded Mary's smiling Irish eyes.

Lysi stroked Mary's hand in an effort to reassure her. Grace grabbed Mary's shoulder and spewed a litany of expletives that would have put a drunken sailor to shame.

Mary crossed herself. "Mother Mary must have been looking after me because one of my regular customers, Thomas Rook, knocked at the door needing a bit of broth for his ailing wife. Kavanagh heard the knock, jumped up and ran out the back door like a terrified weasel. I was saved. May God forgive him for I never will."

Lysi and Grace exchanged hard looks. Then Lysi said, "Mary, that was more than harassment. That was sexual assault."

"That piece of—" Grace stopped herself then finished the sentence. "—belongs in hell. Did you report him to the cops?"

"I didn't for the shame of it. You see, he kept my knickers. The next day he stopped me in front of the pharmacy and made a terrible threat."

"A threat?" Lysi could only imagine what kind of threat he could make.

"He said if I told anyone what he'd done he would spread the word that I had given my knickers to him as a way of saying I would be available whenever he wanted me."

"Bloody hell." Grace slammed her fist on the table spilling some of Lysi's drink.

"After that I made it a point never to be alone with him but his threats didn't stop." Tears moistened Mary's cheeks. "His death saved me. May the merciful Lord forgive me, I'm glad he's dead."

"After his death, did you get your knickers back," Lysi asked, concern in her voice. She knew how it would look if Mary's panties turned up in a police search of Kavanagh's belongings.

"No," Mary said.

"He's probably hidden them somewhere in his house. The police could find them." Grace voiced Lysi's concern.

"If they find them in Sean Kavanagh's cottage my reputation will be ruined. If I report what he did to me, they'll think I killed him. I don't know what to do. I guess I just have to wait and hope they don't find them."

"No," Lysi said. "We can't wait."

"We won't wait," Grace said. Lysi heard Grace say "we" and knew she'd decided to be involved.

All three women knew what they had to do.

Nancy Curteman

Chapter 14

Clouds tinged red by the setting sun filled the sky by the time Maynard and Chess finished dinner in the 1837 Bar and Brasserie. They walked out of the Guinness Storehouse into a moaning breeze that chilled the night air—neither the Californian's nor the Australian's favorite kind of weather.

After the call from Grace, they'd decided to postpone the overnight trip to Hillary Sheep Farm in Galway, and went online to book a night train to Belfast. No luck. The earliest departure available wouldn't leave until 7:35 the next morning.

Needing to wind down a bit they decided to have a nightcap at a pub near their hotel. A taxi driver recommended O'Donoghue's Bar about a block from the Merrion.

Once in O'Donoghue's, Maynard had to raise his voice to talk over a large group of spectators cheering on a Dublin rugby team battering another team on a big screen television. "Let's take a table in that outside area, a bit away from the game." He pointed to an outdoor beer garden that divided the bar into two rooms.

"You're kidding, right?" Chess said. "I'm gonna sit outside in this freezing weather?"

"Don't worry, Ironman. It's equipped with overhead heaters." Maynard slapped him on the back.

Heads turned as the two tall men threaded their way through a jovial crowd toward the beer garden passing a wall adorned with newspaper articles, posters and photographs of famous Irish musicians. Maynard recognized Irish folk singer Christy Moore. From a large colored poster Ronnie Drew smiled at him. Maynard knew the famous lead singer with the Dubliner's, a celebrated band that used to play at O'Donoghue's.

They found a table in the quieter area and ordered two Irish coffees just as traditional Irish music began to boom from a quartet consisting of an accordion, tin whistle, guitar, and a goatskin drum. So much for a quieter area.

A dark-haired woman at a nearby table clapping to the music smiled at Maynard. "Nice accent. From Down Under, eh?"

Maynard removed his Bush hat and nodded with an uncomfortable smile. He felt Chess' grinning eyes on him.

"You're a long way from home, Aussie." The woman flipped a strand of shiny long hair behind her ear and her smile broadened. "Staying in Dublin long?"

Maynard recognized an invitation when he heard it. The woman was not just attractive, she was a Celtic beauty—fair skin, big blue eyes, an alluring sprinkle of freckles across her nose, and a deep dimple in her chin. Maynard couldn't help but notice that her silk blouse revealed just enough cleavage to be enticing. In a previous life he would have leapt at the chance to invite her to his table just to see what might develop, but not now. Now Lysi was his life. He returned the woman's smile and said apologetically, "I'm leaving early tomorrow morning."

"Too bad. Your loss, mate." The woman shrugged and turned back to her friends.

Chess laughed. "Truth. You were tempted, right?"

"Years ago, I might have jumped at the chance," Maynard said. "Not now. Too much at stake. How 'bout you? Tempted?"

"You've got to be kidding this time, right? Hell, I've got all the woman I can handle with Grace." Chess shook his head and blew air through his lips.

Maynard laughed and the two men high-fived. He knew exactly what Chess meant.

After a sip of Irish coffee Maynard decided to tap in Lysi's mobile phone number one more time. He'd already tried four times that evening and gotten no answer. Not even a response to his voice mails. He'd had a bad feeling all through the meal at the Guinness Storehouse about the combination of Lysi, Billy and murder. The bad feeling had grown into serious concern.

He thought back to the day he met Lysi. It was at a crime scene in Sydney, Australia where he was working a homicide case. From her comments and suggestions he concluded she liked to play amateur detective. He was right. Throughout the duration of the case she continually meddled in his murder investigation. He knew she meant well. And he had to admit she did have some investigative skills both natural and learned. On more than one occasion she reminded him about her Criminal Justice course of study at San Francisco State University. She was certainly observant, even intuitive. It was just that she always managed to get herself into a dangerous fix. Now he could tell from Grace's worried tone that Lysi might be heading down a precarious trail again.

Maynard listened to his phone ring Lysi's number. She should have answered by now. Maybe her phone was out of battery power. Unlikely. Lysi's efficient nature would never allow that to happen. Maybe she lost it or left it somewhere. Ridiculous! She would never misplace anything as important as a phone. Maybe it was turned off. That possibility worried him. Why would she turn it off? He looked up at Chess. "She's still not answering."

"I'll try Grace again," Chess said. He tapped in Grace's number. No answer. "Dead or ... "

"Turned off," Maynard said, his tone combining suspicion and worry. Why would both Lysi and Grace turn off their phones? In desperation, Maynard decided to try Billy.

Billy answered immediately. "Hello Maynard, me mate. Bout ye?"

"What?" Maynard said.

Billy laughed. "I see you need to brush up on your Irish. I asked how you were doing."

"I'm not sure. I heard via the grapevine about a homicide in Beechgrove."

"You mean via the 'Gracevine?' She's such a nervous Nellie." Billy emitted a knowing chuckle. "That's right. A guy got stabbed."

"Stabbed?" Maynard's stomach lurched.

"Aye, he was stabbed in his neck, right enough."

Annoyed with Billy's cavalier attitude Maynard snapped. "Where's Lysi? She's not answering her phone."

"Last time I saw her was about 10:30 at Mary McClone's Pub. She and Grace are spending a few nights in a room above the pub. She might be there or … she might be out chasing down a murderer." Billy laughed again.

"Bye Billy." Maynard's stomach tightened. He didn't like Billy's last comment. An ice cube ran down Maynard's back. Billy might be right.

Chapter 15

Michael Doherty stood shivering between two large beech trees across the street from Mary McClone's Pub. The weather had turned raw and damp forcing him to pull his jacket hood over his head against the cold night mist. He watched patrons dribble out the pub door. He had only a slight acquaintance with most of the customers since he, like most Travellers, seldom ventured into village taverns. They kept to themselves only entering town to buy groceries and basic supplies. Michael knew his brother Paddy frequented the pub despite Michael's repeated cautions against it.

As Michael watched he hoped to pick up some idle conversation about Paddy from the exiting patrons or even catch Paddy leaving. He'd considered entering the pub to have a look around, but he'd already enquired three days ago and didn't want to risk antagonizing any villagers.

The kid had been gone for almost a week. Michael felt desperate. He even thought of going to the police but trashed that idea because he knew the police were already well acquainted with Paddy Doherty's antics. Paddy had gotten himself a bad reputation with the villagers as well.

Michael knew more than one pub patron would have a reason to even a score with his brother. He thought about people who might want to harm him. Beat him up or worse. He knew Paddy had broken into O'Toole's Pharmacy and nicked drugs because he found them under Paddy's bed with the labels still attached.

The kid had gotten drunk and smashed the windows of McGarrity's B&B costing Michael two weeks work to pay for the repairs. His brother regularly nicked items from the grocer. More than once village farmers had caught him stealing chickens. Even that nice Mary McClone had to show him the door one evening when he got loud and disorderly.

Michael shook his head. Aye, Paddy was trouble but he wasn't mean. People just didn't know the real Paddy. They only saw the problems he caused. They never saw him playing with the younger kids in the camp or running errands for one-legged Kevin Rook or carrying water for the older Travellers.

Michael felt responsible for his kid brother. He'd cared for him since the death of their parents in a car crash in Derry where the family had lived all Paddy's life. Paddy was twelve and Michael was sixteen when their lives changed forever. Derry social services ruled Paddy should be placed in foster care, but Michael vowed not to let that happen. He joined a band of Travellers and snuck Paddy out of Derry. Now that Paddy was nineteen and always in trouble, Michael wondered if he'd made the right decision.

He watched Mary McClone place a closed sign on the pub door and pull the shades. Disappointed he'd heard nothing about Paddy he decided to call it a night. He'd turned to leave when boisterous banter drew his attention to a group of teenaged ruffians stumbling toward the pub. They stopped in front of the door and blustered about the stupid laws prohibiting underage drinking. Clearly, they were too young to purchase alcohol but from the way they staggered Michael knew they were well and truly blootered.

Michael slipped deeper into the shadow of the two trees and strained to understand the boys' slurred blathering. Had he heard Paddy's name? Did they know where he was? Had Paddy crossed over some forbidden line and incurred their ire?

The teens banged into each other, shoving, nudging and laughing as they moved on down the street. Michael weighed the risks of following them. The two shorter ones and the fat one didn't worry him. The big one who looked like a descendant of the mythical giant, Finn McCool, sent a cold chill of fear through him. Convinced he'd heard one of the boys shout Paddy's name he knew deep inside he could never forgive himself if they did something to his only brother and he hadn't tried to help him.

He'd stepped off the curb to trail the boys when he saw the pub door open. Mary McClone and two tall women exited the pub.

Michael paused. Strange. Where would they be going this late at night?

Chapter 16

Lysi turned up the collar of her all-weather coat and trailed Mary McClone from the pub out into a cold mist. Grace zipped up her down jacket and brought up the rear. Lysi paused on the threshold and turned her head to the left. Male shouting and laughter somewhere off in the darkness had drawn her attention.

"Wait." Lysi grabbed Mary's arm. "You hear that?"

Mary wrinkled her brow and listened then laughed. "Ah that's just a bunch of hooligans letting off a bit of steam on a Friday night. Don't mind them. They're headed toward the square." Mary gestured with her thumb toward a faintly lit church steeple. "If their shenanigans go too far, old Father Lorigan'll give them a bollocking and send them off home with a penance of ten Hail Marys, he will."

"Let's just make sure no one's around," Lysi said. "We don't need company."

"Yeah," Grace said. "We don't need company on an illegal panty raid in the middle of the night."

"No one's out and about at this hour where we're heading," Mary said. "The village hibernates after eleven."

"That's what we should be doing instead of burglarizing." Grace pulled a hood over her head.

Lysi's eyes shifted up and down the street. She saw a few dim streetlights and some hazy nightlights glowing from shops but no car headlights or people with flashlights. "Okay. Which way?"

Mary pointed to the right. Lysi and Grace followed her down the deserted street past a B&B, a small grocery and an even smaller curio shop towards a row of cottages. The streetlights ended before they reached the first cottage and the black pavement disappeared except for the shifting circle of light from Mary's flashlight. Through a few cottage windows Lysi could see flashes from television sets but most windows were dark.

Lysi and Grace both halted when a spray of light appeared a few yards ahead. Lysi moved close to Mary and whispered, "Someone's coming."

"I see. It's a torch." Mary held her breath and stared at the obscure shadows drawing closer.

"Thought you said nobody would be out this late." Lysi stared at the distant light.

Mary kept her eyes on the light. "I can't imagine who would be walking about this time of night."

Mary's words did not calm Lysi's worries. If village people hibernated after eleven as Mary said, then who was behind that light? Troublemakers? Thieves? Or worse, a police officer? Lysi was sure that in a small community like Beechgrove the police would find it curious or even suspicious to see three women walking around in the dark. How would they explain? Maybe they should call off the search of Kavanagh's cottage.

As the light drew nearer, one shadow converted into a large German shepherd followed by an even larger man wearing an Irish flat cap and an Aran Cardigan.

"Why it's yourself, Mary McClone. Good evening to you," a scratchy voice called. "Out for a late stroll are ya?"

With a sigh of relief Mary replied. "Good evening to you Dennis McGill. Right, I'm showing my American friends the loveliness of our village after dark."

"And would you be wanting some company? Me and Kingman just started our walk and would be willing to escort you."

Kingman wagged his tail and licked Mary's hand then loped over to Lysi and Grace, sniffed them meticulously and returned to Mary.

"Ah what a grand gesture on your part. Always the gallant gentleman, you are," Mary said. She turned to Lysi and Grace. "Men like Dennis McGill are proof that chivalry is not dead."

Lysi and Grace nodded nervously.

Mary smiled at McGill. "Thank you for your kind offer, but no need as we'll be heading back in a few minutes. Wouldn't want you to cut Kingman's walk short." Mary patted the dog's head.

"Well, I'll be off then. You'd best be watching for things that go bump in the night," McGill said over his shoulder as he continued on his way.

"Whew, that was close," Lysi said.

"He's a good man and all," Mary said. "Just a wee bit on the curious side."

After they'd walked about twenty minutes Grace said, "Yo, Mary. My dogs are barking. You said Kavanagh's pad was just a five-minute stroll. We've been hiking for an hour. How much farther?"

"Don't exaggerate, Grace. We haven't been walking for an hour." Lysi guessed Grace's stiletto heels weren't the most suitable footwear for long walks on uneven tarmac. They must be torturing her feet.

"Just a wee doddle farther," Mary said.

"A wee doddle farther!" Grace said. "Translation, another hour."

A few minutes later Mary stopped and pointed her flashlight at a small cottage. In the ray of light Lysi could see peeling paint, crooked shutters and a mud-colored front door badly in need of repair. Leggy, overgrown shrubs and tall weeds choked the front yard and an old car with a couple of flat tires stood on a dirt driveway beside the cottage.

Lysi spotted something else she hadn't expected. White police tape with red letters that read Do Not Cross extended the length of the cottage front. A minor obstacle, she hoped.

Gravel crunched underfoot as the women walked the path towards the door.

"Uh-uh." Grace shook her head. "An illegal panty raid is one thing. Crossing crime scene tape is another. Count me out."

Lysi stopped. The minor obstacle wasn't as minor as she'd hoped.

Nancy Curteman

Chapter 17

Michael Doherty's eyes followed the three women until they morphed into shadows in the murky distance. Strange. Why would Mary McClone and two women venture out on a cold, damp night like this? For a moment he considered following them, but to what purpose? Idle curiosity? He had no time for that. He needed to find his brother.

The yobos grabbed his attention again braying and snorting a short distance away. Had he thought or imagined he heard one of them shout his brother's name? Maybe they knew where he was. Determined to find out, he turned and hurried after the dark silhouettes.

Michael knew the roughnecks, like most of the young village men, had no love for his brother. Truth be told, Paddy had created the problem himself with his smart mouth and confrontational behavior. Worse, he couldn't leave off chasing after the pretty young girls of Beechgrove. Michael had warned him time and again that villagers didn't want their daughters fraternizing with Travellers.

Not all Paddy's fault. The lad was a magnet to giddy girls with his curly blond hair, flirty blue eyes, engaging smile and well-toned body. Unfortunately, he also caught the attention of hotheaded young hoodlums resentful of competition. More than once a gang of thugs had waylaid him on an isolated stretch of boreen and sent him home with a fat lip or black eye. Michael knew Paddy didn't pick fights, but he never walked away from one either. Trouble was he rarely emerged the victor.

Michael remembered Paddy laughing about a giant kid who'd threatened to cut off his balls if he ever caught him near a village girl. Michael worried the giant Finn McCool look-alike in the gang he followed might be the kid. Maybe these adolescent testosterone-driven wankers decided to teach Paddy a lesson. Michael's stomach lurched. He had a sick feeling they had a hand in Paddy's disappearance.

He followed them past a dimly lit curio shop, across the grassy town square, past the Catholic church, dark and somber with its fenced cemetery. No streetlights shone on the tombstones because they ended at the edge of the village. Beyond the church, cottages crouched further away from each other, most of their windows dark and silent.

Now he trailed the boys with more caution, keeping a greater distance. The charcoal darkness yawned ahead of him and swallowed them up. He could no longer see the four, but he could follow their boisterous shouts.

Misgivings gnawed at his courage. Was it smart to follow a gang of hotheads alone? What would they do if they discovered him? Could he fight them off—especially McCool? Maybe he should turn back to the safety of the village?

Michael slowed his pace then halted. He squinted into the darkness and listened. Odd. The shouts had ceased. Where were the louts? Could they have reached their cottages and called it a night? Should he waste any more time on them? They had probably already passed out on their beds.

Still, he'd come this far, he may as well go just a wee bit farther. Maybe locate one of the cottages the boys had entered so he could find it when he returned in daylight.

Michael's imagination unleashed a torrent of increasingly more frightening images. Paddy locked in a shed or barn. Paddy tied up in the woods. Paddy buried in a secret grave. He had to find him no matter the cost.

After a few steps, Michael realized the futility of finding his brother or even the cottage tonight. More sensible to return during the day and grab a look around. Deep down he knew he wouldn't be able to find Paddy on his own. He needed help from the police. Would the peelers bother with another Traveller problem? They considered Travellers thieves, drunkards, brawlers and loafers who leeched off the government. True, some fit the stereotype, but not all.

A sound interrupted his thoughts— a shrill squawk—a cat? A barn owl? His imagination? Nothing, he decided, just a night sound.

The shrill noise broke the silence again. This time it sounded more like a falsetto voice. A bad feeling clutched at Michael's chest. Something wasn't right. He paused, listened and peered into opaqueness. A mental picture of the giant kid flashed through his mind. Now sweat ran down his back despite the cold and his heart pounded like a trip hammer.

No, the risk was too great to face them alone. He turned back towards the village, determined to return with the police tomorrow.

Taking longer, faster strides he had arrived at the church cemetery when he heard running footsteps behind him. Before he could turn his head, two boys grabbed him from behind, seizing his arms. He wrenched and twisted his body kicking his legs to free himself from the vise-like holds. The grips just tightened. Fat Boy's face thrust close to Michael's. He turned his head away from the stench of Fat Boy's stale beer breath, and the falsetto almost hysterical laugh blasted his ears.

"Out of the way." Someone shoved Fat Boy hard knocking him aside. A big bruising bulldog of a kid took his place and grasped Michael's chin with one huge hand its fingers digging into his flesh. "Got a message for your pretty boy brother, Traveller. Tell him if we catch him sniffing around our girls again, we'll rearrange his face so even the ugliest heifer will run at the sight of him."

The hulk slugged him in the midsection and Michael doubled over. His breath came in short gasps and when the other two boys let go his arms, he collapsed. The boys sauntered off. Fat Boy's squawk echoed in Michael's ears.

Michael lay on the ground feeling the cold earth dampen his clothes and chill his body. What was it McCool said? He had a message for Paddy. That meant the gang didn't have him. If they did, McCool would deliver the message himself.

So where was his brother?

Nancy Curteman

Chapter 18

Lysi stared at Grace's hard-set jaw and knew it would take some serious cajoling to get her to cross the crime scene tape. Mary stood silent and didn't interfere. Lysi turned back and examined the cottage. Sections of blue and white police tape lay torn on the ground. Footprints in the damp soil led to and from Kavanagh's cottage door. Lysi pondered a moment then it dawned on her how she could convince Grace to enter the cottage.

"Yes, the police cordoned off the cottage," Lysi said. "Yes, they considered it a crime scene. But look." Lysi pointed to the tape. "Judging from the dilapidated condition of the tape and all those footprints they've already done a search. There's no cop posted to guard the scene. It's obvious they're finished here. They just haven't removed the tape yet."

"Lysi, has your pilot light gone out? As long as the tape's there we can't cross." Grace speared her with a sharp glare.

"Drum roll, girlfriend." She beat on an imaginary drum. "We could be hauled off to some Devil's Island type prison for obstructing justice."

"Don't be ridiculous, Grace. Number one, we're not obstructing justice. We're merely retrieving a stolen item. Number two, this is 21st century Northern Ireland not 19th century France. No Devil's Island here. Third, they're not going to catch us," Lysi said, "because, I repeat, they've already been here and searched the place. Trust me. The police are not coming back."

"We're still trespassing," Grace said.

"I'll give you that. So we need to hurry. Come on."

"No."

Lysi took an exasperated breath as an idea crept into her mind. She remembered how Grace, fearing an attack from some nocturnal critter, nearly had a panic attack when they'd had to pass through a wooded area one night near Khayelitsha Township in South Africa. Lysi brushed aside a little sting of conscience and said, "Well then, you wait out here in the dark with all the creepy, crawly nocturnal creatures. Mary and I will do the search."

An eerie harsh scream followed by a long hissing sound startled Lysi and Grace. "What was that?" Lysi looked up in the direction of the sound.

"Why that's one of our wee barn owls it is," Mary said. "It's an endangered species and dear to every Irishman's heart. Special barn owl boxes are common here. I have one myself. There's probably one nearby."

Grace's eyes shot around the dark yard. Her conflicted expression told Lysi the barn owl's scream had been perfectly timed. Grace didn't want to cross the crime tape or trespass, but staying outside alone would be worse.

Lysi couldn't understand Grace's fear of the dark in Beechgrove considering she gave no thought at all to traipsing around the Harlem streets at night, a place much more dangerous than a small Irish village. Her lack of fear in Harlem probably had to do with her legendary father, Big Bill Wright who'd pretty much owned the Harlem streets from the age of eighteen. Grace liked to say no one messed with Big Bill and no one messed with his daughter.

"This is just every kind of wrong." Grace gritted her teeth. "All right. I'll cross but if we get tossed into prison, you better pray we don't land in the same cell. You will not survive."

"Yeah Grace," Lysi said. She turned her face away from Grace and grinned. Mission accomplished.

Lysi tried the doorknob—it turned and when the door opened, she jumped back in surprise. She beamed over her shoulder at Mary and Grace. "There you see, the Lord wouldn't have left the door open if he hadn't wanted us to enter."

They crept into a sparsely furnished living room that smelled of beer, stale smoke, sweat and spoiled food. Mary's flashlight revealed a couch and television.

"My feet are killing me," Grace said. She wrinkled her nose. "I'd sit on that couch but I'm afraid I'd stick to it." She dabbed her index finger at her open mouth in a gagging motion. "Yuk."

A side table held an ashtray full of cigarette butts and a couple of empty Guinness bottles. Belfast Telegraph newspaper pages lay spread-eagled on the floor. A kitchen nook on the left contained a stove, refrigerator, a couple of cabinets and a sink full of dirty dishes.

"Home sweet garbage dump," Grace said through two fingers pinching her nose shut.

Mary flashed a light on two open doors. They saw an unmade bed in one and the other revealed a bathroom.

A small shape skittered through the spray of light from Mary's torch. Lysi startled. Grace recoiled and shrieked. "A mouse!"

"Ah, Grace," Mary whispered. "A mouse is more terrified of yourself than you are of it. The wee thing is racing to hide."

"Grace," Lysi said, "surely you've seen worse rodents in Harlem. What about rats?"

"Yeah, but rats are easier to see." Grace hoisted her pant legs up to her knees. "Our Harlem boys use them for target practice. Keeps the population down."

"Okay." Lysi doubted the effectiveness of that method of rodent control but didn't comment because she wanted to get on with the task at hand.

"In the interest of speed we need to divide the functions." Lysi pulled a penlight from her bag. "Grace, you and I will take the bedroom. Mary, take the bathroom."

Lysi's cell shattered the silence and all three women's eyes jerked toward the door. Did anyone hear it? Lysi yanked it from her pocket and squeezed the mute button. Before the edgy women could take a breath, Grace's phone rang and continued ringing until she'd shuffled around in her purse through lipsticks, compacts, breath mints, gum, a hairbrush and comb until she found it and muted it.

"Let's get this done and get out of here," Grace said, and shot into the bedroom. Lysi bolted into the room at the same moment and they collided at the dresser.

85

"You want the dresser that bad, take it, but open that window." Grace pointed to a small, window above the dresser. "It smells like an old outhouse in here."

"No, it might draw attention." Lysi whispered.

"Draw attention? You're kidding. Our cell phones already sounded reveille for everyone out there in Sleepy Hollow," Grace said as she opened the window.

"Grace, try to focus. I'll take the bed. Sometimes these kinky guys sleep with their trophies. Ick!" She shone her light on the disheveled bed and moved the blanket, sheets and pillow around with the tips of her thumb and middle finger.

Nothing.

She stooped and flashed her light under the bed. Nothing but dust bunnies and smelly socks.

"Got 'em," Grace stage whispered swinging a pair of panties around on her index finger.

Lysi stood, pulled a tissue from her pocket and wiped her fingers. "Go show Mary."

Lysi hesitated before leaving the bedroom. She couldn't resist doing a bit more sleuthing. Maybe she'd find some evidence leading to the murderer.

Grace walked into the living room waving the black lace panties in the dim ray of her penlight. "Nice knickers. They were just sitting on top of the dresser."

"They're not mine," Mary said sticking her head out the bathroom doorway. "That disgusting louse must have assaulted some other woman."

"Grace. Mary. You've got to see this," Lysi called.

Grace and Mary rushed into the bedroom.

"Whoa!" Grace said.

"Sweet Mother of God." Mary grabbed Grace's arm.

"Yeah, that sickie kept trophies all right," Lysi said. "A drawer full of panties."

"Do you think the women reported any of these missing? Some are pretty pricey." Grace held up a purple embroidered bikini. "These are by La Perla. They start at about a hundred bucks a pair."

"No, they wouldn't report. They'd be too ashamed," Mary said. "Strange the police didn't find these."

"Oh, I bet they found them all right. See how they're all scattered around," Lysi said. "They probably got a good laugh over them. Figured Kavanagh was into wearing frilly undies. Figured they had to be his since there were no complaints against him on file."

"Creepy." Grace dropped the panties into the drawer and swiped her hand on her wool jacket.

"Mary, grab a couple of those newspapers," Lysi said jutting her chin toward the pile of papers on the floor. "We'll wrap these up and take them with us. No need for someone to find them and trace the owners."

Mary held the newspapers open while Lysi and Grace emptied the dresser drawer into it. She rolled the newspaper pages around the knickers.

"Let's get out of here." Grace headed for the bedroom door.

"Wait," Lysi said. "Did you hear that?"

The three women froze as a clicking sound followed by a burst of cold air signaled the opening of the front door of Kavanagh's cottage.

"Police," Grace whispered. "I told you. It's the freaking police. We got to get out of here."

"No! Not the police. Police wouldn't creep around they'd march right in," Lysi whispered, almost wishing it was the police. "It's someone else." But who? An irate husband looking for evidence of his wife's betrayal? A father wanting to destroy evidence of his daughter's shameful fornication? A Mother after a victim's knickers hoping to save her child from shame? Maybe it's a desperate killer returning to retrieve something that could incriminate him.

That last thought frightened Lysi into action. Escape. Her eyes shot to the small window above the dresser. Not enough time for all three to squeeze through.

Hide. Her eyes skittered about like a trapped animal in search of a possible spot. A closet? No, just a small wardrobe. No large armchairs to duck behind. No bedroom bathroom. Only one space big enough to hide all three of them. "Quick, under the bed," she said.

Lysi squeezed under the bed followed by Mary holding the newspaper full of knickers. Grace hesitated. "Mouse."

A floor board creaked somewhere in the living room. Grace jumped, bolted under the bed and rammed in tight between Lysi and Mary.

"He'll see us if he looks at the bed," Grace said.

Lysi reached up and tugged a wool blanket down to partially cover their hiding place. All three stopped breathing partly from fear and partly from the sour smell of more than one pair of dirty socks under their noses.

A moment later the intruder's pretense of silence ended with loud, clomping male footsteps racing helter-skelter about accompanied by a cacophony of sounds—the swoosh of cushions thrown off the couch, the thud of chairs tipped over, a metallic clang as a lamp hit the floor. Next the clatter of kitchen drawers yanked open and the clink of cutlery tossed around. Creaky cabinet doors squawked open and dishes crashed to the floor jolting the nervous women.

"Stay calm," Lysi whispered. "He's not searching for knickers in the kitchen." So much for her ideas about jealous husbands and worried parents scouring for panties. Only the 'desperate murderer' theory remained.

She tried not to show Grace and Mary her fear as the lump in her throat dropped to her stomach. "He's looking for something else. The guy sounds nervous, hear how frantically he's racing around. He's desperate to find what he's looking for and get out as fast as he can. Not interested in us." Lysi didn't believe her own words and knew Grace didn't either.

"He'll get to the bedroom," Grace whispered. "Search the dressers, wardrobe, bedding, pillows, mattress, under the—"

"Stop Grace," Lysi said. "You don't know that. Besides, there are three of us and only one of him. We could take him."

"Yeah, right," Grace said. "We could battle him lying on our stomachs under the bed. Maybe beat him with these smelly socks, throw dust bunnies at him. Get real Lysi. We got a problem."

They heard bottles crashing to the tile floor in the bathroom. "Bedroom's next," Grace whispered.

A ray of light flashed on the bedroom wall. "Quiet! He's coming," Lysi said.

Footsteps entered the room and stopped by the bed. The man's flashlight revealed wrinkled pant legs with cuffs that brushed against muddy boots. The boots moved to the dresser. Drawers opened and clothes landed on the floor— shirts, sweaters, undershirts, socks and boxers. The intruder paused at the empty drawer where the knickers had been. Lysi held her breath and her heart thrashed like a frantic bird caught in a trap. What will he do next?

The boots returned to the bed and stood six inches from the women's noses. Lysi could see the boots had morphed into ankle-highs with Cuban heels and a red gusset down the side. Not shiny black cop boots. Not village farmer boots. Fear of the unknown intruder made her long for cop boots.

Blankets and pillows flew off the bed. No longer hidden by the blanket, the women didn't breathe. The intruder bent down and felt under the mattress. This is it, Lysi thought. If he's a murderer we're dead. Desperation swept through her. Maybe she could yank his ankles out from under him. But how could they squirm out from under the bed before he recovered his balance? Maybe if they just stayed still, he might not notice them.

Wrong.

His next search would be under the bed. Lysi had to do something. She tapped Grace's hand and pointed to the left boot. Grace nodded. She pointed to herself and the right boot. Grace nodded again. Lysi and Grace extended both hands towards the man's ankles. A deep-throated dog's bark turned the boot guy and the would-be attackers into statues.

The man stood perfectly still one hand holding a corner of the mattress a few inches above the bed and the other hand holding a flashlight. Lysi's hand rested in mid reach for the man's right ankle. Grace, her hands frozen in a clutch formation, ready to grab the left ankle.

Total silence.

Dennis McGill's shout to his dog, Kingman, shattered the silence. "Damn Peelers haven't got the God-given sense to close a cottage door after frisking it. Lucky no one broke in. What's this world—" The door slammed shut cutting off the rest of Dennis McGill's sentence.

Was McGill inside or outside? Lysi didn't know and hoped the intruder didn't know either.

The man dropped the mattress. The women heard hurried steps heading toward the window over the dresser, shuffling and kicking sounds as the intruder struggled through the narrow window and a thud as he landed on the ground outside.

In silent agreement, Lysi, Grace and Mary remained glued in place listening for the slightest sound, fearful that the intruder might return.

After a few minutes Mary whispered, "I've seen those boots somewhere before."

"Those are Elvis boots. Popular in the seventies in the U.S." Grace said.

"Elvis boots. You mean Elvis Presley?" Mary said.

"One and the same," Grace said. "You can still find them on Amazon and eBay."

"Irish men prefer less showy boots, black or brown," Mary said.

"Talk about showy," Grace scoffed. "Those bright red polka dot print pants screamed bad taste. His butt must look like a neon sign. I'd rather stick pins in my eyes than go out with a guy wearing a clown get-up like that."

"The trouser legs looked worn and dirty," Mary said. "He's single. No wife would allow him to leave the house looking like that."

"And they had cuffs. Way out of style," Grace said. "The guy has no fashion-sense at all. Cuffs went out of style in the nineties."

"In America maybe, but—"

"Not now you two." Lysi couldn't believe this had turned into a chatty Cathy fashion session. "Maybe you didn't notice we're still hiding under a bed in a dark cottage not knowing whether a burglar may return and murder us. We have to figure out how to get out of here."

Worries flooded her brain. Would Kingman, Dennis McGill's dog, sniff out Mary McClone? Would Dennis McGill alert the police? Was the intruder lurking outside maybe with a gun? Would they survive?

Nancy Curteman

Chapter 19

Under a cloudless early morning sky, Maynard and Chess boarded the 7:45 Enterprise train for the roughly two-hour trip from Dublin's Connolly Station to Belfast Central. They settled in beside each other on cushioned seats grouped two by two with a small table between the pairs. A ruddy-faced man took the two seats across from them. He sat in one and placed his briefcase on the other. He doffed his green tartan flat cap, nodded to them, placed a laptop on the table and did not lift his eyes from the screen for the rest of the trip.

Maynard watched the station disappear as the train moved North along the coast of the incredibly blue Irish Sea on its route to Belfast. Beautiful.

While Chess texted Grace, Maynard telephoned Billy and told him they expected to arrive about 9:30.

"You're not wasting any time getting here," Billy said. "Worried about your little amateur detective, eh." Maynard flinched at Billy's irritating chortle.

"Yes. I'm worried. Why isn't Lysi answering her phone? I called last night and this morning. It's not like her."

"Ah Maynard, Lysi's a big girl. Not to worry. She probably shut off her phone so she could sleep late."

Maynard didn't like Billy's answer. Lysi rarely turned off her phone for fear of missing an important call. Why would she do it now? And, why would she need to sleep any later than her normal 7:30 wake up time?

Maynard did not mention his concerns to Billy. Instead he said in as casual a tone as he could manage, "We'd have come to Belfast yesterday but couldn't get a night train out. Had to book an early morning departure. Can you pick us up?"

"Sure," Billy said. "But I've got an appointment at ten. Last maybe an hour. Go have yourselves a good Irish breakfast and we'll pick you up at the station around noonish."

"Fine. Now tell me what's going on." Maynard no longer tried to hide his impatience with Billy's unwillingness to take seriously Lysi's possible involvement in a murder case.

"No big deal. A guy named Liam Maguire almost plowed a tractor over a body in his father's field. Someone stabbed the guy."

Maynard swallowed hard. "How does Lysi fit into all this?"

"She doesn't ... Yet." Billy laughed.

Unable to do anything about their worries, Maynard and Chess ordered coffee from the trolley service and kept their eyes glued to the view from the window. The Enterprise train traveled along the coast then turned inland traversing rolling hills of green fields sprinkled with low-growing shrubs blooming with the golden glow of flowers. "Look at those yellow flowering plants in the fields and along the tracks," Maynard said.

"Furze." A middle-aged woman across the aisle leaned over and smiled at them. "We often use the shrubs to separate fields in place of fences. The blossoms are edible. Smell like vanilla or coconut and taste like almonds. We sprinkle them on salads or pickle them like capers."

"Interesting," Maynard said. "Thanks."

Modest yellow and gray farmhouses speckled the landscape. Stone churches with tall steeples towered over small villages and towns with names like Drogheda and Dundalk. The train passed several small stations strewn with hanging baskets full of flowers. At the Newry stop the woman across the aisle leaned over and said, "You're now in Northern Ireland."

A couple of coffees later they arrived in Belfast and got off the train on Platform 2. They entered a clean, spacious, high-ceilinged building and headed to a row of seats along a wall passing a sign that read, "Belfast Central Opened 26 April 1976."

The station was busy with people rushing, dragging squeaking suitcases on wheels. Tourists stood in line to exchange euros for pounds. Hungry travelers ordered snacks and drinks at crowded concessions.

As Maynard and Chess sat, they both pulled out their phones in unison as if choreographed. Chess tapped in Grace's number and Maynard tried Lysi.

*

Lysi rolled over. Her leg flopped off the edge of the narrow bed yanking her awake. A persistent pinging sounded in her ears. Without opening her eyes, she slapped her hand around on the top of the night stand trying to find her phone to shut off its alarm.

She squinted at Grace sprawled on the twin bed across the room, feet dangling off the end, red toenails sparkling in the rays of sun shining through cracks in the blinds. Ornate silver rings on each index toe added more sparkle. Grace didn't react to her ringing phone. It went to voicemail. No surprise she still slept. By the time they returned from Kavanagh's cottage and chugged a couple of Jamesons to wind down from their misadventure they hadn't gotten to bed until three a.m.

Lysi still remembered the disgusting smell of dirty socks and the musty dust bunnies clogging her throat. They'd waited under the bed for at least twenty minutes after the cottage had emptied, listening for footsteps and watching for a flash of light. They feared the intruder might return or that Kingman's tenacious barking might lead Dennis McGill to inspect the cottage more closely or even contact the police.

When they did crawl out from under the bed, they took a quick tour of the cottage to survey the damage—cushions ripped open, lamps and ash trays overturned, broken dishes and bottles, flatware scattered on the floor. Lysi couldn't stop wondering what the intruder was so desperately searching for. They decided to leave through the back window and take a round-about way home to avoid meeting anyone. Climbing onto the unstable dresser to access a narrow window had presented a challenge especially to Grace in spike heels that she refused to remove for fear of touching any "grungy" surface with her bare feet.

Lysi felt stiff. Her muscles ached and she longed for a shower but she still needed more sleep.

After a moment she realized the pinging wasn't the alarm. It was an incoming call. She picked up the phone and squinted at the screen. Maynard. Why had he called so early? No problem she hoped. Driving all the way to Galway on Irish roads could be risky.

"Maynard? Are you okay?"

"Yes, I'm in Belfast," Maynard said. "What about you? Why didn't you answer your phone last night and earlier this morning? Why didn't Grace answer hers?" Maynard's voice blended relief and suspicion.

Lysi ignored the question because she couldn't think of a good way to explain she and Grace had muted their phones because they'd crossed a cordoned off crime scene, entered a private house uninvited to search for knickers and hidden under a bed while a possible murderer ransacked the bedroom. No, not a good time to share their nocturnal excursion. She changed the subject.

"Belfast? What about your overnight trip to Galway with Chess?"

"We canceled it and caught a train to Belfast. I'll explain more when I see you. Billy has an appointment but will pick us up afterward. In the meantime, Chess and I are going to try an Irish breakfast at a restaurant called George's. A techie guy on the train recommended it. But back to the phone—"

"Those Irish breakfasts are fantastic." Relieved Maynard had brought up food, Lysi continued to distract him. "Wait'll you taste the coddle."

"Coddle?" Maynard said.

"Yes, it's a delicious mix of bangers, potatoes, onions and rashers."

"Rashers?" Maynard said.

"Yes, bacon." Lysi kept up a fast-paced monolog about the dish. "I love the origin of the name coddle. It comes from the slow simmering cooking process. Get it? Coddling. In fact—"

"Lysi, love, you can tell me all about it when I see you."

"Okay. Take your time and enjoy. I'll see you when you get here."

"I'm guessing that'll be around about one or two." Maynard disconnected.

Lysi clicked off, let her head flop heavily down on the pillow, closed her eyes and blew a big puff of air through her lips.

Chapter 20

Billy spotted Liam on a bench across from the Antrim Police Station on Castle Way. "There he is."

Liam sat with his elbows on his knees, hands clasped and head drooping. His jacket and disheveled pants looked like he'd thrown them on in a harried rush. A dry breeze blew old flyers and newspapers across his shoes. He didn't seem to notice.

Billy thought the police must have really worked him over. Liam had probably wanted to get out of there as fast as possible. Maybe that was the reason he'd asked Ryan to meet him outside instead of inside the station.

Ryan slammed on the brakes of his new Volkswagen Golf banging Billy against the dashboard despite his seatbelt. He swerved to the curb knocking Billy against the door. "Sorry, these damnable brakes are grabby and the power steering is awful powerful."

"Grabby?" Billy said righting his hat. "More like you pressed too hard on them. And take a lighter hand on the steering wheel, will you. You're not driving a tractor, you know."

"Maybe I should have driven my old pickup," Ryan said in a defeated voice as he shifted into neutral and set the handbrake.

Billy would have preferred riding in the old pickup to Ryan's bungling efforts to master driving his new car but he kept his opinion to himself out of consideration for his cousin's feelings. He wished he could have taken back the tractor comment. "It's okay Ryan. You just need a little more practice."

Both men bounded from the car and hurried to where Liam sat disconsolately on his bench. Liam jumped up at the sight of them and burst out, "They think I topped him."

"Liam, there's yourself," Ryan said. "Sit down and tell us how you ended up here."

"The bloody, egg-sucking peelers came early this morning, forced me out of bed and dragged me to the Belfast police station. Said I was not under caution, just a volunteer attendee, whatever that means. Am I going to jail?"

"No," Billy said. "It just means you have some involvement in the investigation but you're not under arrest or formally accused of a crime." He pressed down on Liam's shoulders. "Sit. You're not going to jail."

Liam crumpled to the bench. Billy and Ryan sat one on each side of him. Billy smelled the heady scent of daffodils wafting from a nearby garden. He thought the bright yellow harbingers of spring presented a sharp contrast to Liam's dark mood. He liked Liam and didn't want to see him held responsible for something he had nothing to do with. He would do what he could to help him. "There now ... start from the beginning and tell us everything".

Liam took a deep breath. "The peelers came to me da's house before breakfast. They said they wanted to help me because things didn't look good, me finding Kavanagh in me da's field and himself havin' cheated me out of me land and all."

"A reasonable assumption," Billy said. "So they didn't actually drag you out of bed and force you into a police car?"

"No, but it felt like it."

" Hmm. Go on."

"They said it would look better for me if I came in willingly to answer a few questions. But when we got to the station, they accused me and said it would go better for me if I just admitted I'd done it." Liam's eyes moistened and he shook his head several times. "I didn't do it."

"Liam." Ryan touched Liam's shoulder. "We know you didn't do it."

As a former prosecutor, Billy knew there were plenty of reasons to suspect Liam. He had means, motive and opportunity. Deep down in Billy's gut his prosecutorial voice kept insisting that Liam might have done it. "Do you have a lawyer?"

Liam stared at Billy.

"He means a solicitor," Ryan said.

"No," Liam said shaking his head.

"Billy, you're an attorney. Would you be willing to defend him?" Ryan said.

"I'm not licensed to practice in Northern Ireland. I will advise him but not defend him. What we need to do is find proof of his innocence."

Ryan nodded. "But how?"

"We find the guilty party." Billy sunk his teeth into his lower lip. "To do that, we need a skilled homicide detective." Billy paused, raised his eyebrows and focused on some distant piece of space. "I believe I know just the person for the job."

Nancy Curteman

Chapter 21

Lysi and Grace sat at a corner table in Mary McClone's pub feasting on a late breakfast of sausage, eggs and fried potatoes. They'd spent the whole meal brainstorming ways to explain their late-night excursion to Kavanagh's cottage to Maynard and Chess.

"We can't tell them we needed to find Mary's undies. That would embarrass her." Lysi cast a sympathetic glance at Mary behind the counter filling a china teapot with hot water and covering it with a floral tea cozy.

Grace cut off a piece of sausage, held it on her fork and looked at Lysi. "I know. Let's say we heard about a pending estate sale of a nice collection of sexy lingerie and we wanted to get a look at it before the sale? I know men, they'll think we did it for them."

"Too big a lie," Lysi said. "Too easy for them to track down a sale like that in a village the size of Beechgrove."

"Okay. Okay. Uhmm." Grace spoke while chewing the sausage. "I've got it. Some guy was stealing lingerie and hiding it in an abandoned house and we went to get it back. There's a lot of truth in that."

"You're right. There is some truth in that, but not enough." Lysi drained the last of her tepid tea and tried to think.

"How about this?" Grace dabbed at her lips with a lacy linen napkin. "We were taking our evening constitutional when we heard a pitiful mewing sound. We looked around and saw a little gray kitten scratching at a cottage door. We presumed the owner had forgotten to bring it in for the night. Any decent person would understand that it would have been inhumane to leave the poor little creature out in the cold night to freeze to death or get eaten by a vicious carnivore, so we picked it up and knocked on the door." Grace paused and gazed at the ceiling for a beat then returned to her story with even greater enthusiasm. "Oh yeah, the door swung open at our knock because it was ajar. We called out. No response. We couldn't just drop the kitten inside and leave. What if its family had gone on vacation and left it. So we—"

"Grace." Lysi shook her head. "That's a great story for a children's book but way too farfetched to lay on adult males."

"Okay, Lysi. Forget it. I see you hate all my ideas!" Grace stabbed another sausage.

"It isn't that I hate your ideas," Lysi said trying to walk back her harsh comment. "It's just that no one would believe them."

"Says you! Let's see if you can come up with a better one."

"Alright." Lysi perused the white plaster medallion in the center of the ceiling. After a moment she said, "We went out for an evening stroll. We came to the cottage and noticed the door was part way open. We knocked. No one answered so we stepped inside to have a quick look around. We saw the place had been tossed so—"

"Yeah, yeah. I got it." Grace shook her fork at Lysi. "So we crawled under the bed and stayed there for two hours sniffing dirty socks."

Lysi rolled her eyes. "No need for sarcasm. Just say you don't think the idea would work."

Across the room, Mary wiped her hands on a towel, picked up the pot of hot tea and brought it to the table. She refilled their cups, set the pot on a trivet, and sat across from Grace.

"How about this?" She said. "That nice Sean Kavanagh had generously offered some items for our spring rummage sale and we went to collect them? Oh no. Wait. No one would ever believe that because Kavanagh was neither nice nor generous." Mary's eyes sparked. "He's a greedy, rotten chauvinist hog."

Before Grace or Lysi could respond, Mary's mobile chirped. She took a calming breath and picked it up. As she listened her calm expression faded replaced by a deep furrow in her forehead. "It's my friend, Gemma."

Lysi arched her eyebrows in question.

"She's one of the Lowry girls. She's in a bit of a state."

Mary leaned over the table, placed the phone close to Lysi and Grace and pressed the speaker button.

"... and may go to jail." Gemma's voice sounded frantic through the phone. "And we're going to lose our farm."

"Gemma dear. Try to calm yourself and tell me what is going on," Mary said.

"We mortgaged our farm to pay off a loan. And we had to use our savings to pay the mortgage. Oh Mary, the money in the bank was our inheritance. It's almost gone. Now we can't make any more payments on the loan."

"Loan? From—"

"Well it wasn't exactly a loan. I mean there were no formal papers filed," Gemma said.

"Did you sign anything? Do you have a copy of the contract?"

"No." Gemma's voice quavered.

"Does anyone else know about the loan or whatever it was?"

"That's the problem. The police know."

"The police? Why or how did they get involved?" Mary scrunched her face in confusion.

"Our banker noticed large withdrawals from our trust account and asked about them. We told him we were making payments on a loan made to us. When we couldn't show evidence of the loan the banker alerted the PSNI."

"Sounds like the banker tried to help you. He thought you'd been cheated. That's why he alerted the PSNI," Mary said.

"What is PSNI?" Lysi whispered.

"Police Service of Northern Ireland," Mary said aloud.

"I know what PSNI stands for Mary," Gemma Lowry said in a disgruntled tone. "The Police Service of Northern Ireland."

"Of course you do," Mary said and continued to question her about the loan. "There's no proof of a loan, right? Then you shouldn't have to pay anything."

The muffled voices of Gemma and Emma arguing came through the phone. "You have to tell her the truth," Emma said.

"It is the truth," Gemma said.

"I mean the whole truth," Emma said.

"Emma, Gemma, what are you talking about?" Mary tried to hide her growing frustration.

"Oh Mary, please don't hate us," Emma said.

"We did something terrible," Gemma said.

Nancy Curteman

Chapter 22

On the way to the Lowry's Lysi tried to ignore Grace's melodramatic display of attitude as Mary's subcompact Toyota bumped over the muddy boreen. Brooding in the back seat—arms crossed, eyes fiery, teeth gritted—Grace made it clear she did not want to get involved with the Lowry girls' problems.

Lysi had tried to reason with her unreasonable friend. A bonfire flared in her cheeks when she thought about how Grace had totally erupted when Lysi mentioned her legal training to Mary and suggested they go and have a word with Emma and Gemma Lowry. Why did Grace have to go ballistic over doing a tiny little favor for Mary? It would have been heartless not to offer to help Mary's friends after she'd explained about the plight of the Lowry girls. How they were not young anymore and how it would be quite easy for someone to take advantage of them. When Mary added that the Lowry girls might lose the farm, they'd lived on all their lives and that they had lost their mother when they were still in school, Lysi's heart went out to them. All the poor elderly ladies had now was the farm and a small savings their father had left when he died. How could Lysi not help them? What on earth was wrong with that?

Mary parked the car in front of a white wooden trellis. A swinging gate opened onto a gravel path that led to a small cottage. As they approached the house a fat calico cat rose from a sunny spot on the porch, stretched and greeted them with loud purring and circular rubs against their legs. With some relief, Lysi watched Grace's face soften as she bent to stroke the cat. Maybe her temper would soften, too.

Mary leaned on the chiming doorbell and the door swung open. A round lady in a pink ruffled apron greeted them. Lysi thought she smelled like a bouquet of lilacs.

"Emma, dear." Mary encircled the woman in her arms.

Towering behind Emma stood a slim woman almost as tall as Grace. She wore a plaid wool skirt, a knit sweater and sturdy lace-up oxfords. Her no-nonsense facial expression reminded Lysi of her seventh-grade teacher, Sister Delores Marie's scowl when she slapped your hands with a ruler for stepping out of line.

"Oh Mary, we don't know what to do." Emma's eyes watered and her lips quivered.

"Now, now we're here to help," Mary said. "I brought two friends along. Lysi Weston and Grace Wright meet the Lowry girls, Emma and Gemma."

"Pleasure to meet you," Lysi said. Grace nodded and her lips curved into a grudging half smile.

"Lysi and Grace understand the legal system," Mary said.

Grace shook her head and opened her mouth. "We're—"

Lysi cut her off before Grace could object, "—here to help you."

Grace's mouth snapped shut but her eyes torched Lysi. So much for her temper softening. Both Lowry girls looked from Lysi to Grace, their faces radiating respect and hope.

Emma pulled a lace handkerchief from her pocket and dabbed at her eyes. Mary patted Emma's shoulder. "I'm sure it's not as bad as all that, dear."

"Oh, but it is." Gemma insisted. "I'm ashamed to tell you we've been paying a blackmailer."

"Gemma, don't feel guilty for paying a blackmailer," Lysi said. "You're the victim. The blackmailer is the culprit."

"Who is blackmailing you?" Mary asked.

"Sean Kavanagh."

Mary flinched at his name. "Sean Kavanagh was blackmailing you? He's dead now." She smiled. "It would seem to me your problem is pretty much solved."

Emma started to cry again.

"Hush Emma," Gemma said. "Go and put the kettle on."

"Why was he blackmailing you?" Lysi asked.

"We killed a burglar." Again Gemma was succinct and to the point.

"You … " Lysi didn't finish the sentence. Mary's eyebrows popped into her hairline. Grace's head jerked back hard.

"The burglar came to our house in the middle of the night. We woke and caught him filling a bag with our mother's silver. I told him to get out. He startled and punched me in the face," Gemma said, her voice calm as though she was describing a full day of activities.

"So you didn't fall and hit your face on the open oven door as you told the chemist when you bought the Neosporin? " Mary examined the abrasions on Gemma's face. She'd told Lysi she'd learned about the Neosporin purchase from a neighbor who had overheard Gemma tell the chemist about her fall, but she hadn't yet seen Gemma's face.

Gemma nodded and added in an angry tone, "The burglar raised his fist to punch me again. That's when Emma hit him over the head with a cast iron frying pan. She saved my life."

Grace moved closer to Gemma. "Let me have a look at your face."

Gemma pulled back but Grace already had her hand under Gemma's chin. Lysi knew Grace had seen her share of injuries from gang fights while growing up in Harlem and had learned from experience how to determine their level of seriousness. "Well Gemma, honey. You're gonna live, but let me tell you, if I'd have gotten my hands on your burglar, he'd have been begging to die. He'd have thought that fry pan was a feather duster by the time I'd worked him over."

"I had no choice." Emma called from the kitchen and began sniffling again.

"Hush Emma," Gemma said. "Bring a plate of those shortbread biscuits you baked yesterday."

"Emma's right. This was self-defense," Lysi said. "Why didn't you call the police?"

"We didn't need the whole village knowing our business." Gemma frowned.

"Our father would have been devastated if he knew his daughters had committed murder," Emma said. "We had to protect the family reputation."

"There's more," Gemma said as the Virgin Mary smiled down upon her from a gilded frame hanging on the wall above the table. "We stuffed his body into a sleeping bag and hid him in the old barn across the street. We planned to dig a hole the next day and bury him."

Lysi stared at Gemma unable to wrap her head around how a nice, elderly Catholic lady could stuff a body in a sleeping bag and plan to bury it.

"A car passed by," Gemma continued as though sharing plans for the church social. "We found out later it was Sean Kavanagh. He saw us. The next day he appeared at our door and promised he would help us. He said he would get rid of the body. He said not to worry. Everything would be fine." Gemma's features distorted. She slammed one fist into the palm of her other hand. "Lies, all lies!"

"Did he get rid of the body?" Lysi asked.

Emma returned from the kitchen with a plate of cookies, a teapot and cups. She set the cups on the table and started to sob again.

"Calm down pet," Mary said. "Go on Gemma."

"He did get rid of the body but then he started blackmailing us. He said he'd tell the police what we did if we didn't pay him to keep our secret. When we heard he was dead we thought it was over."

"They found Kavanagh's body in Maguire's field. So he can't blackmail you anymore." Mary said.

"Yes, but we got another blackmail letter," Gemma said. "Emma, show them."

Emma went to the sideboard, lifted the lid off a china soup bowl, pulled out a letter and handed it to Mary.

Mary read the letter. "'I know what you did on the night of March 2nd.'" She looked puzzled. "I don't understand. What does this mean?"

"Don't you see? Somebody else knows about the murder," Gemma said. "Now the police will say we committed two murders, the burglar and Mr. Kavanagh."

And Kavanagh's murder won't be self-defense, Lysi thought.

Chapter 23

Maynard's projected two o'clock Beechgrove arrival time had ended up stretching to four o'clock because Billy picked him up two hours later than planned. Obviously, Billy's appointment ran longer than expected, but two hours later? Maynard wondered what kind of appointment could take two hours longer than scheduled. Now at nearly five o'clock, Maynard stood outside McGarrity's Bed and Breakfast and eyed the pink exterior walls of the two-story building with its frame of interlocking magenta quoins.

"Pink," he mused. "I guess there's a first time for everything." He shrugged and followed Lysi through a single door into the B&B, ducking to avoid knocking his hat against the door header. As he trailed her up a narrow flight of carpeted stairs, he watched the soft swivel of her hips just for the sheer pleasure of it. At the head of the stairs they entered the room Ryan O'Rourke had booked for them.

A quick glance around the room told him it lacked the elegance of the Merrion but had a homier more comfortable feeling. The room had a laid-back, lived-in feeling that reminded him of his sheep station homestead. A puffy duvet-covered queen-sized bed dominated the room. He fantasized lying in it with Lysi. Tucked in a corner a small, antique-like makeup vanity perched on skinny legs. Maynard judged its swing mirror might be useful to Lysi, but much too low for him. A well-used mahogany armoire with a bonnet top and three bottom shelves stood like a sentry between two south-facing windows overlooking an English garden. In a corner of the garden on a small patio surrounded by shrubs and flowers sat a reed table and chairs. Nice spot to relax with Lysi and enjoy a cool drink.

Lysi dropped her overnight bags on the patterned carpet and flopped on the bed. She fell back into an ocean of ruffles on an over-sized pillow, and closed her eyes. "Umm, nice."

"Very nice." Maynard winked signaling he did not mean the bed. He'd missed her. Seeing her lying there ignited a desire to show her how much.

She flashed him a weary smile.

"Tired, eh," he said. "Keeping late nights?"

Lysi's eyes flew open. "No. I'm ... I'm ... not tired. I ... I just ... Okay. I missed you. Shed your jacket and get comfortable."

Her strong reaction reinforced Maynard's feeling she was hiding something. Each time he'd asked about her activities in Belfast or questioned why she hadn't answered the phone when he called, she changed the subject. Her evasiveness coupled with Grace's panicky telephone call from the pub restroom and Billy's mention of a village murder added up to trouble. He'd been around that block with Lysi before. It was uncanny the way she managed to sniff out homicide investigations wherever she went.

Lysi kicked off her shoes, wriggled her toes and patted the bed next to her. "Come lie beside me. I need a little snuggle."

Maynard knew what she meant by "a little snuggle" and his body responded with rising heat. He knew he would have to get to the bottom of the Lysi mystery—but not right now. He had more appetizing things on his mind.

"Give me a minute," he said taking off his jacket and hat and tossing them on a chair in the corner. Lysi's seductive signals ignited a testosterone fire in his loins. She had this wonderful way of inviting him to make love to her without asking for it. Something in her eyes, smile and body movements. He couldn't put his finger on it exactly but recognized it when he saw it and it always fueled his desire for her. "I'll be right back. Hold that pose."

Lysi smiled and ran her tongue slowly over her lips. "Hurry back my handsome Aussie."

He slipped into the small ensuite bathroom, closed the door, removed his travel clothes and opened his ditty bag. As he pulled out his toothbrush, toothpaste and cologne, his thoughts strayed to the first time he'd made love to Lysi. It was in South Africa and it was wonderful. There was no holding back, no self-consciousness, no hesitation. Sexual energy raced back and forth without impediment. He remembered thinking it couldn't get any better. He was wrong. Making love to Lysi had just gotten better and better. He adored her. In a few minutes he'd show her how much.

As he washed and dried his face, he spoke to her through the closed door just to hear her voice. "So, Lysi, how do you like Belfast?"

"Umm, very nice. The people are friendly and welcoming." Her low, throaty voice tantalized him.

After brushing his teeth, he asked, "Did you find the city had changed much since you visited with your father?"

"Uh huh."

Her voice sounded so sexy he decided not to take the time to comb his hair. He wanted her in his arms. He wanted to breathe in her warm feminine scent, kiss her, hear her sighs and murmurs. Every nerve in his body longed to touch her.

He opened the bathroom door full of passionate expectation. Already breathing hard, he walked slowly to the bed and leaned over her.

Lysi lay sound asleep.

Nancy Curteman

Chapter 24

The queasy feeling in Lysi's stomach increased as she watched Maynard sit in silence running his finger through the condensation on the outside of a glass of beer, he'd nursed for the past half hour. Private time together in the inn hadn't lightened his mood as she'd hoped. Of course, her dozing off in bed at a most inopportune moment hadn't helped. If she could do it over, she'd stick needles in her feet to stay awake.

Mary's pub hummed with customers crowded at pine tables drinking beer and winding down from a day's work. The jovial group contrasted sharply with the heavy atmosphere at Lysi's table. Like a dog in fear of getting kicked if it barked, Chess sipped his beer without talking. Grace sat stiff and sullen like a chastised toddler. Maynard's eyes seemed to focus inward as if drowning in worry and indecision. Guilt and shame crushed Lysi's chest as she avoided eye contact with the people she cared most about. She loved Maynard and never intended to hurt him. All she wanted to do was help a friend. Why had everything gone so terribly wrong? She almost wished he'd just yell at her and get it over with. Not his style.

Lysi knew it had upset Maynard when she told him about the excursion to Kavanagh's cottage. It upset him even more when Grace opened her big mouth about crossing the police tape, and their close call with the guy who ransacked the house. Then to compound the problem, Grace just had to blab about the visit to the Lowry girls. Yada, yada, yada. Lysi tightened her fist around a napkin in her lap and imagined shoving it down Grace's throat.

Stop! She thought. It's not Grace's fault I wanted to play detective. She didn't want anything to do with the whole thing. I'm to blame.

But when Billy heaped fuel on the fire by chiming in about Liam Maguire's problem Lysi had had enough.

"Billy," she said, a warning in her voice, her eyes shooting sharp darts straight into his Adam's apple. "Maynard's not interested in Liam Maguire."

"Oh, I think he is," Billy said flashing that "gotcha grin" that had infuriated Lysi ever since she could remember. She wanted to smack him the way she'd done so many times growing up. A lot of good it did, he just learned to dodge. She turned her head and blinked back frustrated tears before they could fill her eyes.

As much as she hated to admit it, she had to concede Billy might have a point. Of course, Maynard would feel conflicted about a homicide. On the one hand, he maintained he wanted no part of an investigation while on the other he still loved the challenge of chasing down clues that led to solving a case.

Lysi felt better. If she moved carefully, she could probably enlist his help. A guilty feeling of optimism lightened her mood. After all, wouldn't he be doing something he enjoyed?

When she caught Chess shaking his head and sending Maynard a sympathy message, her optimism waned. What is it with men? They seem to think a small request is a giant imposition and requires a pity party. A little voice in Lysi's head reminded her the request was not small. She checked her irritation.

Maynard took a swallow of beer. After a deep breath he said, "Look, I'm not going to get involved in an investigation, but I am a bit curious about a few things."

Lysi fought back a grin that tickled the corner of her mouth. He's hooked, she thought.

"What are you curious about?" she said, trying to maintain a neutral expression.

"There's nothing to be curious about," Grace said. "We told you everything." Her eyes turned into bullets and she shot them at Lysi. She grabbed her beaded purse and turned to Chess. "Come on, Chess, I'm ready to call it a night and hit that big feather bed at McGarrity's B & B."

Chess' eyes widened and his lips stretched into a wolfish grin. He leaned forward and bounded half out of his chair almost before Grace finished her sentence. Lysi fired a wilting look at Grace. Billy laughed.

"Just a few questions to satisfy idle curiosity. Nothing more." Maynard steepled his fingers and leaned into them staring into space. "First, about the burglar. Did the Lowry girls know him? If not, did the police identify his body?" He paused and looked at Lysi. She shifted in her chair.

"Now about the Kavanagh murder," he continued. "Did the police determine if Kavanagh had been killed in the field or elsewhere? In other words, was the field the actual crime scene? Did anyone else have a motive for killing Kavanagh? Did the police recover the weapon?"

Lysi leaned forward and stared at Maynard. Damn, she hadn't thought of those questions in her urgency to help Mary and the Lowry girls. "Maynard, I don't have any answers."

Billy's face took on the satisfied look of a lion standing over its freshly killed prey. "The only way to find the answers is for a skilled interrogator to question witnesses. A homicide detective." He jutted his chin toward Maynard. "Someone like you, Maynard."

"No," Maynard said.

"Then I'll do it," Lysi said.

"Lysi," Maynard said. "Two murders have occurred. This is serious business. Leave it to the professionals. We don't like amateurs mucking things up."

Lysi latched on to Maynard's use of the word "we." Sounds like he's including himself in this case.

"Ah, don't be so hard on her," Billy said. "She's a smart lass. She could do it."

Lysi knew Billy was baiting Maynard. She knew Maynard worried for her safety. She also knew she would never forgive herself if Mary or the Lowry girls went to jail and a killer went free.

Nancy Curteman

Chapter 25

Michael Doherty hated driving in Belfast especially on Saturday nights when gangs of dodgy, alcohol-soaked louts hung out on street corners looking for trouble.

As the windshield wipers slish-sloshed back and forth in the rain, he thought back to the first time he'd driven to Belfast. He'd scraped enough money together to buy a second-hand Kia and decided to take Paddy to see the Titanic Museum, a memorial to the voyagers who lost their lives when the British luxury liner sank on its maiden voyage.

They both marveled at the magnificent reflective silver surface of the ship-shaped building. They visited all nine galleries that included re-creations of the shipyard where the Titanic was planned and built, passenger cabins and an actual railing from the ship. They stayed until the museum closed then drove around 'til they found a pub where they grabbed a bite to eat—pasties, chips and a beer.

Everything went fine until a group of tanked up hoodies began taunting them with derogatory comments about gypsies—pikies, knackers, sheep-shaggers.

Michael grabbed Paddy's arm and dragged him to the door. When Paddy shouted an obscenity over his shoulder, Michael, aghast, jerked him outside.

Too late.

They heard the guys, like snorting bulls, spring to their feet and stampede after them. Michael and Paddy ran to the car with the bulls gaining on them. Once in the car, Michael locked the doors and fumbled for keys. The bulls crowded around rocking the Kia 'til Michael thought for sure it would topple over. He started the engine and raced away from them.

Michael sighed in relief until at the next intersection from the pub a red light forced him to slam on the brakes. He checked the rearview mirror fearing they were trapped. The louts didn't follow, but laughed and flashed the middle-finger salute along with a chorus of "feck offs."

The memory of that experience had kept Michael from driving in Belfast at night ever since.

Michael entered central Belfast and eased into a parking space on a dark street. As he got out of the car, a drop of sweat dripped down a side of his face and mixed with cool rain. He pulled a hoody over his head and crossed Donegall Square, turned up Pattersons Place and stood outside the Midnight Club. The drab building stood on a narrow cobblestone street littered with trash—beer bottles, empty cigarette packages, tickets, and old playbills. It resembled the kind of back alley dive that sent shivers of fear through Michael's body. He'd never been in the popular nightspot. Notorious for drunks, fights and drugs, it was one of his brother Paddy's favorite hangouts.

He stepped forward, took out his wallet and fumbled for an ID. Well over eighteen, but looking younger, Michael often got carded at bars and pubs. He presented his identity card to a doorman.

The thick-necked, florid-faced doorman, more fat than muscles, examined Michael's photo ID card, flashed a penlight in Michael's face, momentarily blinding him, and with a jaundiced eye, shoved the card back at Michael and motioned him inside. Michael swallowed and paused before entering. He pulled out a tattered photo of Paddy. "Ever see this bloke?"

Without even looking at the photo, the doorman shrugged his mountain shoulders and shook his Cro-Magnon head. Michael assumed it was the doorman's business never to recognize any of the customers who frequented the club.

When Michael stepped into the overheated pub, a mix of odors—beer, smoke, sweat, perfume—wrenched his gut. His feet sticking to the filthy floor and the blur of hot bodies nudging against him on his way to the bar increased his revulsion. His eyes darted about the room. Shouts from above drew his eyes to a creepy voyeuristic balcony filled with men. They leaned on a railing checking out the women on the crowded dance floor below as they thrashed and moshed and bounced to an earsplitting Nirvana video.

Shouting from the middle of the dance floor startled Michael. A big bruiser of a man lunged at a guy with a shaved head. Both men with fists doubled ready to come to blows at any second. Another man grabbed the bruiser's arm before a blow could land. "Catch yourself on there lads. No need to be knocking lumps off each other, now is there?"

Michael wanted no part of that and didn't wait for the outcome. He averted his eyes and hurried toward the bar.

A sharp tug on his arm halted his progress and his heart. He turned his head and almost bumped noses with a woman so bladdered she leaned on him to stay upright.

"Buy me a drink, handsome. I'll make it worth your while," she slurred.

Michael jerked his arm from her grip. Unable to hide his distaste, he clenched his teeth and shook his head. "I'm not staying."

"You can bugger off," the woman said. She gave him a hard shove and staggered away grabbing at people as she stumbled into the crowd.

A slim, red-haired man stood behind the bar. He wore a white shirt, collar unbuttoned, tie hanging loose, and sleeves rolled up above the elbows revealing a tattoo of a lightning strike on one arm and a snake coiled around the other. Michael watched him draw a draught from a tap that had a leprechaun head for a handle. As froth flowed down the sides of the glass he glanced at Michael. "What'll it be, mate?"

Michael pulled out Paddy's photo and held it up to the bar tender. "Seen him lately?"

"You buying or leaving?" the bartender asked.

"A Guinness." If buying a beer was what it took to get him some information about Paddy, Michael considered it worth it.

The bartender set a pint on the counter. "Four euros."

Michael knew the bartender had inflated the price but assumed information costs more than beer. He slapped four euros on the bar and held up the photo again.

"Aye, he's a regular." The bartender turned away.

"When did you last see him?" Michael asked without sipping the beer.

"You say you want another beer?"

Michael cursed under his breath, nodded and slapped four more euros on the counter.

The bartender picked up the money, sucked air through his teeth and looked up at the ceiling. "About two weeks ago. I remember because the little twit bragged about coming into a lot of money."

*

Michael Doherty parked his dilapidated Kia outside the Local Police Station. His palms started to sweat as he surveyed the ominous building—a bomb-proof brick structure with no windows set in a car park surrounded by a chain link fence, a single bullet-proof iron door the only entrance. The building was a relic from the time of the Troubles when local police stations were regular Irish Republican Army bombing targets.

After learning from the bartender at the Midnight Club about Paddy bragging that he'd come into a lot of money, Michael had decided he needed to file a missing person report with the local station of the Police Service of Northern Ireland if he had any hope of finding his brother.

He tried to swallow the lump in his throat and summon courage to enter the station, but his mouth went dry. Like most Travellers, Michael kept his distance from police stations. Although there was no evidence anywhere to suggest Travellers and Gyspies committed more crimes than any other groups, the belief still existed among some police officers and local citizens that they did.

Maybe he should just forget about filing a report. They might give him a bollocking for presuming they'd conduct a search for a "vagrant." It might be a waste of time anyway because the police didn't bother much with concerns filed by Travellers because they received so many complaints about them from community members.

And the money? Where would Paddy get a lot of money? Had he stolen it? If so, filing might help the peelers locate and prosecute him. No, better to continue searching for Paddy on his own.

A vision of Paddy beaten and robbed of the alleged money flooded his mental screen. Michael bit his lip. He couldn't allow that to happen.

Better to file.

The police station door opened on a small room with a row of chairs along one wall. Michael walked to a window at the end of the room and waited until a dark-haired woman wearing a white blouse and necktie looked up from a computer. "Yes?"

Michael set a photo of his brother on the counter. "Me brother's gone missing."

The woman looked through the glass at the photo. Her eyes rested on it for a beat then fixed, unsmiling, on Michael.

Could she tell he was a Traveller from his face? No. Born in Derry, he looked like any other Irishman with his dark hair, fair skin, blue eyes. He didn't have the telltale darker features of the easy-to-spot Roma Gypsies who were believed to have originated in India.

Still, he felt she knew he was a Traveller. She probably inferred it from his accent or the way he had trouble maintaining eye contact.

She turned to a filing cabinet behind her, pulled out a form and picked up a pen. "I need to ask some questions. I know you may not know the answer to all of them but they may help us build a picture of your brother."

Michael determined to answer the series of questions with caution and care as best he could, avoiding any reference to the money or Paddy's previous run-ins with the police.

"Missing person's name?"

"Patrick Doherty. He goes by Paddy."

"Can you describe your brother—age, weight, height, hair color, distinguishing details?"

"Nineteen years old. About 59 kilos. About 170 centimeters. Blonde hair. A tiger tattoo on his left forearm."

The woman filled in some lines on the form and without looking up said, "When did you last see your brother?"

Michael flashed on the night Paddy stood by the road waiting for one of his troublemaker friends to pick him up for what Michael expected would be a night of mischief. "A week ago at our encampment on Tully Road."

There, now he'd done it. With the word 'encampment' he'd stamped Paddy as a Traveller. Would the PSNI even bother with anything more than a cursory search. The woman didn't seem to take note of the slip. She continued questioning Michael.

"How did he seem? Upset? Angry? Scared?"

"No." Michael didn't mention how mad Paddy got when Michael got rid of a small baggie of coke, he'd discovered under Paddy's bed a month ago.

"Does he have any close friends?"

"No." Michael decided not to mention Paddy's good-for-nothing mates. The police probably had their names on reports anyway. Association with them would look bad for Paddy.

"What was he wearing when you saw him last?"

"A black track suit and black shoes."

"Did he take anything with him? Is anything missing from his room?"

"Don't know."

"Does he have any medical conditions or need vital medication?"

"No." Michael swallowed. Not unless you call addictions to spirits and drugs medical conditions.

"Is he dependent on alcohol or drugs (prescribed or illegal)?"

Michael paused long enough for the woman to guess he would lie. And he did. "No."

"Do you know of any reasons he might disappear? Life-changing events that might affect his mental or physical wellbeing?"

Another pause.

He knew from the way the woman squinted at him that she anticipated another lie. "No."

"Okay." The officer spoke in a tone of dismissal.

"Do you think you will find him soon?" Michael asked, immediately wishing he hadn't asked such a stupid question."

The officer frowned at him. "Depends."

Michael waited.

"When somebody disappears, there are usually only four main possibilities: suicide, kidnapping, murder or flight," the officer said in a bored tone. "Depends on the reason for the disappearance."

Michael wanted to question her more but didn't want to upset her.

"We'll get out flyers with this photo and begin making enquiries. Let us know if you think of anything else or if you hear from him." The officer returned to her paperwork.

Michael nodded. "Thank you."

Would the police search for his brother despite his half-truths?

Nancy Curteman

Chapter 26

Maynard stepped from the B&B into a crisp, clear early morning. He stretched and took a deep breath of clean air. No rain yet. Nice. He looked up and down the street deliberating which way to go for a brisk morning walk before waking Lysi for breakfast.

Near the grocery he spotted a man in a black peaked hat, black tie and white shirt with epaulets. Maynard ambled toward him. Drawing nearer, he made out an emblem on the man's hat, a star encircled with the words Police Service Northern Ireland. Interesting.

The officer was tacking flyers on shop doors. The flyers bore the photo of a young man. Below the photo in black print Maynard read the name Paddy Doherty.

Maynard stopped, hoping to engage the officer in conversation and maybe learn a bit about the Northern Ireland police department. He smiled. "Good day."

The man had a freshly laundered appearance when he turned a young, rosy-cheeked face to Maynard and smiled back. "'Good dye' to you, mate," he said imitating Maynard's Aussie accent. Aiden Quinn here. Constable Aiden Quinn, Police Service of Northern Ireland."

"Maynard Christie. Nice to meet you."

"You'd be from Australia, eh?" Aiden Quinn said.

"That's right," Maynard said. "From Sydney."

"Aye. I know it well," Aiden Quinn said. "I've visited me uncle there. He emigrated to Sydney ten years ago. A bonza city as you Aussies would say."

"Aye, that it is, as you Irish would say." Maynard liked the exuberant young officer immediately. "You're at work early."

"We have a person gone missing. I'm distributing flyers throughout the village hoping someone might have seen the lad."

"How long has he been missing?" Maynard asked, his professional curiosity kicking in.

Nancy Curteman

"Over a week. He's a Traveller and his brother didn't report him missing right away. Those blokes don't put much faith in the police."

"Traveller?"

"Aye." The constable moved to the curio shop and tacked a flyer on the wood window frame. "Irish gypsies."

Maynard knew about gypsies. Small bands of Romani gypsies roamed about Australia, even in the Outback. He hadn't had much occasion to interact with them because they preferred to keep to themselves. He knew they had Australian citizenship but lacked the respect of the general population that considered them layabouts and thieves.

"I'm out for a morning stroll," Maynard said. "Would you mind if I tagged along? I'm a retired cop myself. I was a homicide detective in Sydney. I'd like to learn a bit about the Northern Ireland Police Department."

"Would you now?" The constable flashed another affable grin. "Well then, you've come to the right person. Come along. I'd be glad of the company. I don't get to talk to Aussies often."

Maynard could tell the constable was new on the job. His youthful enthusiasm radiated like a flashing neon sign.

As they continued towards a row of cottages on the outskirts of the village's main street, the constable chattered on about the police, making statements Maynard felt sure he'd memorized verbatim from the police manual. The kid must have just graduated from Student Officer Training.

Aiden looked about eighteen years old. Maynard knew he had to be about twenty because the age requirement for preliminary police officer training in the U.K. was eighteen and to complete the program and attain the level of constable took about 2 years. Similar to the Australian program patterned after the British system.

When they reached the edge of the village, Aiden went from cottage to cottage tucking the flyers into mailboxes.

At a picturesque cottage that looked like it came straight from a Thomas Kinkade painting with its rose arbor and gravel path leading to the door, Maynard saw an elderly woman peering out the window. A second later another elderly lady joined her. When Constable Quinn stepped onto the porch, both women disappeared from the window and in an instant the door flew open.

"Aiden ... I mean Constable Quinn, we can explain," the taller woman said. "Won't you please come in for a moment and hear our side of the story."

Noticing the familiarity with which the woman first addressed the constable, Maynard concluded she'd known Aiden Quinn since he was a child.

Constable Quinn looked confused but he turned to Maynard and stuttered, "These are the Lowry girls. They make the best biscuits in town."

Maynard stiffened. Lowry girls! He remembered Lysi said the Lowry girls had committed murder.

"Ladies," Aiden continued. "This is my friend ... uh …"

Maynard saw that in his confusion, Constable Quinn had forgotten his name. "Maynard. Maynard Christie."

Calling the two elderly ladies "girls" struck Maynard as an oxymoron. They had to be in their late seventies or even early eighties.

"Gemma Lowry, I'll not complain if you'd be willing to share a few of your delicious biscuits with us?" Aiden said to the tall woman.

"Yes, yes," Gemma said stepping aside to allow the constable and Maynard to enter. "Emma, please set up tea and biscuits."

The house smelled of lavender and reminded Maynard of the Sydney homes occupied by elderly ladies he'd interviewed during various investigations—overstuffed velveteen couch and matching arm chairs scattered with colorful pillows, crocheted doilies on tables, couch arms and chair backs, frilly lamp shades and a large collection of glass ornaments. A very fat calico cat lay on the back of an overstuffed chair gazing out a window curtained in sheer organza ruffles. The place was too busy for Maynard's taste, but it suited the Lowry girls perfectly.

Gemma with silver hair cut in a bob was almost tall enough to look six-foot two Maynard in the eyes. She wore an Aran jumper over a conservative plaid wool skirt that complemented her sensible brown oxfords.

Emma, short and very round had pink cherubic cheeks almost the same color as her ruffled apron and flouncy dress. Her skirt swirled over shiny patent leather buckle shoes as she turned and hurried into the kitchen.

In no time at all, Emma swirled back from the kitchen and placed on the table a tray that held a delicate bone china teapot, matching milk pitcher and sugar bowl, four cups and a plate of biscuits.

Constable Quinn laid his packet of flyers on the table and took a bite of a butter biscuit. "Mmm." After a sip of tea he said, "Now Miss Lowry, what is it you need to explain?"

Gemma opened her mouth and stared at Constable Quinn's grinning face. Maynard realized the newbie officer knew nothing about the murder Emma had committed. He felt for the young man and did not want to see him humiliated. What to do? He couldn't just blurt out what Lysi had told him the Lowry girls had shared with her. He couldn't say he'd read it in the newspaper or claim to have heard it in the pub. No one knew about it yet. He blinked his eyes several times trying to come up with a solution.

He turned to Gemma. "Miss Lowry, the constable wants to hear the story directly from you, not from a third party. Why don't you share your concerns?"

"It was all my fault." Tears filled Emma's eyes.

"No it wasn't." Gemma spoke in a firm voice. "She had no other choice. We did what we had to do."

Now Aiden Quinn looked even more befuddled. He took another bite of biscuit and turned confused eyes to Maynard.

"I'm sure you did," Maynard said. "I think a bit more explanation would help Constable Quinn understand."

Gemma dropped her eyes to the flyers on the table. Her hand flew to her mouth and with a loud intake of breath, she said, "Holy Sainted Mother Mary! That's himself."

Emma followed Gemma's stare. "Saints preserve us. That is himself."

Constable Quinn's befuddled look increased. He cleared his throat. "You mean you know where to find Paddy Doherty? When did you last see him?"

"The night he burgled our home," Gemma said.

"The night I killed him," Emma mumbled.

Nancy Curteman

Chapter 27

Maynard walked with Aiden to the Police Land Rover parked at the edge of the village where he'd left it when he began distributing flyers. The young constable's unstable gait and chalky face told Maynard the kid could pass out at any moment.

When Gemma confessed to the murder of Paddy Doherty, Maynard had thought Aiden might go into shock. His body had jerked causing him to choke on a biscuit he'd just bitten. The remaining half of the biscuit slipped from between his fingers and splashed into his tea. He grabbed his napkin and held it to his mouth as he coughed repeatedly. His face turned tomato red.

Aiden had probably known Emma and Gemma Lowry all his life. Probably sat at their table even before his feet could touch the floor, legs dangling as he gobbled butter biscuits while listening to the Lowry girls' stories of their long-ago childhoods. Maynard figured their confession must have hit him like a gentle, loving grandmother holding an adoring grandkid on her lap and suddenly announcing she'd offed his grandfather with an iron griddle.

As they approached the Land Rover, Aiden stumbled and grabbed for Maynard's arm. Maynard caught his shoulders. "Breathe, Aiden. Breathe."

Maynard leaned Aiden against the side of the car and held him there with one hand planted in the center of his chest while he opened the door with the other. "Get in."

Aiden obeyed.

"You okay now?"

"Aye, fresh out of the box," Aiden stammered, his face white tending toward green. Clearly, he was not okay.

"Keep taking deep breaths," Maynard said. "That's it. That's it."

After a few breaths Aiden's complexion returned to a less ghostly pallor. "Now," Maynard said. "Feeling better?"

Aiden nodded.

Maynard knew Aiden needed to report the murder confession right away. "Let's talk about how we plan to report this incident."

He broached the subject with caution using the word 'we' instead of 'you.' He'd used this interrogation strategy often with frightened young witnesses in his job as a homicide detective. The word 'we' conveyed to witnesses his desire to work through the ordeal along with them.

"Aye." Aiden looked around the car—shuffling boxes, reaching into the glovebox, rummaging through folders. Maynard could see his confusion.

Wanting to provide some direction, Maynard said, "Let's talk a bit about the Lowry girls' confess—"

"Oh, aye," Aiden said. "The Lowry family has lived in Beechgrove for generations so they have. St. Brigid church cemetery has headstones bearing the Lowry name that date back to the eighteen hundreds."

Maynard realized Aiden had misunderstood his effort to guide him in the logistics of reporting a confession but decided to let him talk out the background of the Lowry girls as a way to calm himself.

"See, back in the day three Lowry brothers owned large farms that joined." Aiden said. "They raised praties."

"Praties?"

"Potatoes. Then in 1845 the Irish Potato Famine struck. A million Irish died and another million emigrated. Two of the Lowry brothers up and took their families to America. Colm Lowry, the youngest stayed on and took over his brothers' farms. The farms stayed in the family.

"Seamas Lowry, Colm's only wean, wedded Colleen McLaney who gave birth to Emma and Gemma. The girls had such a sad life. Their mother passed while they were still in primary school. Then they lost their father when his car got bombed during The Troubles. No one knew which side did it or why because Seamas kept his nose out of the disputes. After her father died, Gemma took over managing the farm. To this day they still raise the best praties in Ireland."

Maynard listened to Aiden without interruption. He knew about the two terrible periods in Ireland's history that Aiden referenced. During the Potato Famine hundreds of Irish emigrated to Australia. Irish immigrants were a boon to Australia. They were crucial to the survival and prosperity of the early Australian colonies because they provided much needed labor.

Maynard remembered Australian newscasts about the period known as The Troubles that pitted Irish against Irish, Catholic against Protestant, and Royalists who wanted to remain a part of the United Kingdom against Republicans who wanted to unite with the Irish Republic. Over 3,600 people were killed and thousands more injured during the 30-year period.

"Ah now, I cannot believe Emma murdered someone." Aiden shook his head and his eyes moistened. "When I was a wee lad Emma would invite me and me friends in for biscuits and tea all the time. She listened to our stories, laughed at our jokes, soothed away our sad times."

Aiden suddenly paused and turned pleading eyes to Maynard. "Ah now Maynard. Sure we know it isn't true. She couldn't murder anyone. She's old. Maybe she's a bit daft. Maybe she only thought she did it. Maybe we shouldn't report until we're sure."

Maynard stared at Aiden. Clearly, he needed a reality check. "Aiden, listen to me. That is not your decision to make. Emma confessed she murdered Paddy Doherty. Report it now."

Nancy Curteman

Chapter 28

Under a leaden sky heavy with the promise of rain, Constable Aiden Quinn pulled the police Land Rover off the road. He parked on a patch of weeds in front of an unauthorized Travellers caravan site and turned to Maynard. The young constable looked miserable. Maynard had advised him to go right from the Lowry girls' cottage to the police station to report the crime, but the young constable wanted to first inform Michael Doherty of his brother's death. He'd asked Maynard to come with him to break the news.

At first Maynard refused not wanting to get involved in a procedural breach but changed his mind when Quinn told him his own brother had died in a barroom brawl four years ago and the first his family learned about it was from the newspaper. He didn't want anyone to go through that pain.

Maynard understood Quinn's reluctance to face Michael Doherty alone when he discovered the young constable had only been on the job for a week and already had to deal with a murder confession. Telling a man his brother had died in the commission of a burglary would be difficult for a veteran officer. Even tougher for a newbie.

May as well get it over with Maynard thought as he opened the car door. "Are you ready?"

Quinn nodded.

They walked into the camp. It consisted of about 20 caravans, some near new others run down and shabby. A large black mongrel tied to a post near one of the caravans barked hysterically and jerked at its rope. Out of the corner of his eye Maynard saw a group of about five young men dressed in track suits glaring at him. They don't have much use for police here, he thought.

Quinn nudged him and motioned with his chin toward the men. "Bad craic. They hate cops."

Maynard and Aiden passed an elderly man perched on a low, wooden bench in the shade of a large sycamore tree. He bobbed his head in rhythm with a melody he pumped on an Irish Concertina. Maynard took in his stringy grey hair and saggy jowls. That skeletal frame would make a scarecrow look like it needed to lose weight.

Quinn stopped in front of the man. "Good day sir."

The man ignored Quinn's effort to communicate with him and continued playing and bobbing. Quinn shrugged and walked on.

In a clearing bordered by a half circle of caravans, shabbily dressed children stopped their jump rope rhymes and soccer games. They stood like statues and stared at the two men.

A woman sitting in a lawn chair with her legs spread around a plastic tub full of scrap metal raised her skull-like face and regarded them with suspicion.

Maynard waited for Quinn to speak. When he didn't Maynard removed his hat and said, "Good day Ma'am, we're looking for Michael Doherty."

One of the woman's gray eyes wandered making it difficult for Maynard to tell if she focused on him when he spoke.

"Don't know that name," the woman said.

"We understand he lives in the camp. Is there someone who might know him?" Maynard asked.

The woman's stable eye shifted left and right. "Don't think so."

Maynard was about to press the woman for more information when a little girl about seven or eight years old, in a baggy dress hanging loosely from her thin shoulders interrupted him.

"I know Michael Doherty," she said twisting a bit of hair between her fingers. "He lives in that caravan over there." She pointed at an old metal trailer with peeling blue paint.

The woman glared at the little girl. Maynard feared the kid would get a sound whipping later.

"Don't beat the wean for being honest," Quinn said.

The woman sneered at Quinn.

Michael Doherty opened the trailer door to their knock. Again, Maynard waited for Quinn to take the lead. No luck.

"Michael Doherty?" Maynard asked the dark-haired man standing barefoot in the doorway, clothes rumpled as if he'd slept in them.

"Aye. Is this about the missing person report I filed?"

"May we come in, Mr. Doherty?" Constable Quinn asked in a quavering voice.

The small trailer's built-ins consisted of cabinets, a stainless-steel sink and a gas stove along one wall. A table and benches that could convert into a bed stood on the opposite wall. Another bed sat on a shelf above a padded bench in the back of the trailer. Plenty of room for two young men to live comfortably. It was clean and well organized.

"Have you found my brother?"

"I think you need to sit down, Mr. Doherty," Maynard said.

Michael sat down and looked up at Maynard through worried eyes.

"We have evidence your brother is dead," Aiden said. "We're so sorry for your loss."

"No." Tears filled Michael's eyes. "How?"

Maynard dreaded that question as always. Never an easy way to answer it. "We understand that he died while committing a burglary."

"A burglary!" Michael shook his head in disbelief. "My brother? Dead? Committing a burglary?" His voice faltered. "No."

Nancy Curteman

Chapter 29

When Maynard climbed out of Constable Quinn's Land Rover, he found Billy Weston standing outside McGarrity's B&B holding a large shopping bag. "Good day, Billy. What kind of mischief are you up to now?"

Billy laughed. "No shenanigans. I'm waiting for me cousin, Ryan. He dropped me off to do a bit of souvenir shopping for me friends back home." Billy opened his bag to show Maynard. Inside were several ceramic leprechauns, damask napkins, keychains, a couple of plaid flat caps and Celtic jewelry. Billy looked at his watch. "Ryan should be collecting me just about now."

Maynard would have found Billy's Irish masquerade amusing if the self-proclaimed leprechaun hadn't irritated him by trying to involve Lysi in a murder investigation.

Billy stared after Quinn departing in the Land Rover then squinted at Maynard. "And yourself? What have you been up to this fine morning?"

Maynard had no intention of revealing anything about his morning with Constable Quinn, the Lowry girls or Michael Doherty. He knew he'd have to come up with some explanation since Billy had seen him get out of the Land Rover with the glaring letters on the front and sides spelling out "Police."

"Consorting with the PSNI. Fancy that," Billy persisted.

"Listen, Billy. It's not what you think."

"Not what I think? You mean that you just got out of a cop car, driven by an officer who might very well be investigating a recent Beechgrove murder? The evidence is pretty overwhelming. Maybe you should explain."

Maynard removed his Bush hat, ran his fingers through his hair and shook his head. He knew he couldn't hide the morning's events from a former big city district attorney for long. Billy wouldn't stop until he'd sniffed out the facts. He also knew it wouldn't be too difficult the way word got around in a small village. "Okay, okay."

Maynard explained how he'd met Constable Quinn on a morning stroll and walked along with him as he distributed missing person flyers, and ended up at the Lowry girls' cottage where they learned about Paddy Doherty's murder. "We informed the victim's next of kin of the death. "That's all there was to it. I was just a tagalong. No further involvement."

Billy's mouth gaped. He tossed his head back, roared with laughter and pulled a handkerchief from his pocket to swipe at teary eyes. "Maynard me lad, you are up to your neck in involvement. Why you've even discovered a second murder. Fancy that!

Maynard clenched his teeth and turned toward the B&B door but stopped when he heard a horn honk.

Ryan O'Rourke skidded his Volkswagen Golf to a screeching stop a couple of feet from Billy.

Billy leapt back and forgetting his Irish brogue shouted, "Ryan, what are you crazy? You almost ran me over."

"Sorry, can't seem to get on with this bloody car. Mainly the light brakes and touchy accelerator."

Ryan waved to Maynard. "I heard you took a ride with young Constable Aiden Quinn this morning. Quite a shock the Lowry sisters knocking off Paddy Doherty. Tough having to break the news to Michael Doherty. Nice lad. Burglary, eh. Clear case of self-defense by my way of thinking."

Billy opened the VW door, turned towards Maynard and raised his brows to an I-told-you-so level.

Maynard didn't even try to hide his amazement that his whereabouts had leaked out so quickly. He wondered who else knew. He hoped the gossipy news hadn't reached Lysi yet. He didn't need her pressing him for details. "I just got back," he said. "How did you find out so fast?"

"Maynard, you're in Beechgrove. You can't sneeze without someone spreading the word that you might be coming down with pneumonia," Ryan said.

"Maynard me mate," Billy said, his brogue back. "Since you're already part of the investigation, would you be willing to just have a wee word with Liam Maguire?"

Liam Maguire? At first the name didn't register with Maynard. He hadn't paid much attention as on the way back from Belfast Billy had babbled on about Liam Maguire's encounter with the police. Another murder suspect.

Maynard's first inclination was an adamant refusal to talk with Maguire. Involvement with the Lowry girls presented enough problem. He didn't need to toss Liam Maguire into the mix. No use compounding his problems with another murder suspect.

Billy got out of the car, leaving the front door open and slid onto the back seat. "You take the front. You need more leg room."

Maynard didn't get in. He debated the best course of action. If he refused to go with them, Billy might obligate him to talk with Maguire anyway. On the other hand, if he went, he might be able to nip things in the bud and avoid any further obligation to investigate the murder of the man in his potato field. Maybe not. No good course of action.

Maynard sighed and folded himself into the car. Ryan pressed on the accelerator and the car lunged forward. Maynard's head banged against the headrest. He glared at Ryan. "What's the hurry?"

"Sorry. I've only had the car a week. Not used to this bloody accelerator. Took a lot more pressure to move my old '87 Ford pickup."

"Relax Maynard." Billy patted him on the shoulder. "Ryan's been practicing. It's the boreens he hasn't mastered yet. You know, those narrow country roads lined with shrubs and stone fences. Almost hit an oncoming car yesterday. Swerved into some bushes just in time. Not to worry we'll only be on a boreen for about twenty minutes." Billy smiled. Maynard didn't.

Nancy Curteman

Chapter 30

Maynard thrust his hands against the dashboard as Ryan swerved to the right onto a short lane and jolted to a hard stop next to a sign that read Maguires Pinks, Pure Balls of Flour, 5 kg €1.99. Maynard read the sign aloud, "Pinks? Pure balls of flour?"

"Praties. Potatoes," Ryan said. "Pinks are floury potatoes and make the fluffiest mash. The Maguires raise and sell Pinks."

Maynard observed Maguire's two-story cottage with its windows framed in brown trim. It looked like many of the gray pebbledash cottages he'd seen while distributing the missing person flyers with Constable Quinn. A stack of turf drying under a corrugated tin roofed shelter next to a large stone barn caught Maynard's attention. He knew the European Union had set restrictions on cutting turf in several peat bogs by designating them as National Heritage Areas. He'd read about the public outcry in rural areas resulting in de-designation of some bogs. He guessed Beechgrove village bogs had been in the de-designated group.

As he followed Billy and Ryan up a gravel path to the cottage, he glanced through the barn's open sliding door and noticed a tractor and plow sitting idle. Strange. Seems like an Irish farmer would take advantage of a fine day like this to work his fields.

Liam Maguire answered Ryan's knock. As soon as he opened the door, a black and white Border collie pushed past him and excitedly snuffled the visitors' pant legs.

"Bridget! Bed!" Liam said. The collie looked with longing at the three sets of pant legs before loping to a large wraparound dog bed. It whined softly before settling down, chin on paws, eyes glued to the three strangers.

"Ryan, Billy, good to see you. Come in. We're main glad you came, so we are." Ryan closed the door and directed them to the living room with a motion of his chin. "Would you take a cup of tea in your hand?"

Without waiting for an answer, Liam shouted over his shoulder, "Da put the kettle on. It's Ryan and Billy." His eyes strayed to Maynard. "And ... "

"Liam," Billy said, "You remember I said that in order to prove you innocent we would need to find the guilty party and that we'd need a homicide detective for that job. Well, here he is. Liam Maguire, meet Maynard Christie, retired Australian homicide detective."

Surprise silenced Maynard a beat "Now wait—"

"Detective Christie, a pleasure to meet you." Liam extended a hand. "I'll be forever beholden to you for your help."

Liam's father called from the kitchen, "Come on in. Tea's almost ready,"

The three men sat around an oilcloth covered table set with mugs and a platter of biscuits.

Maynard could see Liam's discomfort. His demeanor was typical of many suspects he'd interrogated in his cop career. The interviews always went better when he established a rapport before diving into a discussion of the case.

"I have a farm in Alice Springs," Maynard said. He knew mentioning his farming background would establish a common link with Liam and calm him. "I raise sheep. We call it a sheep station. I'm happiest when I'm working on my station."

For a moment Maynard's mind drifted to his Outback station. He felt the joy of rising early under a cloudless blue sky and laboring hard until sunset along with his hired hands—herding sheep with Lizzie, his border collie, maintaining and repairing machinery and water systems with his foreman, and his favorite challenge, joining the shearing team in the annual sheep shearing, a backbreaking "art." He saw himself grabbing a sheep by its front legs and holding the struggling beast while shearing its wool off in less than 3 minutes. He could still hold his own with the best "gun" shearers.

"I love working the land." Liam's facial muscles softened. Maynard saw joy in his eyes.

Liam's father patted his son on the shoulder. "He's a hard worker is Liam."

Maynard pulled a small notebook from his pocket, the detective's tool. He still carried it with him out of years of habit. "Now Liam, I need to tell you I can only act as an advisor."

"I know, I know," Liam said. "The same as Billy. You're not licensed in Northern Ireland. We're lucky to have the pair of you listening to our troubles."

Liam and his father exchanged nods.

"Detective Christie," Liam continued. "I just appreciate whatever you can do. May Saint Michael the Archangel, our patron saint of policemen, bless you for it."

Maynard noticed that Liam and his father spoke with the lengthening vowels and slight sibilance that marked the speech of Antrim country folk.

"Okay," Maynard said. "Let's start from the beginning."

Liam added a teaspoon of sugar to his tea, stirred and sipped it. His eyes desperate he told Maynard about Kavanagh's high-interest loan with his land as collateral, his inability to pay back the loan, and Kavanagh taking ownership of his farm.

Maynard sympathized with Liam. He could only imagine how he would feel if he lost his sheep station, but his professional expression did not betray his feelings. He scribbled a few lines in the notebook and looked at Liam. "I know a bit about your situation from Ryan, but I have some questions that will help me gain a clearer understanding of the case. Are you okay with answering some questions?"

"Aye, I'll answer any questions I can."

"I know you discovered Kavanagh's body in your father's field."

Liam nodded.

"Tell me how that happened."

"I was deep plowing a potato field getting it ready for our March planting when I spied a bit of red cloth a couple of meters in front of me tractor.

"Almost ran over it. I jumped down and walked over to pick it up so I could continue plowing. When I got closer I saw ... " Liam swallowed and his breathing rate increased.

"Take your time," Maynard said.

"I ... I saw a hand just sticking out of the dirt, then a body. I turned it over to see if I could help. It was Sean Kavanagh. Dead."

First mistake, Maynard thought. Liam may have contaminated the crime scene. "What did you do then?"

"I ran back to the tractor and called 999."

"And?"

"I told the police there was a dead body in me field. Two PSNI officers from the Serious Crimes department came."

"Go on."

"Men in white and blue uniforms wearing gloves put Kavanagh in a bag and an ambulance took him away." Liam paused a moment and knitted his brow. "Oh, I forgot. They took photos first then hauled him away."

Liam took a swallow of tea. "Other officers cordoned off an inner circle with red and white police tape around where the body had lain. They used blue and white tape to cordon around a wide outer perimeter." Liam shook his head. "I haven't been able to work in the fields since."

Maynard now understood why the tractor stood idle in the barn. As he considered Liam's vivid recollection of the events at the crime scene he thought it sounded procedurally accurate.

"The PSNI know about Kavanagh taking me land. The whole village knows." Liam hung his head. "Sure and they'll be accusing me of the killing."

Maynard didn't acknowledge Liam's concern but continued to question him. "Did the police determine if Kavanagh had been killed in the field or elsewhere?"

Maynard knew outdoor crime scenes were the most difficult to investigate. Exposure to elements—wind, rain, or heat, as well as animal activity could contaminate the scene and lead to the destruction of evidence. For that reason it was critical to know if the field was the actual crime scene.

"I don't know," Liam said. "I guess so."

Maynard realized that his question had gone unanswered.

"Did the police recover the murder weapon?"

"I don't know. At the police station they asked me if I owned a knife."

"Do you?"

"Yes." Liam shook his head before continuing. "I use it for a variety of things you might do on a farm like cutting twine, topping vegetables, cutting cloth, peeling fruit." Liam swallowed hard and added, "Slaughtering … animals."

"How did you feel when Kavanagh confiscated your land?"

"I was upset. Angry. I begged him for more time."

"Did you at any time threaten him?"

"No! I knew there was nothing I could do. Me and Da planned to save every penny we could to buy back the land."

"Do you know of anyone else who might have a motive for killing Kavanagh?"

"I can answer that," Liam's father said. "Almost the whole village. Kavanagh rubbed on just about everyone at one time or another."

"Anyone in particular?" Maynard asked.

Liam's father looked at Ryan. "He put his hands on O'Malley's young daughter, Kiara. Remember that scene in Mary McComb's pub? "

"Sure I do," Ryan said. "O'Malley knocked Kavanagh on his arse."

"Aye, but Kavanagh's filthy lusting after her didn't stop until the wee Kiara ended up with child," Liam said. "Thank the Lord fate intervened and she aborted."

"Remember the time Kavanagh beat Mulligan's dog nearly to death because it dug a wee hole in his yard," Ryan said. "The poor wee animal had to be put down."

"He carved his initials in the trunk of Dooley's faery tree and laughed in his face when Dooley told him the faeries would have their vengeance," Liam added.

"He paid for that one with his life," Ryan arched his brows.

"What?" Maynard's eyes jerked to Ryan. "Are you saying Dooley murdered Kavanagh?"

"No, no. I don't know that. I do know that if a body desecrates a faery tree his demise will soon follow be it from sickness, accident or murder—faeries will have their revenge. My uncle disrespected a faery tree." Ryan affected a scary tone and dilated his eyes. "He heard the banshee scream that very night, did my uncle. 'Screeeee.' He died of biliousness before the morn."

"That he did. That he did," Liam said.

After listening to several other stories about Kavanagh's behaviors. Maynard consulted his notebook and flipped it shut. "The man was a rake," he said. "I can see how any one of these people could have motive to commit murder."

Maynard believed Liam innocent but knew that wasn't enough to keep him out of prison.

Chapter 31

On the drive back from Liam Maguire's farm, Maynard spotted young Constable Aiden Quinn's Land Rover parked outside a small house. Dilapidated police tape surrounded the yard. Not another case piled on the young constable. Maynard wondered how Aiden was coping after his traumatic morning.

As a senior detective, Maynard always felt sympathy towards the plights of new police recruits. He had even mentored a few in Sydney as well as conducting several police science workshops for them. He liked Aiden and believed he would become a fine officer with good support.

What was Aiden up to? Curiosity got the best of him.

"Ryan," Maynard said. "No need to drive me all the way to the B&B. Just drop me off here. I'd enjoy the walk."

Ryan swerved to a stop slamming Maynard and Billy against the passenger doors and nearly hitting a dog stretched out on a sunny patch of grass at the side of the road. The dog yelped and scuttled under a cottage porch that hid all but his black nose and frightened eyes. Ryan sighed. "Not used to this power steering."

Maynard righted himself and opened the car door trying not to show irritation. "Thanks for the ride."

"Hey, that's Kavanagh's cottage," Ryan said. "It was burglarized a couple of nights ago. I see young Aiden got the job of surveying the damage."

Cold fear swept over Maynard as he stared at the cottage. This is Kavanagh's cottage. This is the house Lysi and Grace broke into Friday night. This is the house a burglar ransacked. Had Aiden found some evidence that might implicate Lysi? He had to find out what Aiden had discovered.

"Maynard," Billy said from the backseat. "You wouldn't be stopping here to see what's going on with your young constable would you?"

"I might have a word with him," Maynard said. "He's still learning. Might remind him of proper procedures."

"Right," Billy said. A grin played on his lips. "Right. Well, see you at dinner tonight. Tally ho."

"That's not Irish. Tally ho is British," Maynard said climbing out of the car. "Don't mix your languages."

Ryan peeled out scattering gravel and dirt on Maynard's pant legs.

Maynard brushed off his pants, and tapped on Aiden's window. Aiden set the report he was writing aside and rolled down the window. "Maynard, 'bout ye."

"I'm fine. What's going on?" Maynard asked.

"There was a break-in Friday night. Dennis McGill reported it this morning. I guess Kingman discovered it first—"

"Kingman?" Maynard worried. The more people involved in a crime, the more complicated it became.

"McGill's dog. I got assigned to sort things out. I surveyed the scene." Aiden sounded unsure. "Now I'm writing up my report."

Maynard glanced at the report on the car seat and saw Sean Kavanagh's name.

"So Aiden, how's the report going?"

"I think okay." Aiden patted the report, looked uncertain and said, "Would you be willing to have a look at it? It's my first report and I'd really like to get it right."

Maynard couldn't believe his luck. He didn't even have to ask to see the report. Now if he could convince Aiden to allow him inside the cottage he could determine if Lysi left any telltale evidence of her presence. "I'll be glad to but I should take a look inside the cottage first to make sure we got everything."

Aiden hesitated.

Maynard's hopes diminished.

"I don't have to go inside ... if it makes you uncomfortable. I just wanted to make sure we hadn't missed something." Maynard tried to ignore a rush of guilty feelings.

"I ... I guess that's okay. Can't hurt anything, I guess." Aiden got out of the car and led Maynard into the cottage.

The living room looked as if a tornado had raged through it—cushions on the floor, end table drawers wide open, lamps turned over. The kitchen was even worse. Contents of cupboards and drawers scattered all over the floor created an obstacle course. Maynard knew Lysi had nothing to do with the condition of the kitchen and living room. She had come in search of Mary's underwear and would not have bothered with those two rooms. She would have gone directly to the bedroom. The burglar had to have ransacked these areas of the house.

Maynard's skilled eyes noted indicators of the burglar's presence—large muddy boot prints. He checked Aiden's report. "Good, you noted the muddy boot prints. What about McGill and the dog?"

"No, because we know neither himself nor the dog entered the house," Aiden said.

"Could the dog have picked up the scent of the intruder?"

"Aye, it's possible," Aiden conceded. "I'll note that."

Maynard scanned the scene. A laptop computer tossed on the floor and the general condition of the room convinced him the intruder was not burglarizing, otherwise he would have grabbed the computer. The bloke was searching for something. What could he have been so desperate to find?

Maynard followed Aiden into the bedroom and surveyed the scene careful not to touch anything. Yes, just as he expected. The disturbed dust under the bed left irregular imprints of three bodies where Lysi, Grace and Mary had told him they'd hidden when they heard the intruder enter. He checked Aiden's report and noted he hadn't mentioned the imprints. Should he tell him?

Muddy boot prints indicating the escape route of the intruder led to the window above the dresser. But imprinted on top of a couple of the large boot prints were smaller shoe prints and even high heels. Aiden had listed the large boot prints but not the smaller shoe prints. Due to inexperience, Aiden had done a pretty sloppy job.

Aiden trusted him. If Maynard didn't point out the problems with his report the young constable could get into trouble. If he did point them out, the police could track the clues back to Lysi, Grace and Mary because he was sure their fingerprints were all over the bedroom. Maynard gnawed his upper lip. He faced a serious dilemma.

Walking back to McGarrity's B&B after Aiden had driven off, Maynard's emotions slammed from anger to worry and back to anger as he fumed over Lysi placing him in an untenable position. At a deep level he regretted not pointing out any of Aiden Quinn's missed clues that pertained to Lysi. Maybe, he rationalized, the police wouldn't even recheck the crime scene. But if they did, he considered it unlikely Aiden would receive much disciplinary action because of his inexperience. Lysi was a different story. If the police did recheck the scene, they'd see what Maynard had seen—small muddy footprints, body shapes under the bed. Worse, they might dust for prints and find Lysi's. If she had to enter the house, why didn't she at least wear gloves? Maybe she did. Crossing the crime tape might not be a problem because it had fallen to the ground. Breaking and entering was another story. Would he be able to come up with a way to keep Lysi and her cohorts out of jail?

Chapter 32

Lysi's eyes shot open at the thunderous pounding on her door. She moaned and tried to nudge Maynard but instead jabbed empty space. She patted the pillow next to her. No Maynard. She called out to him thinking he might be in the bathroom. "Maynard, can you get the door."

No answer.

The knocking continued louder and more insistent. "Up and at 'em. The day's half over." Grace's voice sounded annoyingly cheery.

Lysi knuckled her eyes, dragged out of bed, yawned and grabbed a robe. "Coming!" she called, and muttered "Don't get your knickers in a knot." Since when did Grace become an early riser? She opened the door to her friend. Grace looked irritatingly chipper. "What did I do to deserve this pre-dawn invasion?"

"Top o' the morning to you, mate." Grace eyed her and laughed. "Whoa, honey. You look like you had one hell of a wild night. Didn't that amorous Aussie tiger of yours let you get any sleep?"

"No tigers in Australia." Lysi grinned. She wasn't about to tell Grace about the sizzling night with her torrid tiger.

A thrill rippled through her as she recalled the feel of Maynard's muscular body pulling her close and the hungry flame of desire in his eyes as he ran his hands over her thighs and hips. His kisses still burned on her lips, neck and chest. The memory of reaching the pinnacle of their lovemaking made her legs weak. She caught her breath and said, "Let's just say I had a very satisfying night."

"Hmmm. We'll get to that later," Grace said. "It's a beautiful day. Let's stroll to breakfast."

"Grace, breakfast is downstairs, not what I'd call a stroll."

"Why do you always have to split hairs? Get dressed and let's eat. I'm faint from hunger."

Lysi rolled her eyes, motioned Grace in, grabbed jeans, a shirt and sweater, and disappeared into the bathroom.

"Where's your hunk of prime rib?" Grace said.

"He doesn't like it when you call him that. He's a sheep man not a cattleman."

"Okay. But lamb chop doesn't seem to suit him. Oh, I know. How about erotic ram?"

"Right, Grace. I'm sure he'd love that. Not!" Lysi said pulling on a sweater. She zipped her jeans and added, "I don't know where he is. He got up before you almost knocked the door down. He's probably on a walk about."

"You mean 'a limp about' after you wore him out satisfying your ravenous carnal appetite."

"Give me a break, Grace."

"Hey, I understand. My hunk is still sawing wood. I guess our ferocious lovemaking last night exhausted him." Grace's voice became throaty. "First I put on that red see-through Frederick's nightgown. Then I did a little burlesque show. After that I—"

"Grace." Lysi stuck her head out the bathroom door. "I get the picture. Don't need more visuals."

The B&B dining room had pretty much emptied out by the time Grace and Lysi finished their late breakfast of porridge, fruit and eggs. Lysi looked at her watch. "Eleven thirty. We may as well order lunch."

Grace laughed.

Mary McClone rushed into the dining room. "Lysi! I need to talk to you."

"Good morning, Mary. Have a seat. A wee cup of tea?" Grace said attempting an Irish brogue.

"No. No thanks. It's about Gemma Lowry. Herself called me in a panic this morning. Someone slipped this under her door." Mary handed Lysi a piece of binder paper folded in half.

Lysi unfolded the piece of paper and read the note. She looked up at Mary. "When did Gemma find this?"

"When … when she opened the door to let the cat out," Mary said.

"So we don't know if the writer delivered it last night or in the morning," Lysi said. "That might present a problem."

"So … we don't care because it's not our problem." Grace's voice rose.

"Calm yourself, Grace," Lysi said.

"I am calm." Grace set her cup of tea down hard enough to splash drops out onto the table. "Look at me. This is me being calm."

Mary stared at Grace. "I'm sorry. I didn't mean to … "

Lysi shot Grace a now-see-what-you-did look. Grace lowered her eyes. Lysi could tell Grace was sorry she'd unintentionally hurt Mary.

After a loud sigh, Grace shrugged. "Not that I'm interested, but what does the note say?"

Oh she's interested. Lysi knew curiosity was one of Grace's vices. She also knew well how to exploit it.

The writer had printed in blue ink, the well-formed letters written in neat script. Lysi read it aloud: "I know about the murder. Bring €500 in a brown bag to the old shed at 10:00 tomorrow night or I go to the police. Tell no one."

"This is very fine printing. A woman could have written it." Lysi ran her fingers over the letters. "My guess is the writer wants delivery tomorrow night not tonight because regardless of when she slipped it under the door Gemma would not have found it until this morning."

"The Lowry girls have been through so much. They can't do this alone. I promised to help them," Mary's voice weakened and she stole a glance at Grace.

"Of course, we need to help them," Lysi said.

"We? We? No, Lysi, no!" Grace almost shouted.

"Grace is spot on," Mary said. It's not your problem. I'll just have to manage on my own. I wanted you to have the note in case something happened to me."

Lysi watched Grace's face soften as she listened to Mary. Grace turned to Lysi. "Last time, Lysi. Last time."

Grace was hooked.

"We need a plan," Lysi said. "We can't let the blackmailer know the Lowry girls have told anyone." She picked up her teacup and held it to her lips a moment gazing at a painting of a green Antrim hillside hanging on the wall as if she expected to find the answer there. After a sip she set the cup down and said, "We go to the shed before the blackmailer comes. We hide. The Lowry girls bring the money to the shed at ten. The blackmailer shows up. We nab her."

"Hold on, Lysi," Grace said. "Let's just report the blackmailer to the police. Show them the note. Let them take care of the nabbing."

"First, we don't know who the blackmailer is. Might be a neighbor, a villager, even a police officer. Second, if an officer shows up at the Lowry's the blackmailer will see him. This culprit is smart. Probably watching the cottage and the girls. The blackmailer won't suspect Mary taking a couple of American tourists for a stroll around the village."

"We could sneak around to the old shed through the neighbor's back garden." Mary's voice strengthened.

"Perfect," Lysi said. "What could go wrong?"

Chapter 33

Lysi and Grace sat in institutional guest chairs at the foot of Gemma's hospital bed in Belfast's Royal Victoria Hospital's new Critical Care Center. Lysi glanced out the only window in the room located on an upper floor of the 12-story building, and wished she was anywhere but there. She would prefer a dentist's drill to spending time in a hospital ward. She didn't like the antiseptic smells, the continual pings and buzzes of electronic patient monitoring devices, and the millions of germs she imagined floating in the air ready to attack her.

When Mary telephoned to say she'd received a call from Emma that Gemma had fainted and an ambulance had taken her to the Royal, Lysi guessed it was more serious than a simple fainting spell. Mary had driven Emma to the hospital and discovered Gemma had suffered a heart attack. Lysi and Grace rushed to the hospital to support the Lowry girls.

Emma held Gemma's hand as tears squeezed from the corners of her eyes. Mary held both sisters' free hands. The group resembled a solemn version of a kid's circle game, Ring-Around-the-Rosie.

Gemma's pale face and dry lips spoke of the ordeal she'd experienced, but her sharp eyes warned against any silly you-poor-thing comments.

"The Royal hospital staff will provide the best possible treatment available in County Antrim," Mary said. She explained that the landmark, glass-walled critical care center had its roots in some grand history. Over 30 years ago Frank Pantridge, a cardiac consultant at the Royal, had developed the defibrillator which probably saved Gemma's life. "Thanks to that fine man, you'll be fit as a flea in no time."

Emma smiled through her tears.

A cheery young nurse sashayed into the room. "Good morning Miss Lowry, how are we today?"

Gemma frowned at her and didn't respond as the nurse checked a clipboard.

Undeterred by Gemma's warning frown the nurse persisted in using the wrong approach to a no-nonsense woman like Gemma. In a sing-song voice the nurse said, "I think we need a trip to the loo. Don't you?"

Lysi cringed and braced for the response she thought would come.

Gemma raised her chin to a haughty height. "I do not need a trip to the loo, young lady. If you need a trip, go ahead without me."

The nurse's smile faded. "A ... I don't—a ... Do you need anything—water, more pillows, an extra blanket?"

"No. What I need is some time alone with my guests if you don't mind. Run along to the loo. Ring if you need me. I'll do the same if I need you. Thank you."

Lysi felt sorry for the young nurse as she watched her blink, turn and slink from the room.

Grace guffawed. "Great scene, Gemma. I think you're well on your way to 'being fit as a flea.'"

"Well," Gemma said, "it had better be soon. I've no time to waste lying about." Her voice though weak was adamant.

It was ironic that Gemma, the strong, take-charge sister would end up with a heart attack while the more fragile Emma appeared fine. Lysi wondered if Gemma's worry over both the blackmail note and Emma's pending police interview hadn't triggered the collapse of an already weakened heart.

Gemma turned to Mary. "Not worried about my care. Am worried about getting out of here to meet that blackmailer tonight."

Mary opened her mouth but Lysi spoke first. "You're not going anywhere tonight or any time soon. In-hospital recovery time for your procedure is at least three days— perhaps five."

"Five days! That's daft." Gemma tried to rise but Grace blocked her attempt with an arm barrier across her chest. "Uh, uh. You're staying right where you are even if we have to zap you with a stun gun, tie you into a strait jacket and chain you to the bed. You hear what I'm saying?"

Gemma's mouth hung open. She stared at Grace. Lysi was sure Gemma knew Grace couldn't follow through on her threats, but something in her tone subdued Gemma. The powerful Lowry girl, her voice filled with unaccustomed helplessness asked, "What do we do now?"

"We just won't go tonight," Mary said.

"We can't cancel!" Gemma sounded desperate. She looked hard at Emma. "You have to go tonight to meet the blackmailer."

Emma went almost as pale as Gemma. "I know you're sore tried by all our trouble Gemma, but I—"

"Not to worry, Emma," Lysi said. "We'll be with you and so will Mary."

Grace patted Gemma's leg. "Hey, Gemma, the four of us will reduce that blackmailing swine to protoplasm. I say bring him on."

For a moment, Lysi thought she might have misheard Grace. Of course, she hadn't. Grace always came through when needed. Grace would relish taking on a cowardly man who would stoop so low as to try to cheat two helpless old ladies out of their livelihood.

The question in Lysi's mind was, what kind of monster would they meet tonight?

Nancy Curteman

Chapter 34

As the sun started its slow descent toward the horizon in an extravaganza of red, orange and yellow, Lysi, Grace and Mary left the pub clad in jeans and black hoodies in sharp contrast with the colorful sunset. Lysi considered the black hoodies overkill, but Grace insisted they needed them for camouflage to enable them to blend into the surrounding darkness during their clandestine undertaking.

They turned right and headed through town toward the shed where they expected to encounter the mysterious blackmailer. Lysi had explained her plan to Emma and assured her it couldn't fail. After considerable hesitation Emma, her voice quavering, had promised Lysi she would try her best to do her part. Lysi had little confidence in Emma's ability to follow through on her promise, but there was no Plan B. She had to trust her.

The three women strolled along the road acting out the role of casual tourists as a cover for their night stroll. Lysi reasoned the blackmailer would certainly be surveilling the area to verify that Emma came to the shed alone. Three women discussing historical sites would not interest him or her.

Mary acting as tour guide, pointed out cottages and described their history. "That's the MacGregor cottage built in the 18th century. Note the old stone walls and slate roof. The half door and small windows were typical of the time."

Grace and Lysi made it a point to exclaim with exuberance at each tourist attraction.

"Over there you see the O'Nally house." Mary pointed to a white-washed, L-shaped building. "It served as an inn in the early nineteenth century, and as a Coach Stop on the way to Belfast. See those two cast iron, horse-head hitching posts."

As they walked, Lysi's eyes swept from side to side, watching for any movement. They didn't need company tonight.

Mary continued her tour guide act. "Look just ahead on the right side of the road. See that flat stone with the hollowed-out hole in the center? It's a bullaun, a cursing stone. Quite handy if you want to place a curse on someone."

"Oh yeah! I got a few people I want to curse, like that blonde bimbo at Cadigan's." Grace said. "You can bet I'm gonna hit that rock before leaving Beechgrove."

Lysi rolled her eyes. "Let go of the bimbo, Grace."

Things moved along as planned and Lysi's worries eased. The quiet cottages and the empty road made their job almost too easy.

A loud bark stopped the women in their tracks. Right. Too easy.

In a flash, Kingman appeared tugging on his leash, yanking Dennis McGill forward. "My, my ladies. Out for another evening stroll, are you?"

Kingman nuzzled Mary's hand until she scratched behind his velvety ears. He moved on to Lysi and Grace as if they were old friends and would certainly want to tickle behind his ears as well.

"Good evening to you Dennis McGill," Mary said. "Sure, I wanted to take advantage of this grand weather to show my American friends how lovely the village is just at sunset, so I had Brigid take over the pub and we left a wee bit early."

Lysi admired Mary's quick thinking and easy response.

"I see," McGill said eying Lysi and Grace with what Lysi thought was suspicion. Maybe he didn't believe Mary's story. Maybe he noticed it wasn't much lighter at eight this evening than when they had walked to Kavanagh's cottage last Friday at ten.

"Sure and you're a hard worker Mary McClone and deserving of a bit of a respite now and then. Glad to see you taking a little time off for yourself." Lysi could hear McGill's fondness for Mary in his voice. "Just take care. Did you hear? The peelers say there was a burglary in the Kavanagh cottage."

"No!" The three women exclaimed in disbelief.

"Aye, Friday last. I hear three hooligans got off with a laptop computer, a cell phone, and some very valuable family antiques."

Lysi tried to keep a straight face. She knew as well as Grace and Mary that the burglar had hightailed it through the small window empty handed. Someone had certainly embellished the burglary tale.

"Is that so?" Mary's eyes widened with surprise and fear. "Well thank you, Dennis McGill. We'll be on the watch, so."

McGill tipped his flat hat and continued on his way dragging a reluctant Kingman with him.

"I guess it's true," Lysi said. "Things get blown way out of proportion in small villages."

"Yeah," Grace complained. "Like when Mary said the Lowry cottage was only a wee stroll."

"Only a few more meters," Mary said.

"Uh huh, I guess Irish meters are a lot longer than American yards," Grace said.

After a few more minutes, Mary stopped and pointed at two brightly lit windows a few yards further up the main road. "That's the Lowry cottage on the left. The shed is across the road behind that old farmhouse."

A short distance further, they came upon a narrow lane that jutted off the right side of the main road.

"We'll take this lane and enter the shed from the back," Mary said.

Oak trees lined the narrow lane. Their crowns formed a dense canopy blocking out the moonlit sky and creating a dark tunnel. The women stumbled along deep ruts and through tall weeds lighting their way with one tiny penlight to avoid possible detection. Prickly shrubs reached from the side of the lane and snatched at their hoodies.

A few feet down the lane Grace shrieked. "What was that?" She grabbed Lysi's arm.

"What? What?" Lysi stage-whispered in alarm hoping no one heard Grace's outburst.

"That thing that brushed against my hand. It felt like … like a … a Brillo pad."

"A what?" Lysi said.

"You know, a scouring pad. Except it moved," Grace said.

"Honey," Lysi said. "I think this night antic has gotten to you. Scouring pads don't brush against you on dark paths."

"I know that. I was just describing—"

"Baa-aa."

"Sheep." Mary said as she flashed the penlight on a curly tail as it disappeared among the shrubs.

Lysi laughed.

"Not funny, Lysi." Grace said. "Got a question for you, Mary. Do sheep bite?"

"Can't unless you stick your hand deep into their mouths. Sheep don't have upper front teeth. Same with cows and goats."

"Thanks for the lesson about herbivores," Lysi said, thinking she should have known that having spent months on Maynard's sheep station. "But we need to get moving." She nudged Grace. "Yell if you get attacked by another Brillo pad."

Grace snarled.

The women moved into the shed yard, gravel crunching under their feet. They followed Mary to the old one-story storage shed. She found the entrance, lifted a rusty latch and forced open the sagging wooden door that screeched on rusty hinges. All three caught their breath at the loud noise and looked around before slipping inside.

The shed had one entrance, no windows, and smelled of mildew, rancid animal grain and damp cardboard. Mary swung the penlight around looking for a place to hide.

"Over there." Lysi pointed to a wood workbench built against the shed wall.

Grace scrutinized the workbench. "No way will you get me under that workbench full of cobwebs, bugs, creepy hairy spiders, and slithery snakes."

"No snakes in Ireland," Mary said. "St. Patrick took care of that for us."

"Why didn't the saintly Paddy take spiders with him, too?" Grace wrinkled her nose.

Mary smiled. "I'll ask him when I get to Heaven. Our big problem in here is mice. They feed on the old grain and even the cardboard boxes."

Lysi took a frustrated breath. Mary could have talked all night without mentioning mice. Grace was terrified of the little critters.

"Mice?" Grace said. "I hate—"

"Okay, Grace." Lysi pointed a frustrated finger at her. "You pick the spot to hide."

"I say we hide behind the shed door. Grab the scumbag as he comes through and pound him into a bloody blob," Grace said. "No less than he deserves after trying to pinch money from the Lowry girls."

"Won't work," Lysi said. "We have to catch him in the act of taking the money from Emma or he'll deny he came for it."

Grace grabbed Mary's penlight and waved it around the room.

"Well?" Lysi said.

"Okay, you win. Under the damn workbench."

Mary scrambled under the workbench. Lysi and Grace ducked under after her. "At least it's not as smelly and dirty as under Kavanagh's bed," Grace said. "Roomier, too." She jiggled her hips.

It always amazed Lysi how Grace could complain loud and long about something and then quickly adjust to the bad situation. She wondered if Grace had been forced to learn to adapt because of all the obstacles she'd faced throughout her life—childhood spent on the dangerous streets of Harlem, racism in Mississippi where she spent summers with her paternal grandmother, discrimination in university. And, perhaps most challenging, overcoming the double whammy of being female and black when breaking into the job market. Lysi's heart flooded with affection for her best friend.

"Move your foot, Lysi," Grace said. "You're invading my space."

"Shhh, hear that?" Lysi said. "Douse that penlight."

The sound of slow footsteps crunching on gravel grew louder, approached the shed and paused.

To Lysi the footsteps sounded heavier than a woman's. It had to be the blackmailer. He'd come early. Why? To check out the surroundings? To terrorize Emma when she arrived?

The door squawked on its hinges as it was yanked open. A tall figure stood in the open doorway as if poised to escape. Did he suspect a trap? After a moment the shadow entered the shed and closed the door. Lysi could hear him shuffling around in the dark probably familiarizing himself with his surroundings. What if he pulled out a flashlight and scanned the shed's interior? Would he find them?

Lysi heard footsteps draw close to the workbench. Her heart pounded in her throat. She squeezed Grace's arm and regained some confidence. Could the three of them take him? Maybe. Unless, he had a weapon?

As the blackmailer slinked around the shed, time dragged until the sound of hesitant footsteps padding slowly on the gravel path signaled the arrival of another person. Lysi hoped it was Emma. A latch rattled, the door squawked open and a short round figure entered. Her flashlight found the blackmailer.

From their limited vantage point under the workbench that revealed only the lower half of the man, Lysi, Grace and Mary stiffened. All three gulped a loud intake of air as they recognized the Elvis boots and polka dot print pants. The burglar from Kavanagh's house!

Emma froze, screamed and dropped the brown bag she held against her chest.

The burglar grabbed the bag, shoved Emma to the side knocking her to the floor and disappeared out the door.

"Did you see that?" Lysi asked, scrambling out from under the workbench.

"After him," Grace shouted, scooting out from under the workbench, springing to her feet and racing toward the door.

"Wait Grace," Lysi said.

Grace shot out the door before Lysi could caution her that the burglar appeared desperate and therefore dangerous. He might have a gun or knife. She had to stop Grace.

Mary hurried to Emma and helped her to her feet. "Can you walk?"

Emma brushed at her dress and patted her hair. "I think so. I'm so terribly sorry I failed you and Gemma."

"You didn't," Lysi said. "You did your best."

Lysi, feeling assured Emma was safe with Mary, raced out the door after Grace. She had to reach Grace before she confronted the burglar. How could Grace be terrified of a mouse and yet be willing to risk engaging a desperate thief?

*

Lysi caught up with Grace who stood next to an old stone well. "Which way did he go?" Lysi whispered.

Grace's eyes flitted from the road to the old farmhouse the well to the path behind the shed. "I don't know."

Lysi felt momentary relief until it occurred to her that the burglar might be observing them from a hiding spot ready to attack at any moment. "Grace, let's get out of here."

Lysi knew the only thing to do was alert the police even though it would upset Maynard when he found out the risks they'd taken. "We need to let the police take over now."

"Wait." Grace grabbed Lysi's arm and pointed toward a grove of trees behind the farmhouse. "See that?"

A flicker of light flashed on for a couple of seconds then off. "He's over there."

Without a word, Grace circled around to the left blocking the thief's access to the lane while silently approaching him.

Lysi knew she should not engage the burglar, knew she should run but it was too late. She couldn't allow Grace to face a desperate criminal alone.

She circled to the right blocking the burglar's escape to the road and trapping him between herself and Grace on the left.

Lysi crept closer. A dead branch that cracked under her foot making a thunderous sound in the quiet night. The burglar must have heard it because Lysi caught the sound of footsteps running away from her headed in Grace's direction.

Lysi followed him hoping Grace was near enough to see him.

A moment later Lysi heard thumps and grunts. As she emerged from behind a tall bush, she saw Grace had tackled the culprit. He flopped and flailed, frantic as a fish out of water.

Lysi raced to help Grace, planning to throw herself across his chest and pin his shoulders to the ground. She and Grace would constrain him while dialing 999, the PSNI emergency number.

Grace held on to his hips but his jerking about caused her hands to slip down his legs to his feet.

Before Lysi could pounce, Grace lost her grip. The burglar scrambled up taking the bag of pounds with him and disappeared among the trees leaving one of his Elvis boots behind.

Grace jumped to her feet and held up his boot with a triumphant salute.

Chapter 35

Maynard put his arm around Emma Lowry and nodded reassuringly at Gemma, who, still recovering from her hospital stay, sat in the car wringing her hands. "Don't worry. She'll be fine," he said over his shoulder.

As he guided Emma toward the police station, he heard Lysi add her own encouraging words. "Gemma honey, trust me, Emma couldn't have a better advocate than Detective Maynard Christie. If he says not to worry, then don't worry."

Maynard wished he felt as confident about the outcome of this undertaking as Lysi did. He was familiar with the policing system in Northern Ireland because it was similar to the Australian system—both based on the British model. But he also knew that in Australia procedures varied a bit from state to state, and assumed it might be the same in Northern Ireland. Not knowing procedures could complicate matters. Another concern nagged at him. He didn't like treading on another detective's turf. He would tread lightly.

Maynard rang the bell beside the single bullet-proof door to the windowless Local Police Station. A PSNI officer in a green uniform opened the door.

"We have an appointment with Detective Sergeant Graig. I'm Maynard Christie and this is Emma Lowry."

The officer motioned them straight ahead. "Check in at that window then have a seat." He pointed to a row of four gray plastic chairs lined up against the wall.

A no-nonsense woman in a white uniform blouse ran her finger down a schedule then shoved a log sheet through an opening at the bottom of the window. "Sign in please. Have a seat. DS Graig will be with you shortly."

Maynard and Emma sat and waited for DS Graig to arrive. Maynard watched Emma twist her lace handkerchief into a tight knot. He sympathized with her plight and determined to do his best to help her. Still, he asked himself for the hundredth time why he'd allowed Lysi and Mary to talk him into advocating for Emma Lowry. A combination of things had led to his predicament— Lysi's deluge of reasons why he should help this poor woman, Mary's tears, Billy's insistence that only Maynard had the skills needed for the job and, the final convincing thing, Emma's terrified eyes.

A door opened and a man wearing a tweed sports jacket, slacks, loosened tie and a haggard expression appeared. "Emma Lowry?"

Emma startled. She blinked at the man then looked wide-eyed at Maynard who took her arm and helped her stand.

"Miss Lowry?" the detective repeated.

She swallowed and nodded.

"Detective Sergeant Graig," the man said. "Right this way please."

He led Maynard and Emma down a narrow hallway. Maynard recognized red attack bars along the wall on one side of the hall. He knew the department provided them for the safety of officers conducting violent arrestees. One yank on the bar and cops would flood the hallway and subdue the arrestee. Maynard noticed iron shelves stocked with empty plastic containers of various sizes for storing items from crime scenes— guns, knives, clothing. They passed an open-door framing physicians' implements. An exam room. Another room housed a bank of computers. A well-equipped station.

DS Graig opened the door to a small windowless room and motioned them to a heavy wooden table. Maynard spotted two video cameras mounted near the low ceiling. A banner hung on the wall. It bore the logo of the PSNI— a gold and brown circle with a silver star in the center.

There were five chairs, two on each side of the table—space for an arrestee, attorney and two detectives—and one at the end of the table for an advocate. Maynard tried to pull a chair out for Emma, but it wouldn't move. He glanced down and found the legs locked to the floor with iron clamps. He knew that chair and the others were anchored to prevent a violent criminal slamming a chair into a detective. He glanced at Emma who blinked and trembled. All this must terrify her.

Maynard steadied Emma into a chair across the table from DS Graig and another detective already seated. He sat in the fifth chair at the end of the table he knew was provided for an advocate. Emma's eyes darted around the walls, the ceiling, the floor and lit on the other detective, a young blonde woman with a look of amusement in her brown eyes.

"Miss Lowry, this is Detective Sergeant Shelby O'Shea. She will join us in the interview," DS Graig said. "It looks like we're ready to begin."

Detective Sergeant Graig opened the interview with a statement of Emma's rights, pushed a copy across the table to her and directed her to read and sign. She began to shake and hiccup, wrapping her arms around herself. Maynard touched her arm, handed her the pen and pointed to the signature line. Her trembling turned her signature into a scribble.

DS Graig took the form and placed it in a manila folder. "Thank you, Miss Lowry." He cast a sympathetic glance at Emma then said, "Now calm down a bit. No one's having a go at you here."

A bit of empathy always makes for a smoother interview, Maynard thought. This detective knows his stuff.

"Now tell us about your relationship to Sean Kavanagh." DS Graig said.

At that moment Maynard realized that DS Graig was investigating the Kavanagh murder, not the murder of Paddy Doherty. Either Aiden Quinn hadn't reported Emma's murder confession or DS Graig had not yet been told about it.

"I ... He ... That is to say ... ."

"Yes?" DS Graig sounded impatient.

Emma turned to Maynard.

"May I?" Maynard said to both detectives.

"Mr. Christie, you signed in as Miss Lowry's advocate. You are not a relative but a close friend?" The detective squinted at Maynard.

"That's right. I'm here to provide support as needed," Maynard said.

"I see."

"The interview will go more smoothly if you allow me to provide a wee bit of support to her." Maynard guessed the two detectives probably had other cases to attend to and would like to complete this interview as efficiently as possible.

DS Graig looked at Emma who sat trembling and looking like she might hyperventilate at any moment. He and the other detective exchanged glances and shrugged. When Emma hiccupped again, DS O'Shea whispered in Graig's ear, and he nodded at Maynard.

"Emma, DS Graig wants to understand what occurred between you and Sean Kavanagh." Maynard spoke in a gentle tone. "He already has basic information. He wants you to explain what happened in greater detail. Can you do that?"

Emma grabbed Maynard's hand and squeezed it. She looked up at him through scared calf eyes, swallowed hard and breathed out, "Aye."

"Brilliant." DS Graig said with a heavy exhale.

DS O'Shea lowered her head and grinned.

Emma placed the palm of her hand on her chest and took a deep breath. "After my sister Gemma and I went to bed, she heard noise in our kitchen. She went to see about it. I heard her shout at someone to get out or she'd call the police. I ran into the kitchen in time to see that man punch her in the face. He was a burglar."

"Sean Kavanagh tried to burglarize your house?" DS Graig said.

"No ... No," Emma said. Hiccup. Her confused eyes switched to Maynard.

DS Graig glanced at Maynard. "Okay," he said. "Go on please."

"I grabbed a frying pan and hit him over the head to save my sister. He might have killed her." Tears burst into Emma's eyes.

"You hit Sean Kavanagh over the head with a frying pan because he tried to kill your sister?" DS Graig's mouth hung open.

"No … NO …"

"You just said—"

"Later we hid the body in—" Emma said.

"Wait a minute," DS Graig said. "You killed Sean Kavanagh with a frying pan then buried his body in Liam MaGuire's field?"

"No, no." Hiccup. Hiccup. "I killed the burglar with the frying pan."

"You, you killed a burglar and Sean Kavanagh?" DS Graig and the other detective stared open-mouthed at Emma.

"No …" Emma pulled the twisted lace handkerchief from her purse and dabbed at her eyes.

Maynard knew Emma was confused. She needed time to collect herself. "May we take a wee moment, please?"

"I think we'd best do that," DS Graig said.

"Emma, you're doing fine," Maynard said." Now tell him about what happened to the money in your family bank account."

"Okay. Well Sean Kavanagh found out about the burglar I killed and said he would get rid of the body."

DS Graig sighed and massaged his temple with two fingers. Maynard could tell the senior detective had given up trying to make sense of the interview. "So … ," Graig said, "Did he get rid of the unknown body?"

"Yes, but then he started forcing us to pay him money or he said he'd tell the police what I did."

"I see. You killed Sean Kavanagh because he was blackmailing you?"

"Yes. I mean no. I mean yes, he was blackmailing us. No, I did not kill him."

"I see." DS Graig pulled a large handkerchief from his back pocket and swabbed his brow. "Let's talk about the man you did kill."

Nancy Curteman

Chapter 36

Maynard finished his early morning walkabout and ducked into McGarrity's B&B just as a roll of thunder rocked the sky, turning the light rain into a heavy downpour that promised to douse the village. He turned to the left and entered a small breakfast room where Innkeeper McGarrity had set a sideboard with apples, stewed fruits, cereal, juice and a pot of hot tea on a little warmer.

He poured a cup of tea but took no food preferring to wait for Lysi and Grace to join him for breakfast. He carried the tea to a window table covered with a white linen tablecloth, linen napkins, silverware, butter and condiments. Four place settings invited guests to dine. He sat at one of the settings, sipped his tea and gazed out the window at the street darkening with rain. The wind howled against the window and the delicate curtains shivered in the draft sneaking through tiny cracks around the casings.

Aiden's dripping torso appeared framed by the window. He rapped and waved flashing a broad, toothy grin. Maynard smiled at the eager young face, and proffered a jaunty salute.

Aiden closed his umbrella, gave it a few shakes, ducked through the front door and turned into the breakfast room.

Hanging his coat on a wood rack in a corner he said, "Glad I found you, mate. I have some news that will surprise you."

"Yes?"

"You know the burglary at the Kavanagh cottage?" Aiden brushed wet hair off his forehead. "Well the police found fingerprints."

Maynard caught his breath and his stomach dropped. He had a sinking feeling he knew what was coming.

"They found prints from three different people. They ran all three sets through the database. Now for two of the sets they couldn't find matches. But they found a clear match for the third. Well … You'll never guess who that third set belongs to." Aiden plopped onto a chair across the table from Maynard.

Maynard had been holding his breath and now exhaled loudly when he realized the two sets of prints that had no matches had to belong to Lysi and Grace. He picked up his teacup.

"Are you ready for a grand surprise?" Aiden said.

Maynard nodded. It didn't surprise him that the burglar had left his prints. Why would Aiden think it would surprise him? He decided not to deflate Aiden's excitement. "Who owned the third set?" Maynard said and took a sip of tea.

"Mary McClone."

Maynard nearly choked on his tea. That revelation had indeed surprised him, not that she'd left prints, but that the police had found a match to track her. Why would Mary's fingerprints be in a fingerprint database?

"Aye," Aiden said. "Shocked me too. It seems she used to work as a file clerk at the police station and as part of vetting they took her fingerprints." Aiden paused and squinted at Maynard. "Now what would Mary McClone be doing in Sean Kavanagh's cottage?"

Maynard didn't respond. The only thing on his mind was that he had to get to Mary as soon as possible. He had to find out why she took the risk of going to the Kavanagh cottage just to get back a pair of knickers. He needed to know the answer to that question before the police found out about it from some other source. He puzzled over the question. Had she had a relationship with Kavanagh at one time and it ended badly? Had Kavanagh engaged in a college student panty raid? Or worse, had Kavanagh assaulted her and stolen the panties. This last possibility disgusted him. With the fingerprint match in the hands of the police, he had to find out right away.

Chapter 37

Lysi and Grace bounded into the B&B breakfast room ready to enjoy a big Irish breakfast. Lysi paused when she saw Maynard standing gazing out the window, hair still wet from a morning walk. "Maynard, you went out in this downpour?"

When Maynard turned, Lysi could see his worried expression.

"I did an early morning walkabout and got a little wet before the downpour." He furrowed his brow. "I needed to think."

"Think?" Lysi knew what that meant. Maynard suspected they hadn't told him everything. Over the years she'd found it more and more difficult to keep even little things from him—holiday gifts, surprise birthday parties, involvements in murder investigations. She should know by now he could tell when she hadn't revealed all about something she'd done, particularly when it came to her favorite pastime of sleuthing. The only thing she hadn't mentioned to him was the late-night trip to the old farmhouse shed. She guessed she'd have to tell him about it sooner or later. Or … did he already know? Had Emma told him about her weird encounter with the blackmailer? Not likely. She swore us to secrecy because she didn't want Gemma to know how she'd gotten scared and botched their only opportunity to identify the blackmailer. At any rate, Lysi knew the time had come to come clean.

"Grab some breakfast and have a seat. We need to talk." Maynard pulled out a chair and straddled the seat leaning his arms on the back. Lysi sat next to him, poured a cup of tea, added honey and stirred a bit too vigorously.

"Mary plans to join us for breakfast," Lysi said. "She should be here any minute."

"Good," Maynard said, "I'm going to need to talk with all three of you."

Not good, Lysi thought as she watched Grace go to the sideboard.

"Nice spread," Grace said grabbing a china cereal bowl with a delicate floral pattern, and filling it with stewed plums, canned pears and fruit cocktail. She poured orange juice and grapefruit juice into crystal tumblers and sat at the table across from Maynard.

Lysi recognized the Queen Victoria pattern on the B&B china. Her mother had had a platter in that same pattern. She guessed the tumblers were Waterford from the famous Irish glassmaking city. The pieces were probably treasures handed down from mothers to daughters over the years. Such elegance in a small village inn.

"This fruit'll hold me until the eggs, potatoes and toast come," Grace said pouring a cup of tea.

When Mary walked through the exterior door and stowed her umbrella in the stand, Lysi got up and met her at the entrance to the breakfast room. Before Lysi could warn her, Maynard said, "Good morning Mary. Glad you're here. We have a problem I need to discuss with the three of you."

All three women stared at Maynard, tense with curiosity. Lysi could tell from Maynard's cold eyes, clipped tone and unsmiling expression that they did indeed have a problem.

"You remember that secret visit you made to the Kavanagh cottage?"

All three nodded in unison.

"Well, it's no longer a secret. A man named McGill reported a possible home invasion to the police. The department sent a young constable to check things out."

"Oh God," Grace burst out. "I knew it. We're busted and going to solitary confinement."

"That young constable is still in training and due to his inexperience, his sergeant noted he'd missed some sections of the report," Maynard said.

"Oh, thank the Lord," Grace's hand flew to her chest. "No jailtime."

Lysi wondered how Maynard had gleaned that information and started to ask when Maynard continued.

"So, the department sent a team back to Kavanagh's place to recheck the crime scene. Pretty standard procedure. The team determined it to be a break-in."

"Oh?" Lysi and Grace formed a duet.

"They found fingerprints and sent them to the Scientific Support Fingerprint Bureau in Belfast to run through the police database. I wonder whose prints turned up."

"We didn't break in. The door was unlocked," Lysi said.

"No, like we told you, we just wanted to get back undies that belonged to Mary," Grace said.

Maynard's eyes flicked to Mary. "Why did you think it so critical to retrieve those undies?"

"Okay, okay." Lysi sighed and shifted her eyes from Maynard to Grace and Mary then back to Maynard. She knew they had to tell Maynard everything before they ended up in deeper trouble. Maynard would find out anyway. He always did. May as well fess up now. Without any discussion the three women must have come to the same conclusion because they nodded in assent to Lysi.

Maynard waited, his question dangling in the air.

Mary's neck reddened and the color ascended to her cheeks.

"We had to find Mary's panties because we knew Kavanagh had them," Lysi said.

"I understand that, Maynard said. " Question number one is: how did he come to have possession of Mary's knickers? Question number two is: why did you need to retrieve them?"

"Because," Grace broke in, "that Kavanagh bastard assaulted Mary and stole her panties as a trophy."

Mary's face burned scarlet.

"And … question number two?" Maynard's professional expression did not change.

"That question has two answers," Lysi said. "One. Mary wanted to avoid the shame and humiliation she would face if the village gossips found out about the assault. Two. If the police found her panties and gained knowledge of the assault, they would think Mary murdered Kavanagh."

"Judging from the six or seven other panties we found, none of which belonged to Mary, that Kavanagh pig had assaulted other women," Grace said.

Maynard blinked and swallowed. "Other women?"

"That's what we think," Lysi said.

Maynard paused and focused on a section of space as Lysi had often seen him do while mulling over information.

"There are two issues here," he said. "The first is the home invasion and the second is the assault of Mary."

Again he paused, furrowed his brow and blinked several times. Another problem-solving habit Lysi had often observed.

The three women waited.

"The house was unoccupied," he mused.

The three women nodded.

"I could make a case that it wasn't your intent to burglarize. That you had to retrieve a personal item you needed right away. Maybe the charge could be reduced to a misdemeanor," Maynard said.

"There were also extenuating circumstances given that Kavanagh had assaulted Mary and probably the other women as well. This brings us to the second issue, the assault." He turned to Mary. "Mary, did you report the assault?"

Mary shook her head and dropped her eyes. "I couldn't. You don't understand." Tears dropped on her shirt. "I couldn't bear the shame. The humiliation. I just couldn't do it."

Lysi touched Mary's hand and looked into Maynard's eyes. She saw a flash of empathy instantly replaced by a hard look of unrelenting determination to convince Mary that reporting was her only viable option.

"You have to report," Maynard said in a matter of fact voice. "There is really no other choice. It would help if you could get the other women to report as well. Can you?"

Mary shook her head again. "I don't know who they are."

"It's essential that we find out who those other women are," Maynard said, sympathy slipping through his professional façade.

A heavy silence filled the room.

"We will find them!" Lysi said. "I have an idea."

*

After Grace and Mary left the breakfast room—Mary to finish some bookkeeping at the pub and Grace to go upstairs and drag Chess out of bed—Lysi and Maynard lingered over a second cup of tea. They gazed out the window at the pounding rain that made everything—street, cars, trees, shrubs—look as if they'd just received a coat of clear high gloss paint. People shuffled by with umbrellas high attending to their daily tasks seemingly unconcerned with the downpour while children made it a point of splashing through every puddle.

"I imagine the Irish get used to rain," Lysi said. "It's rained at some time every day we've been here, sometimes a downpour other times a misty drizzle." She spooned more honey into her tea and tasted it.

"I don't mind the Irish rain," Maynard said. "I think of it as more like a drizzle compared to the gully washers that flood Northern Territory Australia."

Lysi hadn't experienced the Australian monsoons but she'd read about them. She continued to gaze out the window. "Of course, the gifts of the rain to Ireland are its incredibly beautiful green mountains and meadows."

"That's true," Maynard said, his face hardening into a stern expression, "but I have something more important to discuss with you. What do you know about Kavanagh blackmailing the Lowry girls?"

Uh-oh. Lysi considered tossing the question back at Maynard—What did he know about the blackmailer? She discarded that idea because it might make him suspect there was more to find out.

Distraction. That sometimes worked. At least it might give her time to think about the best way to tell him about the night excursion to the old shed.

"Maynard, look at that." Lysi pointed to a little girl about five years old struggling to hold an umbrella over a cocker spaniel playfully running in circles around her. "Isn't that cute?"

Maynard glanced out the window. "Cute." His eyes shot back to Lysi. "About Kavanagh blackmailing the Lowry girls."

Lysi sighed. That didn't work. She wondered how much Emma had told him when they sat together at the police station. It didn't matter. She may as well reveal everything that had occurred relating to the blackmailer. Maynard would drag it out of her anyway.

"Well … as you know," she began, "Kavanagh volunteered to get rid of the remains of the burglar Emma had struck with the frying pan. She had to save her sister's life."

"Yes." Maynard said.

"After he got rid of the body, Kavanagh started blackmailing the Lowry girls. When he was found dead, Gemma and Emma thought the blackmailing was over."

"Yes," Maynard said, "that's a reasonable assumption." Lysi noted a slight edge in his voice.

"But it wasn't. They got another note demanding money."

"Lysi, you realize I know all this. It came out at the police interview." The edge in Maynard's voice sharpened.

Lysi paused. Time to stop hedging. She tried to think of the best way to tell Maynard about her attempt to trap the blackmailer in the shed behind the old farmhouse and chasing and tackling him. She knew it would upset him. She also knew his upset stemmed from concern for her safety. He was over-protective because in his profession as a homicide detective he'd seen so many horrible tragedies. She couldn't blame him. Maybe she didn't need to tell him about the blackmailer's shoe Grace had hidden in her closet.

"There's more, isn't there, Lysi." Maynard leaned across the table his sharp eyes focused on her face.

"Well, yes." Lysi dropped her eyes.

"Go on."

"In the note the blackmailer demanded that the Lowry girls put 500 pounds in a paper bag and bring it to an old farmhouse shed and not tell anyone."

Maynard rolled his eyes and shook his head. Lysi could tell he already suspected what she'd done.

Gemma was in the hospital. I couldn't let gentle little Emma go by herself, so I got Grace and Mary and—"

"And you went to meet the blackmailer."

"Well … yes. We hid and waited for him." Lysi spoke faster, her voice strained. "He came. Then a few minutes later Emma came. When she saw him, she got so scared she screamed and dropped the bag. He knocked her down, grabbed the bag and ran off before we could get a good look at his face." Lysi lowered her voice to just above a whisper. "Grace and I chased him. She tackled him but he got away."

"You what? Speak up."

"We chased him and tackled him but he got away."

Maynard gasped and his eyes widened. "You—Crikey Lysi, have you got kangaroos loose in your paddock? Do you have a death wish?"

Maynard planted an elbow on the table and leaned his forehead in his palm. "Lysi, what am I going to do with you?"

"One more thing," Lysi said.

"Not sure my heart can handle more," he said through his fingers.

"The blackmailer was the same man who burglarized Kavanagh's house while we were there."

"I thought you didn't see the burglar."

"We didn't see his face, but we saw his Elvis boots and clown pants. Oh yeah, it was the same guy. What do we do now?"

Maynard didn't answer.

Nancy Curteman

Chapter 38

Lysi tightened her seatbelt and braced for a wild ride as Grace steered the Volkswagen onto Route A1 toward Dublin. Maybe it wouldn't be too bad at least Grace was in a good mood. After bumping over those boreens, Grace's rocket-like driving would feel like a sleigh ride on new snow. Wouldn't it?

Lysi looked over her shoulder at Chess, seated in the backseat, iPad in hand frantically asking Siri for driving directions from Belfast to the Merrion Hotel in Dublin. "Chess, trust us. We got this." Lysi tried to sound confident.

Maynard winked at Lysi from his seat in the back next to Chess. He gave Chess a friendly punch on an arm. "They found their way to Belfast from Dublin, they can find their way back to Dublin."

Chess didn't look convinced. He continued querying Siri without success. He kept getting the wrong answers.

"Siri, directions to the Merrion please."

"I didn't quite get that," Siri said in an annoying voice.

"Okay, Siri, where is Dublin?" He enunciated each word slowly.

Siri replied, "Dublin is in California."

"No," he moaned. "Dublin in Ireland."

"That is correct," Siri said.

In a frustrated voice he said, "Siri, just connect me with Bing Maps."

Siri replied, "Sorry, I'm an Apple personal assistant."

"Give it up Chess," Grace said sniggering. "Maynard's right. We made it from Dublin to Belfast. We can get you back to the Merrion. We'll take A1 to N1 to M1. Pretty much all the same motorway. Only the names change. No sweat."

But Chess was sweating. Wrinkles furrowed his forehead and his lips had tightened.

Grace switched on BBC Radio Ulster. When Bruno Mars burst into his hit song, Uptown Funk, she turned up the volume and started tapping the beat on the steering wheel while bobbing her head in rhythm with the music.

"Grace honey, please turn the radio down. I can't hear Siri," Chess said.

Lysi sucked air. Whoops. She knew Grace would overreact to Chess' need to verify her directions with an annoying digital voice on a computer. Lysi didn't blame her. So much for Grace's good mood. Strike one.

Grace didn't turn the radio down. Instead she hit the gas and swerved around a slow-moving pickup truck, knocking Chess hard against the armrest.

"Grace, have you noticed the speed limit signs?" Chess dragged himself upright and straightened his jacket.

Lysi shook her head. Strike two.

"Not to worry," Grace said. "You know what the Irish say, 'You're not speeding unless you get caught.' Now sit back and relax to this easy listening station."

"Easy listening?" Chess' tone broadcasted his disdain for the Funk music. "Just get me to Dublin in one piece so I don't lose my account," Chess said.

Strike 3.

"Enough, Chess," Grace said, "unless you want to walk to Dublin."

Time to intervene, Lysi decided. "I'm with Chess on that one," she said. "We got a presentation to make tomorrow. We don't want to do it on crutches."

It surprised Lysi when Maynard jumped in on Grace's side.

"Compared to riding with Ryan O'Rourke this is a leisurely Sunday drive. He hasn't mastered that new VW yet. Still thinks he's driving his old pickup—jerks the power steering, stamps too hard on the accelerator, slams on the power brakes. A ride with him at the wheel is like riding a mad bull."

"Sounds like Grace," Chess mumbled.

"I heard that," Grace said, and lead-footed the accelerator.

Two hours and several heart-stopping near misses later, Grace pulled the VW to the curb in front of the entrance to Dublin's Merrion Hotel. Lysi, Maynard and Grace hopped out of the car. Chess opened the car door and dragged unsteadily from the back seat, tottered across the sidewalk and plopped onto the bottom step of the hotel entrance. The doorman moved toward him, a concerned expression on his face.

"Grace, you'd better tend to Chess," Lysi said. "I think he might have a touch of car sickness."

Chess' condition didn't surprise her. Anyone not accustomed to Grace's kamikaze driving style would experience nausea brought on by sheer terror.

Grace took one look at Chess and hurried toward him nearly colliding with the doorman who grabbed his toppling derby hat and jumped out of her way. She sat next to Chess and put an arm around him. "Chess, honey, are you okay?"

"Fine, fine. I just needed a moment to thank St. Christopher, you know, the patron saint of travelers, for helping me survive that horrifying ride."

Grace yanked her arm back, and her body rigid, her eyes like a tiger's, said, "Stop whining. I got you here, didn't I? A thank you would be nice."

"What, a thank you for not killing me?"

Lysi and Maynard exchanged glances and suppressed grins. The doorman, big-eyed mumbled, "Luggage?"

Nancy Curteman

Chapter 39

Lysi and Grace entered the Cadigan Construction Tools' lobby.

"Back in Macho land," Lysi said.

"Uh-huh." Grace rolled her eyes.

Lysi frowned as the bottle-blonde receptionist looked up, spotted Grace, dropped her eyes to the fashion magazine on the desk next to her phone and started frantically flipping the pages.

She remembers the "Chessie" ordeal with Grace last week. Not good.

"Good morning, Miss ... " Lysi glanced at a gold plate on the receptionist's desk that read Candy Caine. " a ... Caine. We have an appointment with Caitlin O'Connor. Please let her know Lysi Weston and Grace Wright are here."

"Ms. O'Connor is expecting you, Ms. Weston. Please wait in Mr. Murphy's office." She pointed to an open door. "It's on the left. I'll let her know you're here."

"Thank you." Lysi noticed Miss Caine did not acknowledge Grace's presence with even a glance. Uh-oh, Lysi braced for trouble.

Grace's lips stretched into an icy smile. As they walked to Killian Murphy's office she chided over her shoulder, "Hey Lollipop honey, lose the brassy blonde hair. Doesn't do a thing for you. Turns your face puce."

"My name's not—" Candy Caine didn't finish the sentence. Lysi judged Candy had made the right decision. It defused an explosion.

"Grace!" Lysi said.

"What? Just trying to be helpful. That hair color is terrible. And that can't be her real name. Candy Caine?" Grace said. "That's not a name, that's a sticky thing kids eat at Christmas time."

"Maybe, but Lollipop? Come on." Lysi tried not to smile.

Grace grinned with satisfaction.

"Lysi, Grace. Welcome back. So good to see you." Caitlin O'Connor stood at the open door. Lysi observed the stark contrast between Caitlin in her pearl grey business suit, and Candy in her cleavage revealing magenta fluff blouse. Grace could pull off flamboyant and sexy, too but at work she always dressed professionally .

"The lunchroom is ready with all the materials and equipment you requested for employee training," Caitlin said.

"Perfect." Lysi looked around the office. No materials. No equipment. "I thought we scheduled two days of management orientation in this office starting today followed by the three half days of employee training in the lunchroom. Is there a change of venue?"

"A ... yes." Caitlin's neck turned as red as her silk blouse. "Killian arranged a different venue for management. It's off campus. Only a short drive from here. The SUV is out front."

Lysi raised her brows at the change but nodded. Any place would be better than this smelly office that reeked of stale cigar smoke.

Ten minutes later the SUV stopped in front of a pub with the name Bath Tub strewn across the front in big letters surrounded by bubbles. Lysi and Grace stared at the venue with open mouths.

"Here we are," Caitlin said. "Your trainees await you."

"It's a bar," Lysi said.

"Oh," Caitlin said, her tone apologetic. "Killian booked the small banquet room in the back for ten o'clock. The pub doesn't open until later."

The pub door opened on a room filled with tables and a long bar. CEO Killian Murphy, DO Dylan Doyle and three other men sat at the bar. Killian Murphy turned when the door opened. "Lysi, Grace good to see you." He sniggered and said to the three men, "Lads, meet the little ladies who will teach us about sexual harassment."

The three managers lecherous eyes slithered slowly over Lysi and Grace's chest, hips and thighs. Then laughter burst from the group.

Lysi, Grace and Caitlin did not laugh.

Murphy smiled benignly. "So, girls, before we get started on our session, we need a wee warm up. You know, get acquainted. Grab a stool. Drinks are on me."

"Nothing for me. We need to get started." Lysi didn't like Killian's stalling tactics.

"Mmmm, maybe one drink." Grace scooted onto a stool, struck a little-girl pose with a finger pressing her lower lip and perused the bottles on the top shelf behind the bar. "I'll take a glass of that whiskey up there. The one on that cute little glass pedestal. Midleton." She smiled her sweetest smile at Killian. "Is that how you pronounce it?"

All heads turned towards Killian, including the over-time-duty bartender. Killian swallowed and nodded his okay.

"I'll take it neat," Grace added in a naive tone. "Oh, and let's make it a double."

Killian's jaw dropped.

Lysi grinned. Grace wasn't naive at all. She was well acquainted with the €150-a-shot Midleton Very Rare. She'd coveted it in bars all over the world explaining that it was a rare and expensive Irish whiskey and that someday, when she got rich, she planned to try it. Guess the day had arrived and the money would come from someone else.

The surprised bartender pulled over a chair to stand on and carefully removed the Midleton from the rarely used bottles on display. He poured the Midleton and Grace took a small sip. "Delightful. Taste it, Lysi."

Lysi tried it and managed to suppress a cough. "Not bad."

"I love its golden color," Grace said.

"Why it's almost the same color as my scarf." Lysi held up the end of a gold scarf.

"Oh look." Grace read the label. "Brian Nation signed his name. Says here he's the master distiller. How sweet is that?"

"Nice label," Lysi said.

Grace perused the label. "Could use a bit more color." She thrust the bottle toward Killian Murphy. "What do you think, Killie?"

Sweat beaded on Killian's forehead. He grabbed the bottle and handed it to the bartender. "The label's fine."

After a couple more sips Grace raised her glass and said, "Down the hatch." She smacked her lips and smiled. "That Midleton really warmed me up. How about another double?"

Again, all eyes turned toward Killian as the bartender raised the Midleton bottle ready for another pour.

"Some other time, Grace," Killian said shaking his head emphatically and holding up his hand to stop toward the bartender from refilling Grace's glass. "We'd best get on with the training session."

As the managers filed into the banquet room, Lysi winked at Grace. Her little ploy had worked perfectly. It might be a bit more difficult to train a half-lit management team in the art of identifying and eradicating sexual harassment in the workplace, but watching Killian Murphy sweat, turn pale and then green as he forked over €300 to the bartender's open hand was well worth it.

Chapter 40

Lysi stood beside Grace next to a large screen on which the first PowerPoint slide projected the words, "Sexual Harassment in the Workplace." She hoped this presentation would go better than the management seminar where a couple of the men dozed off after a boozy lunch. The venue wasn't much better. The employee lunchroom looked like an old converted warehouse—gray walls, high ceilings, industrial-style fluorescent lights, concrete floors. Employee comfort was not a Cadigan top priority.

Lysi watched Cadigan employees file into the lunchroom. After a moment her eyes widened, and she nudged Grace. "Look at that."

"Holy crap!" Grace's mouth hung open as she followed the scene unfolding before her.

"Well that's a first for me." Lysi blew a puff of air. "This might end up a suicide mission."

"Hey, we're gonna demand double pay for this fiasco." Grace guffawed.

Lysi and Grace waited in silence while all the women settled into seats on the right side of the room under high windows with open transoms. The men shuffled to the other side next to the cafeteria kitchen. It reminded Lysi of the "No Girls Allowed" boy's clubhouse in her neighborhood when she was a kid.

The juxtaposition of body language on the two sides of the room created a cartoonish picture. Most of the men sat arms crossed and chins tucked with bored expressions. Lysi remembered that same kind of behavior from the redneck males when she'd conducted a sexual harassment seminar in Sage Deer, Montana.

In contrast to the men, the women readied notepads and pens, and looked with anticipation at the two presenters. It was clear which group had the most to gain from the training.

Caitlin sent Lysi an eye message full of apology and frustration.

After Caitlin's introductory words, Lysi clicked to the next PowerPoint frame. Large red letters shouted: Ignoring Sexual Harassment in the Workplace is Expensive. Below were some examples: Firm required to pay €54K after sexual harassment suit. Girl wins €30,000 in sexual harassment case. Company forced into bankruptcy following sexual harassment payout. This was one of the slides that had caught the attention of the executives during the management seminar.

Lysi paused to allow time for the audience to read the data then said, "As you can see, sexual harassment costs companies a lot."

Women scribbled on their pads. Men rolled their eyes. It'll take a bit more convincing to get these Neanderthals' attention. Lysi advanced to the next slide titled:

The Irish Supreme Court Confirmed "Vicarious Liability"

The men shrugged and muttered things like: "So?" "Never heard of it." "Nothing to do with me." "Can you move it along girls."

The women continued to write on their pads and looked up expectantly.

"This court ruling made organizations liable for sexual harassment by its employees even if the company had put anti-harassment measures in place," Lysi said. "In short, the company is responsible for the actions of its employees."

The men grinned and nudged each other. Lysi expected that reaction. They imagined they could harass all they wanted without being held accountable. After all, the company would be responsible. Not them.

The women looked concerned and murmured to each other in disappointed tones. If the men were not accountable for harassment, why should they stop harassing? Lysi knew they assumed the same thing as the men. Her next comment wouldn't help the situation, but she needed to cover all the bases.

"Furthermore, the court declared that harassment does not have to occur in the workplace or during the victim's normal duties for the organization to be liable."

Grace stepped forward. She looked hard at the men's side of the room. "Sounds like you're off the hook for harassment. Right boys?"

Laughter from the men's side.

"Uh uh." She switched back to the court-awards slide. "The question is this: How long do you think a company will take to fire the ass of a dumb oaf who costs them big buckos?"

Lysi thought Grace's comment was a bit too graphic, but it certainly made an impact.

The room lapsed into silence.

Grace smiled sweetly as she answered the question, "As fast as a cheetah leaping for the kill. You all hear what I'm saying?"

Lysi looked out at raised brows and tight lips. Now she had their attention. "Let's talk about how you can avoid losing your jobs," she said.

"Let's talk about eliminating sexual harassment in the workplace," Grace said and switched to the next slide titled: What Does Sexual Harassment Look Like, followed by a series of slides explaining how men as well as women suffer sexual harassment, how to report offenders, how to bring suit against an unresponsive employer.

In giant red letters the last slide listed names and phone numbers of Ireland's victim support services.

The men kept their eyes glued to the women as they nodded to each other and took copious notes on the services information listed on the last slide.

Lysi switched off the computer. "Questions?"

Nancy Curteman

Chapter 41

Lysi and Grace high-fived as more than twenty women crowded into Mary McClone's Pub for a lingerie party, probably the first one ever in conservative Beechgrove. Lysi's plan to use a lingerie party to search out which women Kavanagh had assaulted looked as if it would work.

As the women streamed in Lysi thought back to when she'd first approached the rather unconventional idea with Mary and Grace. Mary's cheeks had blazed, and she shook her head. Lysi remembered blinking in surprise. She'd assumed she'd get a negative response from Grace, but not from Mary. She'd assumed Mary would want to cooperate. After all, Lysi had planned this whole scheme to help her. At Mary's response, Lysi had fortified herself for a battle with both Grace and Mary.

Lysi smiled when she recalled Grace's response. "Fantastic! A panty party. Right up my alley." Grace slapped her hands together as she spoke. Lysi could hardly believe what she'd heard. Although it shouldn't have surprised her. Of course, Grace would love everything about a lingerie party especially shopping for designer undies.

Even after both Lysi and Grace had explained the critical need to find Kavanagh's other female assault victims if Mary wanted to avoid becoming a murder suspect, Mary still vetoed the party. Feeling frustrated, Lysi had asked Mary if she could suggest a better way of finding the other victims. Mary had no other suggestions and after what seemed like endless coaxing, had agreed and promised to do her part to make the lingerie party a success.

While Lysi and Grace presented their sexual harassment training in Dublin, Mary's job was to create an invitation on her computer. It would read: Lingerie Party, Mary McClone's Pub 10:00 A.M. Saturday. Women only. Grace had created a rather risqué title for the invitation that Lysi suspected Mary might balk at—Hidden Delights Panty Party. Put more zip into your love life.

When Lysi and Grace returned from Dublin, they were delighted to find that Mary had created the invitations on her computer. In fact, she'd outdone herself. She used a fancy font and printed out ultra-feminine invitations on glossy pink paper with sweet peas twining around the border. She'd already distributed them to female pub customers. She'd even incorporated Grace's titillating title only substituting lingerie for panty.

Lysi observed the women as they settled onto chairs, expectant expressions on curious faces. She estimated the ages to range from eighteen to fifty. Dress varied from skinny pants with long tops to conservative pant suits to fluffy dresses. Some of the women were familiar to her. One in particular caught her attention. In the back row close to the exit sat a slim, conservatively dressed woman, her hair pulled into a tight bun—the minister's wife. She looked interested but a bit edgy, maybe worried about word getting back to her husband.

Lysi tried to guess which of the women would have suited the vulgar taste of a rag like Kavanagh.

Two boxes covered in elegant pink brocade adorned with satin bows and faux pearls sat on a table at the front of the room. Grace had spotted the boxes in the gift department of Brown Thomas Department store in Dublin and insisted no well-planned panty party could do without the over-priced gift boxes.

One box contained several pairs of expensive panties that Lysi and Grace had purchased in the stylish Lingerie Room of Brown Thomas. Grace bought more La Perla and Stella McCartney designer pieces for herself than for the party.

At Grace's insistence, Lysi purchased one La Perla on sale. "Buy it for Maynard," she'd said. Grace's personal purchases came to more than seven hundred American dollars.

The other pink box on the table held the freshly-washed panties retrieved from Kavanagh's cottage.

The logistics of the plan were simple and focused on the Kavanagh box. While Grace presented pieces of lingerie, Lysi would act as the observer noting any stressful reactions on the part of individual attendees to panties shown from the second box. She would alert Mary, who would record their names and track them down later.

"Welcome, Ladies. I'm Lysi Weston. Please help yourself to a glass of pink lemonade and some cookies. We will begin the program in a few moments. First a couple of logistics. My colleague, Grace Wright, will present the lingerie pieces. After all the pieces have been presented, they will remain on display for you to select the ones you'd like to purchase. Mary will take cash or checks. Ready Grace?"

Grace reached into the first Brown Thomas box and pulled out a pair of fire-engine red La Perla briefs. "Fire up your lingerie wardrobe with this lacy panty in inflammable red."

Giggles sounded from the audience as attendees tittered to each other behind open palms.

Grace pulled another pair from the same box. "Consider this virginal white lace thong finished with a petite bow at the navel." With a mischievous gleam in her eye she added, "It'll drive the man in your life crazy."

Several women put hands to their mouths, giggled and averted their eyes. One Rubenesque woman in her fifties wearing a dress printed with large sunflowers shouted from her seat in the front row, "I'll take it."

"Black is a bewitching color," Grace said as she held up a shiny black satin French cut hipster studded with tiny pink silk rosebuds. "Wear this beauty when you want to bewitch him."

Lysi hoped Grace wouldn't get too graphic. Her concerns lessened when she noticed the audience seemed hang on Grace's every word.

When Grace emptied the first box, she moved to the Kavanagh box and pulled out a pair of black lace panties with a single pearl at the waist and held them up. "Now this beauty will have your man begging you to come to bed."

Laughter erupted from the women. Some slapped their knees and nodded their heads enthusiastically, except for one woman whose eyes sparked and lips tightened. Lysi nodded to Mary who scribbled a name on her pad.

Grace reached into the Kavanagh box and took out a pink pair of basic briefs with the initial M on the left side. The women scowled and Lysi heard words like, "Too plain," "Skip it," "Boring."

In the front row a dark-haired woman's hand flew to her mouth. She uttered a high-pitched squeal then looked around as if checking to see if anyone heard her.

Mary did and wrote down her name.

After Grace emptied the second box, Lysi invited the women to peruse the panties and purchase their favorites. Several of the women gathered at the table, but some including the dark-haired woman from the front row whose name Mary had recorded, slipped out the door without saying goodbye.

Lysi watched women purchase from the Kavanagh group. She guessed they were purchasing their own undies because most of them were women whose names Mary had recorded on her pad after observing their strong reactions to the panties as Grace presented them. Each time one of those women made a purchase Mary tried to catch her before she escaped out the door.

Mary took the women aside and spoke quietly to each one separately. As planned, she explained to the women that she and her American friends had found their panties in the Kavanagh cottage and that they suspected the women were victims of assault. Mary revealed her own victimization. She shared that she planned to report the assault to the police and urged them to do the same before the PSNI found evidence of the crime and questioned why they hadn't reported it and whether it was a motive for murder.

Lysi knew it took a lot of courage for Mary to reveal her own assault by Kavanagh in an effort to convince the women to come forward of their own accord, but it had to be done.

Would the plan work? Would other victims come forward? Or would Mary suffer village disgrace or worse would she find herself the prime suspect in the murder of Sean Kavanagh?

Chapter 42

A fine mist in the air felt good against Maynard's face as he stepped from McGarrity's B&B and turned toward Beechgrove's town square. He heard the soft chimes of St. Brigid Church bells tolling six o'clock Mass and wondered how long the old church had served the Beechgrove Catholics. He thought it looked like 19th century construction rebuilt with its steeple and arched stained glass windows.

Maynard found he enjoyed quiet early morning walks in this small village and had formed the habit of taking one every morning before Lysi woke. The solitude provided thinking time. God knows he had plenty to think about—the Kavanagh case, the burglary and homicide at the Lowry girls' cottage, Liam Maguire's strong motive for murder, and his biggest worry, Lysi's involvement in all of it.

His long strides brought him to the town square in less than ten minutes. He found a bench, wiped the dew off with a handkerchief and sat. As the sun vanquished the clouds, he removed his jacket under its warmth, leaned back, stretched his legs and listened to a chorus of sparrows perched on the church wall greeting the new day with their soprano tweets. The distant baritone lowing of hungry cows provided a curious kind of harmony with the birds. Sweet scents from the church rose garden reminded him of Lysi's favorite perfume. He emptied his mind of all thoughts and allowed himself to just be for a few minutes.

A little boy about six years old appeared out of nowhere and plunked down on the bench next to Maynard. The boy's plaid jacket drooped a bit at the shoulders but his dapper flat hat fit perfectly. Freckles danced across his nose and cheeks.

"Well hello there, young mate." Maynard looked around for an adult. The square was empty. "Are you waiting for someone?"

"Just me mum. She's over there in church." He pointed to the gray stone building. "She goes there every morning."

"You have to wait outside?"

"Naw, I just get tired of churchin'." The kid's feet didn't touch the ground. He swung them back and forth to some private rhythm inside his head.

"So, what do you do out here while you're waiting?"

"I look around for leprechauns."

"You don't say. Are there many around this square?"

"A few. Not as many as around my house." The boy looked up at Maynard with big round eyes. "I caught one once."

"Really, how did you do that?" Maynard enjoyed the kid's enthusiastic approach to the tall tale he was about to tell.

"Easy." The boy jiggled into a position from which he could look straight into Maynard's eyes. "You see, one night when it got dark, I cracked our door open a wee bit and put a wee bowl of porridge just inside. I hid behind the door and waited."

"How long did you have to wait?"

"Not long because Leprechauns love porridge and can smell it from a way off. When it came and started nibbling at the porridge, I grabbed it."

"That's bonza! I'd really like to see that Leprechaun."

"A ..." The boy paused and looked nervous. Maynard watched his eyes shift about as if searching for a response. After a moment he said," The next day after I caught it, I put the poor wee thing in me pocket to show it to me mates and on the way to school I fell down and it got squashed."

"Well now, that was a sad ending." Maynard grinned. This kid would carry on the great Irish tradition of telling tall tales.

The rumble of an engine distracted Maynard's attention from the boy. He looked up to see young Constable Aiden Quinn step from a police Land Rover and stroll across the dew-covered lawn toward him. "Morning Detective Christie."

Aiden's eyes shot to the boy next to Maynard. "Conner, get back into church. Your mammy will be looking for you. Go on with you now."

"Ah ... Aiden." The boy grinned at Aiden and scampered off. Maynard figured Aiden had caught Conner skipping church on more than one occasion.

"Aiden, good to see you, mate." Maynard said. He motioned to the spot on the bench where the boy had sat. "Have a seat. What brings you out so early?"

"I'm heading to Antrim Local Police Station to meet with the Detective Chief Inspector. I have to check in with him each Monday. Kind of a pain to get up so early, but I have to meet his schedule. He's a good guy." Aiden checked his watch.

Maynard observed Aiden. The young constable reminded him of his first year as a police officer—brand new shirt, razor-sharp creased trousers, spit-polished shoes and always an eager-to-learn expression on his face.

"Any news on the Kavanagh case?" Maynard tried to sound casual. He saw Aiden as a willing source of information but felt a little guilty about quizzing him too much.

"Aye," Aiden said. "I have a copy of the autopsy report. I'm not really working the case, but the DCI—that's the Detective Chief Inspector—let me have a copy to review. Part of my orientation. It's one of the things we'll be talking about this morning." Aiden hesitated. "I guess it's okay to show it to you because you're a copper, too."

"We'll keep it between us just in case," Maynard said. He felt another sting of guilt, but he needed enough information to keep Lysi out of trouble.

"Okay. I do have a couple of questions about the report. Maybe you could help me figure out the answers," Aiden said.

Maynard's eyebrows rose. He couldn't believe his luck. He could get a look at the autopsy report and help Aiden at the same time. He followed the young officer to the Land Rover and slipped in beside him. The spic and span interior of the Land Rover looked and smelled new.

Aiden reached into the back seat and grabbed a black leather briefcase complete with gunmetal hardware and a mobile phone pocket. The briefcase was as shiny and new as Aiden. Maybe a graduation gift from proud parents. Aiden searched through it and pulled out a manila folder labeled Kavanagh and handed it to Maynard. "The report took a while to get here because we send all bodies off to Belfast for autopsy."

Aiden watched and listened with total attention as Maynard skimmed the pages of the report making periodic comments. "Rigor mortis put time of death between 12 and 48 hours from discovery. Body muscles had already begun to relax." That seemed about right to Maynard since the body had probably lain in the field for a time.

Three points in the report grabbed his interest. On the body the ME found Caucasian hairs not belonging to the victim. Two different blood types on the victim's clothes, one belonging to Kavanagh and the other to an unknown person, indicated that a fight might have ensued. "The ME found evidence of defensive abrasions on the victim's knuckles. That could mean the victim tried to fight off his killer," Maynard said.

Maynard knew those three findings would provide excellent evidence but only if the police found a viable suspect.

"The cause of death was a stabbing wound from a six-inch blade though no weapon or fingerprints were found." Another complication, Maynard mused.

He read further, then commented more to himself than to Aiden. "The manner of death was declared a homicide. That's pretty obvious."

Aiden waited until Maynard had finished browsing the autopsy report then said, "That part about the kind of death is a wee bit confusing. I mean what is the difference between manner of death and cause of death? They sound the same to me."

"The cause of death refers to the specific injury or disease that led to death. In Kavanagh's case, the cause of death is the knife wound." Maynard tried not to sound too scholarly. "The manner of death is the determination of how the injury or disease led to death. There are five manners of death—natural, accidental, suicide, homicide and undetermined. In Kavanagh's case the manner of death was declared a homicide."

Aiden squinted and thought for a moment. "I think I get it."

"Good." Maynard handed the folder back to Aiden and reached for the door handle. He wanted to jot down what he'd learned from the report while it was fresh in his memory. He patted his jacket pocket to assure himself he had the notebook he always carried with him out of years of habit. He'd just opened the door when Aiden popped another question.

"About rigor mortis," Aiden said. "It stiffens the body, right?"

Maynard nodded.

"Then why were the muscles relaxed?"

"Because rigor mortis sets in about two to six hours after death and the body stiffens, but after about 12 or more hours the muscles relax again."

"Wow, Maynard, you should be a teacher. You make things so clear."

"Thanks," Maynard said. He slapped Aiden on the back. "You're a fast learner and you're already a fine police officer."

Aiden blushed. "Away off," he said.

Maynard got out of the car and waved as Aiden drove off. He walked back to the bench, pulled out his notebook and scribbled what he'd learned from the autopsy report. He sat a few minutes before heading back to the Inn and pondered the new developments.

Now a new worry invaded his mind. Would the autopsy evidence clear Liam Maguire, the Lowrys and Mary McClone or convict one of them?

Nancy Curteman

Chapter 43

The small PSNI local police station reception area had no windows, low lighting and dull, institutional gray walls and ceiling. Lysi felt claustrophobic when the bulletproof door slammed behind her. She and Grace sat on folding chairs and watched Mary and Maynard leave the room through a side door opened by a police officer.

Maynard had convinced Mary she needed to report Kavanagh's assault before the police discovered it and drew their own conclusions. Mary had reluctantly consented on the condition that Maynard act as her advocate if the police required her to come for an interview.

Both Lysi and Grace worried the police would deem the assault of Mary a strong motive for killing Kavanagh. Both women sat without talking, gazing at the closed door through which Maynard and Mary had disappeared.

Lysi's eyes strayed from the door and settled on a dark-haired woman behind a glass window at the opposite end of the room from the exterior door. She nudged Grace. "See that clerk? I recognize her from the lingerie party."

Grace scrutinized the clerk. "Right. But I can't quite place her. Is that the minister's wife? Grace's eyes turned mischievous. I saw the Reverend whistling and grinning in the pharmacy yesterday. Must have been those red silk panties the Mrs. Reverend clandestinely purchased at the panty party." Grace snickered.

"Really?" Lysi's eyes crinkled in amusement. "No, she's the woman who reacted to the pink panties with the 'M' monogram embroidered on them. Remember? She left right after your presentation."

"Oh yeah, one of Kavanagh's victims." Grace rolled her eyes. "A cop, yet! That vile piece of filth had the gall to assault a cop."

No surprise, Lysi thought. Kavanagh reasoned he'd get away with it given the village women's fear of incurring ostracism if they revealed an assault. Lysi recalled passing some of the assault victims on her way to the B&B the day after the lingerie party. They wouldn't make eye contact with her. There had to be a way to help these women conquer their fears and stand up for themselves. Her eyes shifted back to the figure behind the window. She might be the answer.

Lysi walked over to the window where the woman sat sorting and filing papers into folders. She didn't look up right away so Lysi tapped on the glass.

The woman raised her head. "What can I do—"

The woman's eyebrows shot up and her mouth dropped open.

"Hello," Lysi said. "Maureen isn't it?"

Lysi imagined what must be racing through the stunned woman's mind—Does she remember me? Does she suspect I was assaulted? Has she told anyone? What if the whole village finds out? What will my parents say? Lysi noticed Maureen's hand shaking. She waited a moment to give the woman a chance to calm down, then got right to the point.

"Maureen, I know what Sean Kavanagh did to you." Lysi spoke in a soft voice.

Maureen swallowed hard but didn't say anything. She stared at Lysi.

"I also know the fear you have of people finding out."

Still no response from Maureen.

"I hope you understand the assault was not your fault. You were the victim of a criminal act."

No response except a flicker of her right eye.

"What you don't know is that Kavanagh was a seriel rapist. He assaulted six other village women. Those are the ones we know about. There may be more."

"Six? Maybe more?" Maureen whispered. "A serial rapist?"

"Probably more," Lysi said. "We found proof of the assaults."

Lysi told Maureen about the panties they'd taken from Kavanagh's cottage in an effort to keep the other women from being found out by the police. She realized that removing the panties was tampering with evidence and that it was risky to admit it to Maureen, a police officer, but she saw no other choice. "He assaulted Mary McClone and she reported the assault."

Lysi saw a mixture of fear and sympathy in Maureen's eyes. She hoped sympathy would triumph over fear.

"Maureen, Mary needs your help. She needs you and the support of the other six victims."

Maureen didn't respond. She glanced toward the door to the interview rooms then wrote something on an index card and slid it through the opening in the bottom window. Without looking at Lysi, she lowered her head, picked up a sheet of paper and began filing again.

*

In the interview room, Maynard sat in a chair at the end of a small table. The same place he'd sat a week ago when he advocated for Emma Lowry. Two detectives, a man and a woman sat on one side of the table. Maynard recognized them as the same team that had interviewed Emma. Mary sat across from them.

Maynard thought it a bit unusual that the police had requested an interview after Mary had already reported the Kavanagh assault. Maybe it was a procedure in Northern Ireland with which he wasn't familiar.

One of the detectives, DS Graig glared at Maynard. "You again. You planning to set up housekeeping here."

Maynard smiled. "Not in my plans."

DS Graig introduced the female Detective DS O'Shea and turned to Mary.

It caught Maynard's attention when the detective went through the preliminaries of reading Mary her rights and having her sign a paper indicating she'd received them. Maynard knew this procedure normally took place before interviewing a suspect. Was Mary a suspect?

"Now Miss McClone, you say Sean Kavanagh assaulted you."

"That he did." Mary didn't look at the detective, her head bowed, she spoke to the table.

"That's a serious accusation. When and where did the assault occur?"

"I've already explained all this to the other officer when I reported the assault."

"Bear with me, Miss McClone. I'm just reviewing information to make sure you didn't leave out any details," DS Graig said.

"It took place on February 15th at two in the morning in my pub."

Maynard knew Mary's definitive statement was typical of assault victims. She would never forget the time and place of the humiliating invasion. In every assault case he'd investigated the victim always remembered the exact time and place of the painful event because they were permanently seared into their minds.

"Tell us how it happened."

Mary turned to Maynard. Her eyes told him she didn't want to relive the experience. He nodded to her as if to say I know it will be difficult, but it has to be done.

Mary took a deep breath, her eyes sparked, and she looked directly into the face of the male detective. "I was alone in my pub counting up receipts and making entries into my account books when that animal burst through the back door." She swallowed a sob. "He grabbed me and threw me to the floor. He tore off my knickers." A tear slipped down Mary's cheek. "I was saved from the worst by the arrival of Thomas Rook needing a bit of broth for his sick wife. He scared Kavanagh off."

"Would you answer another question now? Are you sure he assaulted you? Maybe he thought you invited his advances," DS Graig said looking down at his tablet instead of at Mary.

"No never."

"I believe we know the answer to that question," DS O'Shea commented. "From the description Miss McClone just gave of the assault, it does not sound as though she invited it."

Detective Graig looked sheepish and didn't press the question.

Maynard glared at Graig. "DS O'Shea is correct. That question was out of order." He guessed the rebuke would provoke a reaction, and it did.

"Mr. Christie," DS Graig said. "We are conducting this interview, not you."

Graig turned to Mary. "Miss McClone, you must understand our goal is to get the facts. We need to ask difficult questions to do so."

Mary nodded.

"We found your fingerprints in Kavanagh's cottage which made us wonder." He paused before asking the next question. "Were you having an affair with him?"

"No. God no!"

"Is it possible he rejected you?"

"No."

"Maybe you couldn't stand the humiliation? I could understand how painful that might be—you love someone and he rejects you. You'd be hurt."

"No. I hated him."

Maynard pursed his lips. He wished Mary hadn't said that. Hate is a strong motive for murder.

"That hurt turned to hate. Did you hate him enough to murder him?"

Mary stared at the detective in speechless shock.

"Sergeant O'Shea sighed. "I think Miss McClone has made it quite clear that she had no affection for Sean Kavanagh."

Maynard didn't like the direction the interview was taking. Was Graig accusing Mary of murder? Was it time for a lawyer? He decided to try to reason with the detective.

"May I ask a question?" Maynard spoke respectfully. He realized he'd overstepped his bounds with his previous comment and wanted to err on the side of caution.

The detective scowled. "It's not standard procedure. Make it brief."

"I understand Kavanagh's body was found in a field, buried in a shallow grave," Maynard said.

The detective squinted at Maynard. "How did you know that?"

Maynard gulped. "I … I must have read it somewhere. I …"

"Get on with your question?"

"How could a woman the size of Mary McClone dig a large hole in the middle of a field and move the body of a big man like Kavanagh into that hole?"

"That is something we intend to find out," Graig said.

Chapter 44

Lysi and Grace stood on the gravel path that circled the town square, and peered at the church with its dark cemetery. The nebulous tombstones resembled a ghostly gathering of meditating angels among Irish crosses. Night sounds caught Lysi's attention. An owl hooted followed by a shuffling of wings. Had a mouse seen its last day? The yowl of a distressed cat pierced the night. Frogs croaked throaty duets. Sounds of unseen things scampering about. Sounds she never noticed during the day.

She knew Grace didn't like the country night sounds. She was used to city night sounds—cars honking, buses squealing, music streaming from bars and nightclubs, people talking. She expected a caustic comment from Grace, and she got it.

"Lysi," Grace said. "What is it with you? Always creeping around at night like … like bats and frogs and mice and worms and—"

"Save it, Grace."

Lysi took out her penlight and reread the card Maureen had slipped her at the police station. The woman had scribbled, "Be at St. Brigid at 10:00 tonight." She checked the time on her cell phone. "Ten o'clock."

"Yeah," Grace said looking around. "Where is she? It's hecka creepy around here."

A faint light flickered from behind a gravestone in the cemetery.

Grace grabbed Lysi's arm. "Did you see that. A ghost. Probably pissed at us for invading his territory."

"That's more likely Maureen signaling us. Come on. Let's check it out." Lysi disengaged her arm and stepped toward the cemetery gate.

"Hold on, that's a zombie zone," Grace said. "No way am I going into that marble orchard with all those dead people."

Lysi cast an incredulous glance at Grace. "You're kidding, right? The girl who roamed the streets of Harlem surrounded by gangs is afraid to venture into a village cemetery?"

"It has nothing to do with the village. It has to do with ghosts."

"Get off it, Grace. No such things as ghosts."

"How do you know? Ireland's full of ghosts like shrieking Banshees, evil fairies and sea monsters. And haven't you ever heard of poltergeists?"

"Grace, please. Banshees don't live in cemeteries. Sea monsters live in the ocean, and poltergeists are German." Lysi gave herself a mental slap for engaging in such a ridiculous discussion. "Besides, don't you want to get help for Mary?"

The light flashed from the tombstone again. A loud whisper followed. "Over here."

"There she is," Lysi said. "Behind that tombstone with the angel on top of it. Come on."

Lysi walked over to Maureen. Grace followed reluctantly behind.

Maureen's face looked pale, almost ghostlike in the darkness. Her eyes kept switching around the area. Lysi understood her caution. Decent women in Beechgrove didn't wander about alone after ten o'clock at night. How would she explain meeting two Americans in the local cemetery?

Lysi extended her hand. "Thank you for meeting us, Maureen. I know it took a lot of courage."

"I want to help Mary." Maureen spoke in a small tremulous voice. "But if I report, people will think I encouraged Kavanagh."

"Will they think that Mary and the six other women Kavanagh assaulted encouraged him?" Lysi asked.

Maureen shifted her gaze to the concrete angel and stroked its wings.

"In my job I deal with sexual harassment all the time." Lysi pointed to Grace. "My colleague and I understand how difficult it is for women to cope with an assault or harassment. We'll stand with you throughout the ordeal."

"Who are the other women?" Maureen stopped stroking the angel's wing and looked at Lysi.

"Before I tell you, I need to know if you will help Mary."

Maureen sighed. "I … I'm willing to try."

"Excellent. Here's what we want you to do."

Chapter 45

Mary McClone had finished wiping down the bar in the pub, removed her apron and sat at a table bent over an accounts journal entering the receipts for the day. When the clock struck two a.m. she looked up and pressed cramped fingers against her throbbing temples. Fatigue from a usual day's work and worry over being a suspect in a murder case had exhausted her. She stretched and massaged a knot in her neck before returning to her task.

At a light knock on the pub's back door her head jerked up, shoulders rigid with fear. She certainly hadn't expected anyone at this late hour. She touched her hand to the base of her throat where her pulse hammered. Had she locked the door?

A memory of Kavanagh's assault froze her to the chair. Had word gotten out about Kavanagh's attack? Did people in the village think she had invited it and would welcome male advances? What if a man viewed her as fair game now, considered her tainted goods? She couldn't go through another assault.

The door. She had to check if she'd locked it. What if she hadn't? What if someone tried the knob, found it unlocked and now waited for her in the dark kitchen? Panic forced her to her feet. After a deep breath, she tip-toed to the bar, grabbed a full bottle of whisky and started toward the back door. If an intruder opened the door, she would attack him before he could pounce on her. She would rather spend the rest of her life in prison than allow some brute to hurt her again.

Heart thundering in her chest, she walked on past the bar and ordered her limp legs to carry her through the swinging door to the dark kitchen past the stove, sink and large walk-in cooler. At the back door she tried the handle of the heavy-duty deadbolt she'd installed after the Kavanagh assault. Locked. "Thank you, God," she whispered, her legs weak with relief.

She stood listening for more raps. None came. Either she'd imagined the knocking or the person gave up and left. She turned to head back to complete her accounting task but stopped when a quiet voice called to her. "Mary, it's Ryan. May I have a wee word with you?"

Mary hesitated. She knew Ryan felt fondly toward her but now if he as well as the whole village knew she'd been assaulted he wouldn't have the same feelings toward her. There would always be that lingering suspicion that she'd encouraged Kavanagh. What if Ryan thought he could now have his way with her since she was already stained. No, she would not become a village tart. "Ryan, it's late. Come back tomorrow."

"Please Mary. Allow me a few moments of your time."

Mary took a deep breath. She knew Ryan was a good man. He always treated her with respect and kindness. Holy Mother knows if things were different, she could have returned his affection. Too late now.

"I'm begging you Mary. Please allow me a moment." Ryan's voice sounded urgent but Mary couldn't risk allowing him in at this hour. "Ryan, you know the kitchen is closed."

"I don't want food."

"Why come in the middle of the night?" Mary asked.

"I saw your light. I wanted to talk with you in private. Mary, I have to tell you what I'm feeling."

Mary's hand moved to her chest. He sounds sincere. Should she allow him a moment? Should she risk opening the door? Blessed Mary guide me.

She opened the door and looked into Ryan's moist eyes. "I'll not come in if you prefer. I can talk here."

"Come in Ryan. Sit a moment."

They sat across from each other at a small food-preparation table in the dimly lit kitchen. Ryan reached across the table and touched her fingertips. "Mary, it's no secret how I feel about you. Sure the whole village knows. I—"

"Ryan, there's no need—"

"Please, let me finish while I have the courage. I know what that son of a bitch tried to do to you. Forgive my language." He hung his head. "I just wish he were alive so I could kill him with my bare hands."

"Ryan please." She pulled her fingers away from him and placed her hands in her lap.

"I know you didn't murder him."

"Ryan, I—"

"Please, I'm still not finished. This is the hardest part. Give me your hand, will you?"

Mary saw deep affection in Ryan's eyes. She moved a hand from her lap to the table.

Ryan took Mary's hand in both his. "You know I've been a bachelor for many years since my wife Abigail died. I'm probably set in my ways and habits. I know I haven't much to offer a fine lass like you."

Mary squeezed Ryan's hand. "You're a good man Ryan O'Rourke. Any woman would be proud to have your attention."

Ryan leaned forward. "Mary, can you not see? I ... I ... love you. I'm asking you to be my wife."

Nancy Curteman

Chapter 46

Lysi and Grace shepherded a group of 12 nervous but determined women through the door of the PSNI station. They lined up along the waiting room wall. Their ages ranged from early twenties to late forties. Some tall, others short. Brunettes, blondes and redheads. Assault by Kavanagh was the one thing they had in common.

The women surveyed the stark waiting room with big eyes and anxious expressions. Some held hands. Some whispered to each other. Lysi guessed most of them had never had reason to enter a police station.

Lysi went to the registration window and winked at Maureen. "Are you ready?"

Maureen nodded. To Lysi, she looked confident, almost eager.

At the meeting in the cemetery Maureen had agreed to follow Lysi's plan to help Mary.

Lysi assured Maureen the plan would work even though she hadn't completely convinced herself and feared Maureen would not have the courage to follow through. She was wrong. Maureen told her she'd met with a couple of her friends whose names were on the list Lysi had generated at the lingerie party. Those women contacted their own friends who were on the list and discovered some victims who were not on it. The group met with Maureen in the back room of Mary's pub. They all knew each other. When the women disclosed their victimization by Kavanagh and realized how many women he'd hurt, their anger ignited. On hearing that Mary McClone was now suspected of murdering him their anger burst into a wildfire. The women had consented to help, some fearfully, some angrily, some tearfully. Now they stood united in their determination to expose Kavanagh and exonerate Mary.

"Good morning, ladies," Maureen said and gave an encouraging thumbs up to the waiting women. "Welcome. I'll let DS Graig know you're here." She grinned as she pressed the intercom button.

The waiting room door swung open and DS Graig stepped briskly through it. He started to speak but instead stared open-mouthed at the herd of women staring back at him. He tugged at his collar and cast a questioning glance at Maureen who said nothing. He looked back at the women.

"Good morning, DS Graig." Lysi stepped forward. "My name is Lysi Weston and this is my colleague, Grace Wright. We are management trainers with Stellar Corporate Development. We train clients in strategies for identifying and eradicating sexual harassment in the work place."

She waited for a response from the detective who raised his brows in confusion. He simply nodded and shifted his eyes to the crowd of waiting women.

"In short, DS honey," Grace said. "Our job description includes advocating for male and female victims of any form of sexual assault."

"Maureen," Lysi said. "Please take over."

DS Graig whipped his head around to Maureen.

"Each one of these women wishes to report an assault by Sean Kavanagh," Maureen said. "How would you like to handle this?"

The detective sergeant surveyed the long line of women staring back at him, and swallowed hard. He turned to Maureen. "Distribute report forms, please."

"Already did." Maureen had provided a form to each woman when they met at Mary McClone's pub. "They're filled out and ready for interviews." She picked up a stack of papers from the window counter and handed them to him. "I put them in alphabetical order. You can start with Brigid Carrigan."

She motioned to Brigid. "You're first, honey. We've got your back."

"Wait," DS Graig said. "Maybe DS O'Shea should handle this. You know … a … gentle feminine touch."

DS Shelby O'Shea, standing behind Graig tapped him on the shoulder. "You're right. I'll be sitting in with you."

The reporting women smiled when they recognized O'Shea. Some waved, others called out to her using her first name. "Hi Shelby."

DS Graig's eyes flicked from the women to O'Shea. He swallowed and tugged at his already loose collar again.

Maureen had invited O'Shea to participate in the meeting with the women in Mary McClone's Pub as a way to assure them of O'Shea's support. She had also arranged for Lysi and Grace to meet with DS O'Shea ahead of the pub meeting.

Since joining the PSNI two years ago petite, curly-headed, blond-haired Shelby O'Shea had advocated for a more encouraging reporting environment for women. She consented to cooperate fully with Lysi's plan. In fact, when she learned Lysi and Grace conducted sexual harassment seminars, she jumped at the chance to schedule a workshop for the PSNI station.

Grace patted Brigid Carrigan on the shoulder. "You take charge girl. Give 'em hell."

Six hours and four boxes of tissues later all the tearful women had described their ordeals in detail to the two detectives.

DS Graig looking haggard and exhausted entered the waiting room. "That's the last one. Right, Maureen?" he asked hopefully.

Lysi grinned at the thought of DS Graig trying to cope with 12 women each with a possible motive to murder Kavanagh. Now maybe Mary would no longer remain a prime suspect.

But what about Emma Lowry?

Chapter 47

Lysi stood in the middle of the 66-foot long Carrick-a-Rede Rope Bridge waving her arms and urging Grace to follow her. She could hear the wild waves swirling and crashing against the already eroded cliff sides 100 feet below. A pungent smell of fresh seaweed rose from the chasm. The creak of the bridge's wooden slats in the rushing wind did unnerve her a bit but she determined not to let it show. She avoided looking down for fear of losing courage.

Ryan had insisted on taking the four Americans on a tour of two of County Antrim's famous sites, the Rope Bridge and Giants' Causeway. The Sunday trip was a good idea since there would be no movement in the Kavanagh case while DS Graig was busy verifying 12 women's alibis. An added bonus of the trip was that Lysi's fear on the bridge took her mind off the case for a little while.

"Come on Grace." Lysi couldn't understand why Grace would forego crossing the bridge after enduring the exhausting 45-minute walk from the parking lot, navigating up and down slippery gravel paths and rough uneven stone steps. Maybe the morning visit to the Giant's Causeway had worn her out.

"Come on, Grace," Lysi repeated. "You'll feel like you're floating above the world."

Chess had taken a few steps onto the bridge and extended an encouraging hand to Grace while Maynard, having completed the crossing, waited on Carrick-a-Rede, the tiny fishing island the bridge had connected to the mainland for 350 years. He didn't join in the cajoling effort to persuade Grace to venture onto the bridge but just observed.

Grace stared down at the rugged rocks and crashing waves below and shook her head. She turned away from the bridge and pushed past the line of tourists waiting their turns to cross. She trudged up metal steps to the cliff above the bridge entrance, glanced back and waved. "I'll meet you at the Weighbridge Tea Room," she shouted over her shoulder ignoring the urging from the line of strangers that she just try the bridge since she'd come this far. Lysi knew what Grace would do in the Tea Room. She'd grab a sweet cake and browse the gift section for souvenirs.

Disappointed that Grace hadn't joined her, Lysi turned and continued across the bridge. When she reached the end, Maynard took her hand and guided her up the steps to the summit of Carrick-a-Rede Island. Beneath the haunting cries of seabirds soaring and diving they stood gazing out across the water at the Scottish coast and the L-shaped Rathlin Island. "It's ruggedly beautiful," Maynard said.

"Lovely," Lysi said. "They say Robert the Bruce, the Scottish king, took refuge on Rathlin when Edward the First drove him from Scotland. Rathlin is where Bruce took courage from watching the perseverance of a spider spinning its web. Courage that enabled him to continue his own fight despite losses, and to regain his Scottish kingdom."

Maynard smiled at Lysi. "Glad to have a history major at my side."

Lysi kissed his cheek, happy to see him less preoccupied with her amateur sleuthing. At least for the moment.

*

Inside the white pebble-dash Weighbridge Tea Room, Grace sat at a table with Ryan who had elected not to cross the Carrick-a-Rede Rope Bridge as he'd done it once and that was enough.

Next to a cup of rich hot chocolate Grace had piled her gift shop purchases—a leather passport wallet for Chess, two pebble necklaces, a blue one for Lysi, a coral one for herself, one scarf, and a pair of bee earrings.

As she spread lemon curd and cream on scones for herself and Ryan, he regaled her with stories about the origin of the Giants' Causeway they'd visited earlier in the day. Grace had marveled at the Heritage Site in which she walked among hexagonal-shaped basalt pillars that seemed to tumble down into the Atlantic Ocean just as they had done during the volcanic eruptions in the Paleocene period. She liked the lore associated with the unusual geological formations. Ryan's stories reminded Grace of her mother's tales of Puerto Rican lore—Coqui the tiny frog created by a Goddess, El Chupacabra the creature that sucked the blood from small animals, Taroo whom the gods turned into a hummingbird that flits from blossom to blossom seeking his lover whom the gods had changed into a flower.

"Irish giant, Finn MacCool, and Scottish giant Benandonner loathed each other." Ryan's voice reeked of hatred. "One day Finn built a path of boulders to use as stepping-stones to reach Scotland. In anger, Brenandonner ripped up that path. That's how we got Giant's Causeway."

"Why did they hate each other?" Grace asked.

"Because they were rival giants."

Grace understood the basic problem—a common testosterone battle. Still happens today.

By the time Lysi, Maynard and Chess had returned from the Carrick-a-Rede Bridge, Ryan had filled Grace's head with tales of the various rock formations of the Giant's Causeway—The Giant's Boot lost by Finn as he raced back home to Ireland, Finn's Camel that was turned to stone, and most fascinating to Grace, the Wishing Chair, that so many people had sat on so often that the basalt stones were mirror shiny and smooth as glass. A part of Grace wanted to believe that wishes were granted to those who sat on the stone throne.

*

The drive back to Beechgrove along the Causeway Coastal Route presented a visual feast of stunning sea and land. Maynard thought that Ryan's command of his new car had improved somewhat and the well-maintained highway presented less of a challenge to him than the narrow country roads. Lysi sitting in the backseat with a dozing Grace and snoring Chess, kept reading facts from her guidebook to Maynard who sat in front with Ryan.

Maynard breathed a sigh of relief as Ryan pulled to a stop in front of McGarrity's B&B. From his vantage point in the front seat he had witnessed Ryan's near misses that the backseat passengers had not. He figured he had a few choices to ensure he would survive his visit to Beechgrove—persuade Ryan to allow him to drive, sit in the backseat when riding with Ryan, or stop riding with Ryan altogether. None of them were likely to work. Prayer was his only option.

Chapter 48

Maynard leaned back on the bench in the town square and gazed at the dark, ominous clouds that seemed to bear down on him. The sunny morning was turning into a rainy day. "Rain again."

Constable Aiden Quinn sat next to him peeling an orange. "Aye. There's an old Irish saying: 'If cows are lying down it's raining. If they're standing, it's going to rain.'"

Maynard sighed. How true. It seemed as if had rained at least some time during every day since he'd come to Northern Ireland. No wonder it was so beautiful and green. So different from his sheep station, dry and golden most of the year. As the first misty droplets landed on him, he stayed seated hoping the sun would break through the clouds and evaporate the droplets in midair.

"A bit of drought would be nice right now," he muttered.

"What did you say?" Aiden held the orange out to Maynard, offering him half .

Maynard accepted half, broke off a section and bit into it. The sweet, juicy flavor reminded him of the Navels grown in the sunny Riverina groves of New South Wales. He could do with a dose of the warm dry climate.

"Nothing important," Maynard said. Not wanting to offend Aiden with his drought comment he changed the subject. "How goes the Kavanagh investigation?" He had developed a keen interest in the case because down deep he felt sympathy for the suspects Mary McClone, Liam MaGuire and Emma Lowry, and wanted to see them cleared. "Any new developments I can help clarify?"

"Aye, it's a wee bit confusing. After scouring a goodly part of the field, the police found the weapon—a knife."

"Not so confusing. Murderers usually dispose of the weapon in the vicinity of the murder," Maynard said.

"I know. I know. That's not the confusing part."

"No?" Maynard said, gazing up at the darkening clouds. "Were the fingerprints readable?"

"Clear enough so they could see two sets of prints."

That fact got Maynard's attention. "Were the prints clear enough to identify?"

"Aye, one set belonged to Kavanagh. The other set will surprise you as well as what I'm about to tell you." Aiden popped a section of orange into his mouth and chewed slowly.

"And that is?" Maynard said.

Aiden finished chewing and swallowed the orange section. "Well, you remember the blood they found on the victim's clothes?" Aiden popped another orange section into his mouth and looked at Maynard while he chewed.

Maynard took a breath and tried to hide his growing impatience. "I do."

"They ran the two blood samples through the DNA Database and got definitive hits."

"DNA? Sounds pretty clear to me. Why do you think that's confusing?"

"That's not the confusing part. It seems the timing is all off. It seems the murderer, as identified by DNA, couldn't have committed the murder when the autopsy report stated the time of death to have taken place."

"Time of death isn't always precise. There are lots of things that can impact it."

"I know. I remember what you said. Temperature, weather, location. But it wouldn't be off by over a week."

"Aiden, what are you getting at?" Maynard's impatience came through in the question. He popped the remainder of the orange Aiden had given him in his mouth and waited.

"Well now, are you ready for a weird wrinkle in this case?"

Chapter 49

The soft lighting from antique table lamps in the sitting room at McGarrity's B and B along with the soothing piano strains of Debussy's "Clair de Lune" and the plush 19th century style burgundy couch and side chairs created a relaxing ambience.

The four people seated around an English oak cocktail table, Lysi, Grace, and Mary were not relaxed despite the soothing glasses of Bailey's Irish Cream they'd been sipping.

Maynard sat quietly listening to flurry of reactions to his sharing of Aiden's "weird wrinkle in the case."

"My first thought is that it's impossible. My second thought is that there is always a logical explanation," Lysi said.

"I knew I didn't want any part of this." Grace clenched her teeth and slammed one fist into the palm of her other hand.

"I just don't see how it could be possible." Mary knitted her brows and shook her head.

"Are the police certain about the time of Kavanagh's death?" Lysi asked.

"If it's true, it contradicts everything we've learned so far about the Kavanagh case," Mary said.

"A match of the suspect's DNA from previous arrests came from the Northern Ireland DNA Database," Maynard said. "There are some variables, however."

"And they are?" Lysi leaned forward toward Maynard who sat across the table from her.

"DNA is not a hundred percent accurate. Samples are sometimes imperfect. DNA breaks down. It doesn't have a timestamp on it. It may have been left at the crime scene weeks before the crime occurred. And, labs can make mistakes when processing the DNA sample,"

The group kept their eyes glued to Maynard. Lysi frowned and said, "Then we don't know for sure who the killer is."

"There's more." Maynard held up his palm signaling Lysi not to jump to conclusions. "The police found the knife and it had fingerprints on it that confirmed the source of the DNA."

"Could the murder of Kavanagh have taken place a week before the official time of death?" Lysi asked.

"Possible but unlikely. A few hours earlier maybe," Maynard said. "The medical examiner used the three most important indicators of time of death, algor mortis or body temperature, rigor mortis or postmortem rigidity, and livor mortis or the discoloration of skin due to pooling of blood. His time of death determination is probably pretty accurate."

Lysi looked fascinated. She remembered learning in her criminal justice courses about the procedures for determining time of death but had never witnessed their application in a real crime.

Maynard paused. "I don't mean to get too technical. Don't want to bore or confuse you."

"No," Lysi said. "We're not bored or confused at all." She turned to Grace and Mary. "Are we?"

Grace looked bored and started filing her nails. Mary looked confused and kept shaking her head.

"If you can bear with me," Maynard said. "Two interesting findings struck me: lividity indicated that the body was not moved post mortem. So, the murder probably did take place in the field."

"Interesting," Lysi said.

"And," Maynard continued. "They found Kavanagh's prints on the knife. This could mean a struggle ensued and the murderer tried to defend himself. That could mean self-defense."

"That's all well and good," Lysi said. "But the tine of death is the bottom-line issue."

Mary nodded in agreement.

Grace stopped filing her nails and looked up. "Sounds like an avenging ghost to me."

"Get real Grace," Lysi said. "This is serious. We have to determine how the impossible happened."

Chapter 50

The crowded tables in Mary McClone's Pub buzzed with the jovial sounds of people winding down at the end of a work week. Lysi grinned at Billy who had just ordered another round of pints for the table. She slapped him on the back. "I guess you're not as bad as everyone says, Billy Boy."

"Nope," Billy said. "Worse."

Ryan raised a pint to the four Americans sitting across from him. "Here's to the impossible."

"To the impossible?" Billy said raising his glass and his eyebrows. "A ...You want to explain that a bit more?"

"Well now, Beechgrove not only has a murder, we have a ghost that did the dastardly deed."

Lysi and Maynard exchanged glances. How did Ryan find out about the ghost murder? They both looked at Grace.

Grace elbowed Chess. "There, you see? What did I tell you? Ghosts, spirits and fairies abound in Northern Ireland."

"Please Grace, honey," Chess said. "Let me unwind a bit from my Dublin trip before you start with the weird stuff."

Grace ignored his caustic comment, and pointed to the black night outside the window. "You'd better hope no spirits are lurking out there waiting to grab nonbelievers."

Lysi rolled her eyes. Could her sophisticated friend really believe in spooky spirits? Since the return from Carrick-a-Rede Rope Bridge, Grace had prattled on about all the ghosts Ryan had filled her head with while they waited in the Weighbridge Tea Room.

"Grace, honey, for the last time, I don't believe in ghosts or fairies or spirits," Chess took a big gulp of Guinness and banged his mug on the table to emphasize his point.

"Ah now, Chess," Ryan said. "You'd best not be saying that too loud. Grace is right, himself might be lurking about. You wouldn't want to offend him."

"Offend who?" Chess asked.

Lysi squeezed Maynard's thigh under the table to get his attention and sent an eye message. Chess had just given Ryan the opening he needed to embark on one of his Irish ghostly goings-on as he liked to say.

"Who? You're asking who? I'll tell you who." Ryan's eyes sparkled. "Now did you not hear tell of the wee Faery Island located between Rathlin Island and mainland Ballycastle? It surfaces only once every seven years."

Chess shook his head and took a big swig of beer as if fortifying himself for a long spiel.

Lysi sighed. Save me. This mythological monologue could go on for hours.

"Well in the waters of Faery Island dwell the beautiful Merrows. Maidens with long golden hair and voluptuous figures from the navel up." Using his palms, Ryan fashioned a female figure in the air.

All eyes now shot towards Ryan. Billy broke the silence. "From the navel up, you say?"

"Aye, Merrows are among the most lusciously desirable creatures on earth. Lucky for us they find mortal men irresistible and are uncontrollably promiscuous in their relations with them." Ryan winked at Maynard who grinned back.

"Sounds pretty good to me." Chess jiggled his brows and clicked his tongue a couple of times.

"Hey, are we talking about a fish here?" Grace said. "Chessie, are you saying you'd like to get it on with a fish?"

"A mermaid," Lysi said. She didn't add that she considered a mermaid to be a mythical creature.

"Aye, a mermaid. They travel through the sea wrapped in sealskin cloaks. In order to come ashore they abandon their cloaks and take on the form of a human. Men lust after them for their beauty which surpasses that of any mortal woman."

"Now hold on." Lysi and Grace exclaimed in duet.

"Not counting you." Maynard put his arm around Lysi's shoulders.

"Or you," Chess added.

232

"Some mortals have even married Merrows not just for their beauty, but for the wealth of gold they've plundered from shipwrecks," Ryan continued as if he hadn't noticed everyone's skepticism. "Why they've even had children with them. In fact, they say the O'Flaherty, O'Sullivan and MacNamara families claim to have descended from those unions."

"Do any of those families live in Beechgrove?" Lysi asked. "Do you know any of them?" She tried not to sound dubious.

Ryan downed the last of his pint. "Well, no."

"Let him finish the story," Grace said.

"Now the drawbacks to these unions are the Mermen." Ryan pause long enough to signaled the bartender for another beer.

"Mermen?" Chess burst into a loud belly laugh. "Ryan, maybe you've had enough beer."

"Chess!" Grace glared at him then turned to Ryan. "Go on, Ryan."

"Aye, Mermen. You rarely see them, but they've been described as exceptionally ugly. Scaled, with pig-like features and long, pointed teeth." Ryan wrinkled his nose and bared his teeth.

"So why are they drawbacks?" Lysi asked.

"They've been known to murder a mortal who has taken up with a Merrow."

"What does this have to do with the Kavanagh ghost murder?" Billy asked.

"Ah, now. You know Kavanagh was a letch. He would naturally be drawn to a wealthy, beautiful woman." Ryan paused and squinted at Maynard. "I'm thinking he took up with a Merrow."

Grace leaned forward. "And?"

"And … a jealous Merman murdered him."

"Ryan," Maynard weighed in. "The evidence doesn't support that theory. In Australia our Aborigines speak of yawkyawks or mermaids that live in fresh water. Shenanigans of water creatures take place in water not on land. Kavanagh died from a knife wound on land. He was not murdered by a water creature which would most likely involve drowning."

"Well then, how about Púkas?" Ryan said, persisting with his ghost murder theory. "These ghost shape-changers live on land."

Lysi sighed. No use trying to dissuade Ryan from his ghost murder theory.

"These creatures can shape-shift into humans." Ryan lowered his voice until it was just louder than a whisper. "Some shift into terrifying creatures and hunt down, kill and eat evil people. Now would you be willing to agree Kavanagh would qualify as evil?"

No one disagreed with that.

Ulster is a land of folklore and myths that often have their roots in fact, Lysi thought. Maybe the theory of a ghost murderer could have some merit. She shook her head and scowled. No. Ridiculous! Fairy tales are fine, she thought, downing her beer. But real murders require real murderers.

Chapter 51

Michael Doherty sat on one of two aluminum lawn chairs under a tattered awning outside his caravan and watched the sky darken as the sun plunged below the horizon. He nursed a Guinness and turned his gaze to the empty chair next to him. The one his brother used to sit in.

Michael beat on himself for not having done enough to stop Paddy's downward spiral. He'd done this every night since the police informed him of Paddy's death.

His heart ached for his brother. His head filled with visions of Paddy as a happy kid—playing catch with his father, munching his mother's fresh baked biscuits, romping with the family dog. The memories brought a lump to his throat.

After the death of their parents in a car accident something in Paddy had died. He changed—didn't care about anything except a good time, ran with a bad crowd, got into all kinds of mischief. Michael swallowed. Why hadn't he done more to help his brother? The thought brought searing pain to his dry eyes. It was his fault his brother was dead. He swore never to forgive himself.

A rustle alerted Michael to a presence. The black mongrel tied to the post outside the Walsh family caravan lifted its head but didn't bark. Must be a camp Traveller noving about because strangers always sent the dog into an impotent rage of yapping and growling.

Thankful he didn't have to listen to that bloody hound's frantic yapping, Michael leaned back in his chair, stared into some inward space and listened to the multitude of night sounds in the rural camp—owls hooting, crickets chirping, wind whispering, leaves rustling. Comforting sounds.

A crunch of gravel disturbed Michael's soul-searching. He leaned forward, glanced around, and saw nothing.

He relaxed again, took a sip of beer and pondered the human noises that were not unusual this time of evening—the footfall of a restless Traveller taking a walk. A lad heading off to join his mates. A couple returning from a pub.

None of his business. He tuned out the sounds, zipped up his jacket against the cooling breeze, downed the last of his beer and tried to clear his mind of painful thoughts.

As the sound crunched closer to his personal space without so much as a "How ya?" a slight feeling of discomfort intruded on his self-recrimination. He leaned forward and squinted into the darkness. A fleeting shadow caught his eye. The outline of a figure began to materialize. Michael jumped up from his chair, eyes wide, mouth agape. "Mother of God."

Michael Doherty blinked hard trying to make the shadowy figure before him disappear.

"Shhh, it's me."

"I … I … You're dead." Michael stumbled backward and tipped over his chair.

"Not dead." The figure reached out and tried to touch Michael. "See?"

Michael flinched, picked up his chair and positioned it in front of him like a shield. He'd heard stories about the return of the penitential dead who must remain earthbound until they fulfil obligations they had incurred in life. Could this be one of those penitential ghosts? If so, he knew this ghost certainly had any number of obligations what with his brawling and drugging and stealing.

Michael also knew earthbound ghosts could be released by human intervention. He just didn't know how.

"Paddy, if that be yourself can you tell me what you want of me?" Michael's voice trembled.

"I'm not dead I tell you," Paddy said. "Don't be daft." He yanked the chair from Michael and set it down. "Could a ghost do that?"

"But the police—"

"The peelers are eejits. They don't know what they're talking about."

"You got killed attempting a burglary."

"Did I now? And you viewed my lifeless remains did you?" Paddy's laugh sounded bitter.

Michael thought for a moment. Not only did he not see a body, the police had not asked him to identify the corpse. "No," he said.

"That's because I stand here as alive as you, Michael."

Michael stared at Paddy for a long beat. "Then where have you been?"

"I've been hiding. I'll soon be leaving the country. I've got money." Paddy flashed a wad of pounds. "I want you to come with me."

"Where'd you get all that money?"

"Doesn't matter. I earned it."

Deep down Michael knew Paddy had not earned the money. He remembered the bartender at the Midnight Club telling him Paddy had bragged about coming into a lot of money. "How did you earn it?"

"It doesn't matter. Listen, I got a bloke who can get us to Scotland but he needs a few days to arrange it. Michael, I'll be needing a place to hide."

"Why? Who from?" He hoped it wasn't the police. When he'd reported Paddy missing, they'd tried to help.

"I did something bad."

"You stole that money. You have to give it back." Michael felt desperate. "Just give the money back. We'll get a solicitor. It'll be okay. You'll see."

"Worse, Michael. I did something much worse."

Michael's heart battered his chest. "What are you saying?" Michael's legs turned to water and he dropped onto the chair.

"I need to know if you're willing to hide me until I can get away?"

"I don't know," Michael said. "What if the police come looking for you?"

"In the name of Jesus, Michael. I'm your brother."

Michael looked into Paddy's eyes. He saw a little boy who'd lost his family, his home and the life he'd known. God help me, he's my little brother.

Nancy Curteman

Chapter 52

After leaving the pub, Lysi and Maynard strolled to the town square before returning to McGarrity's B&B for the night. The sky was cloudless and the night air unseasonably warm, so they sat on Maynard's favorite bench across from St. Brigid Church.

"Is this where you come on your early morning walkabouts?" Lysi asked.

Maynard nodded. "Yes. It's a good place to think. The square is empty and it's quiet—that is until early mass lets out at about 7:00. From that hour on the square stays busy with people moving in and out."

Lysi gazed at the old church. It reminded her of St. Mary's Cathedral and School where, as a student, she attended 7:30 mass every Friday before class.

"Sometimes," Maynard continued, "young Constable Aiden Quinn joins me on his way to the PSNI station to meet with the detective who's supervising his training."

"Constable Quinn." Lysi thought for a moment. "Kind of a young guy with carroty hair and a quick smile, right?"

"That's him," Maynard said.

"Yeah," Lysi said. "I've seen him around but never really talked to him. Just nodded a greeting is all."

"He likes to talk about his cases," Maynard said. "I give advice if he asks for it."

"He's lucky to have someone like you to talk to." Lysi took his hand and smiled at him with pride. He squeezed her hand and smiled back.

Lysi looked around the square. It did seem restful. A large old beech tree dominated the grassy square opposite the church. She estimated its height to be about 50 feet. She knew beech trees grew slowly. At that height, the tree had to be at least 80 years old. Wood benches flanked the perimeter of the square. A small, carefully attended flower garden of blue crocus and yellow daffodils provided a pretty circle of early spring color in the center of the lawn. Lysi knew Maynard would seek out a place like this. He loved nature and she loved that side of him. "I can see why you would choose this spot. It's beautiful."

Maynard leaned back, stretched his long legs and put an arm around Lysi. "Having you here makes it perfect."

Lysi smiled and snuggled closer to him. They sat in comfortable silence as night birds warbled softly.

Maynard looked up at the pincushion of stars beginning to appear in the night sky. Lysi glanced up at him and realized he had something on his mind. She waited.

"You know, Lysi, I've been thinking about Ryan's ghost murderer theory. I can see where he's coming from."

That comment coming from practical, evidence-based Maynard surprised Lysi. "Yes?"

"Emma Lowry killed Paddy Doherty to save her sister. Kavanagh got rid of Doherty's body. A week later, Liam Maguire found Kavanagh's corpse half buried in his potato field. The police found the dead Paddy Doherty's fingerprints on the murder weapon and his DNA in the blood on Kavanagh's clothes."

"So you said."

"Of course, the police couldn't reveal their findings about Paddy Doherty because they can't discuss an ongoing investigation. Since Doherty had already died at the hands of Emma Lowry, police officers might have labelled the case as a ghost murder—just among themselves."

"Right," Lysi said. "I've heard police officers sometimes nickname killers like the Zodiac Killer and Dr. Death."

"True. Now I figure someone let the words 'ghost murderer' drop in a casual conversation somewhere outside the police station. Maybe in a pub. After that, it spread throughout the village.

"When Ryan heard about a ghost murderer his imagination, already steeped in Irish myth, went wild."

"Yeah," Lysi said. "And he took Grace's imagination right along with him."

"Now about Paddy Doherty's death." Maynard paused and looked up as if in deep thought. "Aiden told me the police hadn't actually recovered Doherty's body. They assumed Kavanagh had hidden it in a shallow grave in a forest area or cast it into the sea."

Maynard turned excited eyes to Lysi. "What if Emma Lowry only thought she killed him? What if she only knocked him unconscious with that frying pan? What if Sean Kavanagh told the Lowry girls he'd hidden the body but in reality he'd found Doherty alive? What if instead, he seized the opportunity to blackmail them?"

Lysi focused complete attention on Maynard. When he paused again she asked, "If Paddy Doherty is still alive, where is he?"

"That's one question that baffles me. I would have thought he would seek out his brother Michael, but he didn't. His brother had filed a missing person report on him. When we reported his death to Michael, his shock and grief were real."

"How terrible." Lysi felt a stab of pain at the memory of losing her parents.

"The other question I'm grappling with is—what motive would Paddy Doherty have for murdering Sean Kavanagh?"

Nancy Curteman

Chapter 53

Michael Doherty's body stiffened, his eyes fearful as he watched a white Land Rover with large checkered yellow and blue squares painted on the sides pull off the boreen onto the grassy field in front of the Travellers camp.. A car with no markings pulled in behind it.

Peelers. Michael gripped the arms of his aluminum chair and his heart pounded so hard he couldn't swallow.

He could hear Paddy moving around inside the trailer. He had to alert him but how? He couldn't call out to him or rap on the window or greet the police in a voice loud enough for Paddy to hear without rousing suspicion. He regretted hiding him but knew he'd had no other choice. Paddy's problem was his fault. He should never have dragged him into the Travellers' caravan. The kid would have been better off in the Derry social services system.

Several Travellers stopped what they were doing and watched as two officers, one woman and one man, in green PSNI uniforms got out of the Land Rover. Two men in plain clothes exited the unmarked vehicle. All four marched through the caravan lot arrowing straight for Michael's trailer.

A sense of disaster crept up Michael's spine. Somehow he managed to stand as the men approached his caravan.

"Good morning officers," he said trying to keep his voice steady. He risked speaking a bit louder than necessary in hopes that Paddy would hear his warning.

"DS Graig, PSNI," a tall red-haired officer said flashing his warrant card. "I'm looking for Paddy Doherty."

"Paddy's dead. He is … was my brother," Michael said.

"He's as alive as you and me," the officer said.

Michael made a great effort to look surprised. "But they told me he was dead."

"Did they now. Well we'll be having a look about just the same." The detective motioned the uniformed officers toward the caravan door.

Michael, in desperation conquered his fear of the police. "Would you be showing me your search warrant first?"

DS Graig produced a paper with the words WARRANT TO ENTER AND SEARCH printed in bold capital letters across the top of the page. Michael read the entire search warrant stalling for time hoping Paddy managed to scramble out one of the small windows in the back of the caravan or crawl into some hiding space inside.

"Are you satisfied, Mr. Doherty?" DS Graig sounded impatient.

Michael exhaled. He couldn't stall any longer, he had to consent to the search. He nodded, opened the caravan door and the two uniformed officers and DS Graig entered. He followed them inside as the female officer circled around to the back of the trailer.

No Paddy. Thank the Lord.

The officers opened cabinets, looked under a stainless-steel sink and shuffled clothes about in a closet. No Paddy. Michael began to think Paddy had escaped through a window.

The male officer walked to the back of the trailer and opened a storage unit above a bed. He shuffled the blankets and pillows. Michael caught his breath when he saw a foot and knew the officer had seen it at the same moment.

"Well now, would this be Paddy Doherty himself taking a rest on these pillows?" The officer flashed a self-satisfied grin.

"Come on down, lad," DS Graig said. "You have good color for being dead."

Paddy crawled out of the storage cabinet, dropped to the floor and stood in resigned silence before DS Graig.

"What are you going to do with him?" Michael asked.

"We'll take him to the station. After that, we can't say."

Chapter 54

Lysi and Maynard staggered out of Ryan's new Volkswagen. Lysi took a deep breath. Maynard shook his head and clenched his teeth at the sound of tires screeching as Ryan torpedoed away.

"Well that was exciting," Lysi said.

"I can do without that kind of excitement," Maynard said. "I don't know how that guy has survived as long as he has what with his crazy driving on these Irish roads."

"I meant the tour of Carrickfergus Castle," Lysi said. "What a treasure trove of history! I learned so much from that visit." She held up the information booklet she'd bought in the Visitor Center.

"I guess the trip was worth it since it distracted you from meddling in the murder investigation at least for a little while." Maynard frowned at Lysi.

"Come on, Maynard. You know you enjoyed the tour. I saw you examining those 17th century cannons."

"I did enjoy the tour. It's just that suicidal drive that unnerved me. I don't care if I ever get in a car with Ryan again," Maynard said.

"Right, but we survived." Lysi wanted to talk about the castle not Ryan's death-wish driving style. "Can you imagine the Normans built that castle in 1180? Even more astounding, Ryan told me that twelfth century castle housed an air raid shelter during the First and Second World Wars? Pretty sturdy construction. Amazing! And later on—"

"Maynard," Aiden shouted, interrupting Lysi. He skidded up on his bicycle, stopped next to Maynard and nodded at Lysi. "The police found the ghost murderer."

"Ghost murderer!" Maynard looked surprised. "Aiden, don't tell me you believe in ghosts and fairies."

"No, of course I don't believe in ghosts." Aiden paused and glanced around. "Faeries are another story. They—"

"They found the ghost murderer!" Lysi said. It interested her that the ghost murderer gossip had now become a common reference for the Kavanagh murder investigation. She forgot all about Carrickfergus Castle and focused her full attention on Aiden. "What do you mean they found the ghost murderer?"

Maynard cast a warning scowl at her. She got the message—'Stay out of this!'

"Well not a real ghost murderer. A person," Aiden answered her.

"Go on, Aiden," Maynard said.

"Paddy Doherty," Aiden continued, his voice pitched high. "They found him. Alive. His brother Michael had hidden him in his caravan."

"I'm not surprised they found him alive," Maynard said. "His body never turned up. I am surprised the lad stayed in the area after the murder instead of escaping to … say Scotland. Why risk staying?"

"Good question," Aiden said. "Maybe he had no money? No wheels? No friends?"

Lysi had been attentive to the conversation between Maynard and Aiden. "Maybe the ghost murderer … I mean Paddy Doherty had no place else to go. Ryan told me Paddy was just a troubled kid. It's only natural he'd go to his older brother for help."

Maynard glanced at her. She saw in his expression an acceptance of her observation despite his desire to keep her out of the case.

Aiden shot a sharp look at Lysi. "He was old enough to commit murder."

"I'd like to know what Paddy's motive was for murdering a man like Kavanagh?" Maynard said.

Lysi admired Maynard's willingness to look at all sides of a situation instead of jumping to a quick conclusion.

"I don't think they even knew each other," Aiden said. "I never saw them together and I never heard Kavanagh speak of him."

Maynard paused, folded his arms and looked toward the sky. After a moment, he posed some questions. "Could Paddy have had a relationship with one of the women Kavanagh assaulted? Did Kavanagh disrespect Paddy or Michael? The Lowry girls stated that Kavanagh had promised to dispose of Paddy's remains. Obviously he didn't. The question is, what did he do with Paddy?"

"He's in custody now. We'll find out the answers to those questions after the detectives interview him," Aiden said.

Nancy Curteman

Chapter 55

Michael knew he had to swallow his fear of the police for the sake of his brother. He had to advocate for him—communicate to the police that Paddy was a good lad, that he never instigated fights. Paddy's only problem was the hoodlums he ran with.

Michael entered the police department's small interview room and took a seat next to Paddy who sat hands folded and eyes round with fear. So young and vulnerable. The same look he had when the officer came to their door in Derry with the terrible news that their parents had died in a car accident. Michael's stomach felt like it had been twisted in a vise and his eyes stung with suppressed tears for his brother.

After providing Paddy with his rights, DS Graig wasted no time getting on with the interview. "Well now, Paddy Doherty, you understand the serious situation in which you find yourself?"

Paddy nodded without looking up from the table.

"This interview will go easier for both of us if you answer my questions fully and honestly to the best of your knowledge. Do you understand that?"

Paddy nodded, his eyes still glued to the table.

Michael wished Paddy would at least look at the police officer when he answered a question.

"You know this man?" DS Graig shoved a photograph across the table to Paddy.

Michael flinched when he saw the crime scene photo of the dead Kavanagh his chest covered in dirt mixed with blood.

Paddy gasped and looked away.

"Do you know this man, Paddy?" DS Graig repeated, his voice firm and void of empathy.

Paddy licked his lips and nodded.

"Tell us how he died."

Paddy turned to Michael, a scared kid. All bravado gone from his pale face. Michael knew he had to speak up. "Paddy didn't mean to kill that man. My brother's a good kid."

"Is he now?" DS Craig opened a manila folder and pulled out some papers. As he scooted the pages across the table to Paddy he read each one: "Arrested for a street brawl. Arrested for stealing drugs from O'Toole's Pharmacy. Restraining order for stalking young Róisin Reilly." The sergeant paused and looked at Paddy through hard eyes. "Shall I go on?"

Paddy shook his head.

"Now, I ask you again. How did Sean Kavanagh die?"

Paddy dropped his eyes to the table again.

Michael started to speak. He wanted to relate to the officer what Paddy had told him. "Officer, he—"

The officer's hand shot up in the universal signal for stop. "Let the lad speak for himself."

"I … I stabbed him."

Michael jerked forward. "But—"

Graig's hand flew up again. He reached into an evidence box and withdrew a plastic bag containing a knife. Holding it up, he said to Paddy. "You stabbed him with this knife?"

"Yes," Paddy said. Tears flowed from his eyes onto the table.

"Why?" DS Graig demanded giving no indication he cared about or even noticed Paddy's breakdown.

Paddy didn't raise his eyes from the table. Didn't reply. Michael knew that for Paddy the interview was over. He'd seen Paddy clam up like this in the past when Michael grilled him about his unsavory friends and mischievous activities. He knew Paddy would say no more, would not tell his side of the story, would not defend himself, would just remain silent. Michael wanted to shake him, make him understand the dire consequences of his not speaking on his own behalf. He clinched his fists. "Officer, please—"

Again, the silencing hand.

Desperate, Michael opened his mouth determined to reveal what Paddy wouldn't but something in the officer's expression stopped him. Had the hard lines on the officer's face softened? Had his voice changed—no longer so brittle and harsh?

"Paddy," DS Graig said. "We know you stabbed Sean Kavanagh with this weapon because we found your fingerprints and his blood on it. However, we also found Kavanagh's fingerprints on the handle of the knife. In addition, we found your blood on the blade. Do you know what this tells us?"

Paddy didn't raise his head or reply.

Graig shouted, "Look at me lad."

Paddy startled, jerked his head up and stared at DS Graig.

"I said, 'Do you know what this tells us?'"

Paddy shook his head.

Nancy Curteman

Chapter 56

Michael knew what the evidence showed. Why couldn't Paddy see it too? If only he would meet DS Graig halfway. If only the sergeant would allow Michael to speak.

"Well Paddy Doherty," DS Graig said. "The evidence tells us you may have killed Sean Kavanagh in self-defense."

Paddy blinked and his eyes lost their hopeless dull color.

Michael slumped in his chair as the terrifying tension drained from his body. He looked at DS Graig through eyes brimming with gratitude. The sergeant had given Paddy a reason to tell his story.

"Now, would you be telling us what happened, Paddy lad?"

Paddy looked at Michael. He took a deep breath and turned his gaze to Graig. "I … I … "

"Come on. Spit it out, boy. I don't have all day," DS Graig said. "This is no time for spluttering."

"I tried to rob the old girls. I'm ashamed for it. If I could undo it, I would. They were right to defend themselves against me." Paddy sniffled and tears escaped his eyes.

Michael wanted to put his arm around him and comfort him as he had done when Paddy was a child.

"Enough sniffling," DS Graig said. "Get on with your story."

"The one old girl knocked me on the head. I saw stars I did, but it didn't kill me. The next thing I remember I was in Sean Kavanagh's cottage. He had a plan to make some money. He told me that for it to work all I had to do was stay out of sight so people would think I was dead. If I did, he'd give me half the money. He cheated me. He kept all the money for himself."

"What did you do about that Paddy?" DS Graig asked.

"I telephoned him and told him I wanted to meet or I'd come out of hiding. He said to meet him in Liam Maguire's field at midnight when no one would be about."

"You met him and then what?"

"I said I wanted my share of the money or the deal was off. He laughed at me and asked me what I was going to do about it? He said I couldn't do nothing about it."

"What happened next? " Graig asked.

"I got mad and punched him."

"So you had a bit of a scuffle, but that wasn't the end of it, was it?" DS Graig glowered at Paddy.

"He pulled a knife," Paddy said.

"This one?" Graig pointed to the knife in the evidence bag.

Paddy nodded. "I guess."

"You guess? You have to do better than that."

"Yes, that's the knife." Paddy looked away from the knife.

"Go on."

"We struggled. The knife cut my hand." Paddy rubbed the scab on his palm. "I guess I stabbed him."

"No lad." DS Graig pounded the table. "I just told you not to guess."

Paddy jerked.

"Now let's try again. What happened next?"

"I did it. I stabbed him because if I hadn't he would have stabbed me."

"That's better," DS Graig said. "And?"

"I went to his cottage to try to find my share of the money."

"And, did you find it?"

"Some of it."

"Aren't you leaving something out? What did you do with Kavanagh's body after you stabbed him?"

Paddy paled and dropped his eyes to the table again.

"You buried him in Liam Maguire's field." DS Graig said. "Why?"

"I was afraid the police wouldn't believe he tried to stab me first. I was afraid they would hang me. I didn't want to die."

"Capital punishment was abolished in Northern Ireland in 1973, Paddy." DS Graig said. "But some punishments are worse than death."

Chapter 57

Lysi surveyed at the jovial faces seated around the long oak dinner table in the home of village doctor, Ronan McStarran, Ryan's third cousin twice removed. She had no idea how distant her relationship to Dr. McStarran might be even after Ryan tried to explain that their shared ancestor would be a great grand uncle. She would research that cousin business when she returned to San Francisco. Not important right now. Not while a celebration was happening, a grand hooley as Grace called it—another word from the Irish phrase book she carried in her purse.

Fifteen people including Maynard, Grace, Billy Weston, Mary McClone, Ryan O'Rourke and several distant relatives she had just met raised their glasses to toast Dr. McStarran, coach of the primary kid's Camogie team that had just won their first game. Dr. McStarran had invited several of the O'Rourke and McStarran clan and friends to a Sunday barbecue to celebrate the young team's great start of the season.

Through the glass patio doors Lysi watched a gaggle of children romping on a grassy slope under a clear blue sky. She planned to ask Dr. McStarran if any of the girls on the slope played on his team.

Over a delicious homemade dessert of Pavlova, the celebrants relived the first Camogie game.

"Ah now," Dr. McStarran said, "you should have seen young Rosie Fitzgibbon. She shot that wee sliotar under the bar more than a few times."

Ryan pointed to the group of children at the slide. "She's that wee bit of a red-haired lass just coming down the slide."

Lysi spotted a slight child whizzing down the slide and wondered how her matchstick-thin arms could possibly have the strength to lift the hurley much less hit a ball across a field with it.

"What a sight it was!" Dr. McStarran continued to gush. "Picture this. It was the last half of the game, only seconds remaining. Tie score. Out of nowhere that little bit of a lass raced up with that hurley and slammed that sliotar and sent it careening right under the goal bar for the three grand points that won the game." He slapped his hands together. Wham! She hit that ball so hard she nearly lost her helmet."

"No surprise with a name like Fitzgibbon," Ryan chimed in. "Sandie Fitzgibbon was awarded the 2013 District Hall of Fame Award for her outstanding success as a camogie player."

Lysi remembered Rosie's last second hit in the game Ryan had taken her and Maynard to see the day before. The game moved so fast she had difficulty keeping track of the ball. "So that's the little heroine who won the game," Maynard said. "I've read about the Western Swans, a camogie team out of Perth, but yesterday was the first time I'd seen an actual game. Quite an experience."

After another clink of glasses Billy said, "Lysi, tell this fine group how you solved the Kavanagh case."

"I didn't solve it, but Grace and I may have helped."

"We almost solved it when we tackled Paddy Doherty at the old farmhouse," Grace said. "At least I got a great item to sell on eBay, an Elvis boot."

Laughter greeted Grace's comment.

"I meant we helped to take suspicion off Mary," Lysi said.

"Oh yeah," Grace said. "The panty party did the trick."

"The lingerie party proved that if Kavanagh's assault was Mary's motive for murder, then over a dozen other women had the same motive," Lysi said. "After poor DS Graig's grueling interviews of twelve of Kavanagh's assault victims, Mary was no longer a person of interest in Kavanagh's murder."

"Great Irish police work solved this murder," Maynard said. My source tells me—"

"And who would that be?" Billy asked.

Lysi feigned shock. "Billy, surely you're not asking Maynard to reveal his source, are you?" She knew that in his days as District Attorney Billy had several unsavory sources.

Maynard smiled at Lysi and continued, "The Lowry girls acted in self-defense so no jail time for them. Paddy Doherty also acted in self-defense, but he'll have to serve time for two attempted burglaries and conspiracy to extort money from the Lowry's."

"Two burglaries?" Billy asked.

"Yes," Maynard said. "First the one at the Lowry's. The other one took place after Kavanagh's death. Paddy went to Kavanagh's cottage to try to find the money he believed Kavanagh owed him for cooperating with the extortion scheme."

"Trouble seemed to follow that lad," Dr. McStarran said. "I heard from O'Toole he stole drugs from the pharmacy."

"Paddy's young—just nineteen," Maynard continued. "The Irish penal system doesn't require him to do hard time. He'll serve his sentence at the Hydebank Young Offender Center in Belfast. The Center has a Secure Training College that provides educational and vocational training aimed at preparing young men for employment when they finish their terms."

"Kavanagh had no relatives so the land was returned to Liam according to my source." Mary cast a conspiratorial grin at Maynard. "The Lowry girls were given the money in Kavanagh's account."

"Michael Doherty moved to Belfast and got a job as a cleaner at Pizza Express," Ryan said. "He got that job because of Mary." He looked at her fondly and patted her hand.

"I felt kind of sorry for Michael Doherty," Mary said. "I told my cousin, Rory about him. Rory manages a Pizza Express. He needed a cleaner and Michael made a good impression on him during the interview. Rory also helped him rent a room in a home not far from Hydebank so he could be near Paddy."

"The Kavanagh case would make a terrific mystery novel with all its twists and turns," Lysi said.

"Just the kind of case you love, eh Lysi," Billy Weston said.

"I still swear I heard the banshee shriek the night before Kavanagh left this mortal plane," Ryan said.

"You sure that wasn't Mary McClone screaming in terror when you proposed marriage to her?" Dr. McStarran burst into a robust belly laugh.

"You laugh now, Ronan but you'd best be starting to save your money for our wedding gift," Ryan said.

"Will you tell us what took you so long to gather the courage to ask the lovely Mary to be your bride?" Dr. McStarran asked.

"There's two things too serious to joke about, matrimony and potatoes. I wanted to wait until I knew she would accept."

"The wedding's kind of old news," Dr. McStarran said. "Everyone in the village knew Ryan was daft over Mary and would soon pop the question. Even Mary knew."

Mary nodded and squeezed Ryan's hand. "I wondered that it took you so long."

"Now, will you lift your glasses once again and we'll toast our local Don Juan," Dr. McStarran said.

Ryan's face turned crimson and he quickly changed the subject. "So," he said turning to Grace and Lysi. "What's next for you two sleuths?"

"I'll be joining Chess in Dublin while he finishes his contract," Grace said. "We're going to see a little more of Ireland and maybe trip over to Scotland. Then I'm off to Harlem to visit my family for a couple of days before my and Lysi's next assignment."

"Lysi and Maynard, any plans?" asked Ryan

"Back to San Francisco," said Maynard.

"In September," Lysi said. "Grace and I will return to Beechgrove to be bridesmaids.

"After Ryan and Mary's wedding, Maynard and I will return to Australia to spend six months on Maynard's sheep station near Alice Springs."

"As for me," Billy said. "I'll be staying in Beechgrove for a wee bit. Want to get in touch with me Irish roots."

Emma Lowry's Favorite Irish Butter Biscuits

Ingredients:
2 cups flour
½ tsp baking powder
¼ tsp salt
2/3 cup sugar
8 oz Irish butter (Kerrygold)
2 egg yolks beaten
1 tsp vanilla extract
24 pecans

Instructions:
1. Preheat oven to 325 degrees
2. Cream butter and sugar until fluffy
3. Add vanilla and eggs to creamed butter and sugar
4. Sift together flour, salt and baking powder
5. Slowly add the flour mixture until the dough is stiff
6. Form the dough into two logs each one 7 ½ " long and 1 ½ " wide
7. Wrap in plastic wrap and refrigerate at least 2 hours or overnight.
8. Cut into 1/4" circles.
9. Place 1 inch apart on a cookie sheet and place a pecan on each one.
10. Bake about 12 minutes until edges and bottoms are light brown.

Makes 2 dozen

Nancy Curteman

About the Author

Nancy Curteman has lived most of her life on the majestic Pacific coast. After graduating from San Francisco State University she studied at the University of Nice in France.

She has a Masters in French literature and a Masters in Administration. She has taught college French and worked as a school principal.

Curteman's passions are reading, travel and writing. She loves to read mystery novels so of course she loves writing them. She is currently working on her eighth novel.

Curteman sets her novels in the countries she has visited. Her novel, Murder in a Teacup, set in Montana, placed second in the California Writers Club Jack London novel contest. Murder Casts a Spell, set in South Africa, was voted 2013 Best Mystery by The Readers' Poll. Murder on the Seine, set in France was rated in the 2015 Top Ten Best Mysteries by The Readers' Poll. Murder Down Under, set in Australia, and Lethal Lesson were released by Solstice Publishing. Murder Lurks in the Fog is set in San Francisco, California.

On her blog, Global Mysteries, Curteman posts writing and travel tips.

www.ingramcontent.com/pod-product-compliance
Lightning Source LLC
Chambersburg PA
CBHW052032260626
47163CB00006B/174